Murder Most Sacred

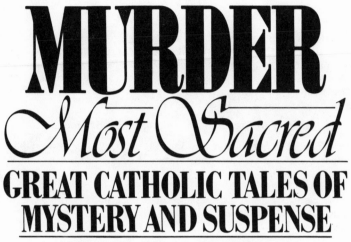

MURDER
Most Sacred
GREAT CATHOLIC TALES OF MYSTERY AND SUSPENSE

**Edited by Edward D. Hoch &
Martin H. Greenberg**

DEMBNER BOOKS • New York

DEMBNER BOOKS
Published by Red Dembner Enterprises Corp.,
80 Eighth Avenue,
New York, N.Y. 10011
Distributed by W. W. Norton & Company, Inc.,
500 Fifth Avenue,
New York, N.Y. 10110

Library of Congress Cataloging-in-Publication Data

Murder most sacred : great Catholic tales of mystery and suspense / edited by Edward D. Hoch and Martin H. Greenburg.
    p.   cm.
    ISBN 0-942637-09-7 : $16.95
    1. Detective and mystery stories. 2. Short stories—Catholic authors. 3. Catholics—Fiction. 4. Catholic Church—Clergy—Fiction. I. Hoch, Edward D., 1930–   . II Greenberg, Martin Harry.
PN34448.D4M825   1989
808.83'872—dc19   88-38749
                                                        CIP

Designed by Antler & Baldwin, Inc.

Acknowledgments, permissions, and additional copyright material to be found on page vi.

CONTENTS

INTRODUCTION

A number of historians of the mystery story, notably Dorothy L. Sayers, like to trace its origins back to the Bible, especially to the Old Testament history of Bel in the *Book of Daniel*, which appears in Catholic versions of the Bible, but is relegated to the *Apocrypha* in the King James version. Certainly this would make the prophet Daniel the first religious detective in literature, and the nefarious sixth century B.C. priests of the idol Bel the first villains to be unmasked by a detective.

But I think we must turn to the twentieth century for the real origin of Catholic influence on the mystery-suspense tale. Certainly Arthur Conan Doyle was born a Catholic, and Sherlock Holmes once assumed a clerical disguise, but neither Doyle nor Holmes contributed anything to the Catholic mystery. One might say that the French playwright Paul Anthelme (Paul Bourde) made a contribution of sorts with his 1902 drama titled *Nos Deux Consciences (Our Two Consciences)*. It was the first known use of a favorite plot device of later writers, in which a murderer confesses his crime to a priest who is bound by the seal of the confessional to keep silent—even when he himself is accused of the crime! The play was updated and filmed in 1952 by Alfred Hitchcock—another born Catholic—under the title *I Confess*.

But Paul Anthelme's priest did not function as a detective and the plot was resolved by other means. It was not until the September 1910 issue of a British monthly called the *Storyteller* that the Catholic mystery story really came into being with the publication of G. K. Chesterton's "The Blue Cross," the first adventure of Farther Brown. Five collections of Father Brown stories followed over the next two decades. Chesterton also produced a religious allegory in the form of an intrigue novel, *The Man Who Was Thursday*, which actually predated Father Brown by two years, but it was the priest detective who was to capture the public's imagination and become one of the popular characters of detective fiction.

Considering the popularity of the Father Brown stories at the time, it's surprising that no other clerical sleuth appeared on the mystery scene until 1940. Even Monsignor Ronald Knox, a Catholic priest who became a mystery writer, limited his puzzles to non-religious themes. It was not until Anthony Boucher's novel *Nine Times Nine*, first publisher under the name "H. H. Holmes," that detective fiction had a character who was almost a match for Father Brown. She was Sister Ursula of the fictional order Martha of Bethany, and our only regret is that she appeared in only two novels and three short stories.

Perhaps the first mystery novel with a Catholic priest functioning as a detective was *A Gentle Murderer* (1951) by Dorothy Salisbury Davis. Later in the same decade author Jack Webb produced a series teaming up a Catholic priest and a Jewish detective sergeant. A nun detective was featured in three French novels by Henri Catalan, and other priestly sleuths were forthcoming in series from Leonard Holton, Alice Scanlan Reach, Ralph McInerny, William X. Kienzle, Andrew M. Greeley, and me. McInerny also created a series about a nun detective under the pseudonym of "Monica Quill," and an actual nun, Sister Carol Anne O'Marie, has begun a series of novels about a nun detective. Medieval monks have figured in a series of novels by Ellis Peters and in the international best-seller *The*

Name of the Rose (1983) by Umberto Eco. Information about these and other titles may be found in the bibliography at the end of this volume.

The stories that follow will introduce readers to some of the authors and characters I've mentioned, as well as to other mystery writers who have used Catholic themes from time to time. Not all of the authors represented here are (or were) practicing Catholics themselves. (Of the two editors, I am Catholic and my co-editor is Jewish.) But almost everyone here has a Catholic background of one sort or another. You'll know it in their portraits of Catholic schools and churches, their depictions of priests and nuns and altar boys, their points of Catholic doctrine.

But first of all, these are good stories—good mystery and suspense stories. I believe they can be enjoyed by any reader, regardless of religious beliefs.

—Edward D. Hoch

A FACE TO REMEMBER

Mary Amlaw

🦋 "May I speak with you, Mother?"

Small and stooped with age, Sister Gabriela paused respectfully by the prioress' desk. Normally she wore a smile that radiated joy, but she was not smiling today. On the contrary, she seemed unusually agitated. An ordinary person might not have detected Gabriela's emotion, for the Daughters of Elias had learned in pre-Vatican II days to conceal anything that seemed negative, but Mary Dominic noticed the line that kept reappearing between Gabriela's eyebrows and the small sigh that escaped her unsmiling lips.

With a small gesture Mary Dominic invited Gabriela to sit down. Mary Dominic was the elected superior of the community, changed not only with the care of souls but with the overall

Mary Amlaw's short stories have been appearing in *Ellery Queen's Mystery Magazine* and *Alfred Hitchcock's Mystery Magazine* since August 1974, when her first story was published by *EQMM*. Many of her stories, like that first one "Farewell, Beloved," have had Catholic backgrounds. She has done public relations work and has been a schoolteacher, social worker, and classical musician. This story, her most recent, is one of her best.

1

well-being of the nuns. Keeping eighteen women in harmony—
Mary Dominic already thought of little Sharon Diaz as one of
themselves— taxed her innate understanding of people far more
than handling the needs of scores of retreatants. They returned
to the outside world within a few days. The community remained.

Mary Dominic smiled at Gabriela. "Yes, Sister?" Gabriela
was ninety-two, a meek soul tending towards scruples. A gifted
artist, her eyes were still sharp and her hands still able to wield
the brush, although more slowly than before.

Gabriela whispered, "Mother, I've sinned against charity.
Oh, such a stupid offense! I hardly know how to tell you."

Mary Dominic had never known a scruple in her life. A
vibrant woman, she embraced life whole-heartedly, and had a
knack for restoring minor difficulties to their proper perspective.
But she had a soft spot for Gabriela, so timid and loving, and
nodded to encourage her to speak.

"I was assigned to one of our retreatants, Mrs. Prestavolta.
Mother, I've been praying earnestly for guidance on how best to
help her. Her face struck me the moment I saw her, when she
registered. There is no peace in it. I went to her room this
morning to inquire about when she would like to make an
appointment for spiritual discussion. Her door was partly open,
and music was coming out."

Gabriela unconsciously wrinkled her forehead in dismay.
"Not religious music, Mother. That loud noise the youngsters
seem to enjoy. She didn't hear my knock, but it made the door
swing open wider. Poor Mrs. Prestavolta—poor thing!—" Gabriela's eyes filled with tears of compassion. "She was *shaving*,
Mother. I had a relative once with the same problem, and it
made her life a misery. I understood then why Mrs. Prestavolta
has been so withdrawn. She doesn't want her secret known,
poor woman."

Mary Dominic was more amused than she wanted Gabriela
to know. "did she see you, sister?"

"Oh, no, Mother. I drew the door nearly shut, as it had
been, and left without speaking to her. But I clumsily intruded

on that woman's privacy, Mother and now I know her secret which I have no right to know."

Mary Dominic managed to sound as solemn as the situation warranted. "Dear sister, please do not upset yourself so. Our dear Lord would not desire it. Who knows, perhaps He allowed you to learn this secret for some purpose of His own. I know you won't say anything of her affliction. That would be truly uncharitable."

"But there's more fault on my part," Gabriela said. "I had meant to instruct her about our regard for silence. I understood too late that she had the radio playing so loudly to cover the noise of the razor. If I hadn't been so quick to judge—"

"Life is full of ifs," Mary Dominic soothed her. "Put it behind you, sister. You meant no harm, and where there is no ill intent, there is no sin."

Gabriela left Mary Dominic's presence only partially consoled. Tact suggested she avoid Mrs. Prestavolta unless the woman approached her; conscience urged that she keep a watchful eye on Mrs. Prestavolta from a distance in an effort to anticipate any of the poor woman's desires. Mrs. Prestavolta had little to say to her fellow retreatants. She had not requested spiritual guidance and didn't seem drawn to the chapel, but she did spend many hours on the grounds by herself. Gabriela considered that Mrs. Prestavolta was communing with God among the trees, alone and in silence. That was what a retreat was for—solitude and silence with God. Mrs. Prestavolta was surely in need of God. Her features haunted Gabriela. So shallow a face! No peace, no joy, no love resided there.

Perhaps God had allowed Gabriela to blunder because He wanted to reach the woman in His own way. He would touch her, and then she would wish to speak to Gabriela. Until then, Gabriela would remain at a distance, watching and praying.

Sharon Carmelita Diaz sat at the small desk in her narrow cell. The community had informed her after morning prayer that she had been accepted. She had been with the Daughters of Elias twelve months; first as a retreatant, then as postulant and novice. Now she was to choose her profession day, when she would dress like a bride to make her solemn vows. Then she would retire and be dressed in the dark blue habit of the sisters. Thereafter she would be called by her name in religion, Sister Mary Magdalen—a name she had chosen as being eminently suitable.

She had won. Twelve months of prayer, of obedience, of uninspired meals. Twelve months laboring without pay, without crossing the iron gates of the convent into the outside world. Twelve months of behaving like the most docile applicant ever to approach a community.

At first she barely survived from hour to hour. Only the thought of Big Luke's vengeance had helped her persist. He thought she had agreed to testify against him when he was picked up for the murder of a local politician who had been making trouble for Luke and his colleagues.

She would never doublecross a man like Luke, but he had been looking for a scapegoat and he would never believe her. He picked her up six months before when she was working Las Vegas as a stripper, and he was already tired of her.

Sharon never knew her mother. Her grandmother died when she was five, and her father, a migrant farm worker, had no way to raise her. By the time she was fourteen she'd lived in seven foster homes and two residences. Her body was her fortune. She took to the streets, then to the lounges. She'd been doing just fine when Luke picked her up. If he hadn't been arrested, the affair would have fizzled out without any danger. As it was, she thought flight her best chance to live, even though she knew it sealed her guilt in Luke's eyes.

She went to the Daughters of Elias, a continent away in Boston, Massachusetts, as an ordinary retreatant. The scores of weary people seeking the peace and solace of God made her feel safe. Three days after arriving, she lied, saying that she felt an attraction to the religious life; would the Daughter of Elias accept her as a postulant?

The nuns seemed like children to her. They accepted her

lies as truth, and she assumed the outward shell of their life as a protective disguise.

A year had gone. Luke must have forgotten her by now, or given up the search. She knew she could leave for the city at last. She had five hundred dollars and jewelry the nuns didn't know about. That was nothing given the way she spent in the old days, but it would get her a room for a few days while she found an income. With her dark eyes, creamy skin, and sexy figure that wouldn't be hard. Twelve months of convent life hadn't killed her skill with men, she was sure.

Time to resume the excitement of her old life. The habit of prayer would soon be overcome by pleasure, the remembrance of solitude and silence swamped by headier joys.

She had played her part perfectly for twelve long months, amused and then intrigued by the existence of such an un-worldly thing as a community of women who took God so seriously they had vowed to devote their lives to Him.

Maybe she had played her part too perfectly. The lie had become truth: she was attracted to this life. But in spite of the morning's good news, she was most certainly not acceptable; the nuns thought her an orphan who had been a good little mouse from birth. Would they want her if they knew she had been a hooker, a stripper, a criminal's girl?

There was only one way to find out. Sharon pulled a piece of stationery towards her and began to write. "Dear Mother Mary Dominic, I have not been honest with you and the community."

She wrote quickly, without pausing to phrase her words more tactfully, sealed the letter without rereading it, and took it at once to Mary Dominic's cell. Then she went to her work in the garden.

Once Mary Dominic read that letter, Sharon feared she would be asked to leave. She did not want to leave. And others had applied who were not very good material on the face of it; at least one boasted a past nearly as colorful as Sharon's. The nuns made her welcome, to Sharon's surprise. "Some of God's greatest saints began as notorious sinners," Mary Dominic told her. "If God calls souls here, we must give them their chance." But the life proved too foreign and she left within weeks.

The white rhododendron needed attention. Sharon concentrated on debriding the leaves of last year's dead stalks. She made a perfect target as she stretched to reach the top of the bush.

White rhododendrons, Ouzo noted. Expensive. The Daughters of Elias must have money somewhere.

He looked around carefully. The retreatants were attending the late morning conference, the nuns were at their household tasks, the garden below was empty except for Sharon. A wall surrounded the grounds, and trees grew near the wall, protecting him from the street. He was on the fire escape outside the women's wing, just beyond the lilac hedge that separated the retreatants' garden from the small area reserved for the nuns.

He aimed without hurry. The bullet had only to graze her. It had been treated with a nicotine solution that would poison her after he had gone. The bullet reached its mark; she slapped at her neck and looked about as if a bee had stung her. Good. Maybe she'd realize Big Luke had caught up with her before she died. He watched her resume breaking the spikes of the dead flowerets as if nothing had happened and smiled, a lengthening of the upper lip and glint in the eyes that boded no good. Soon the poison would work; she might feel faint and excuse herself from recreation, or keel over unexpectedly in choir. She might think it was flu. The nuns might never know otherwise; and if they came to realize it was murder, they would surely want to hush it up. From what he had learned, that Mary Dominic had the clout to do it.

It had gone well. Luke would be pleased.

Ouzo slid the gun into the purse at his feet. Now he would leave by the front gate in the same guise in which he had entered—a retreatant. At the corner he would walk boldly into St. Anthony's church. Only the side door nearest the rectory was left open nowadays—symbolic of the neighborhood's deteriorating respectability—but he could leave by any door; it would lock behind him. An old lady or two might be huddled in one of the pews, saying her beads. He would walk by, lock himself in the restroom near the sacristy, shed wig and dress, and emerge as a male. His disguise would join the bundles of clothes collected monthly for the poor.

Purse in hand, he turned to find two dark eyes peering at him from the wall. A black kid, about eight or nine. The child gave a startled gasp and leaped for the ground. Ouzo heard him pounding down the sidewalk.

How much had the kid seen? Was he there when Ouzo fired? No. He had checked. At most, the kid had seen an aging woman fumbling with her purse. Even if he had glimpsed the gun, what harm would it do? This was a neighborhood where people kept shootings and brawls and drugdealing to themselves. If Ouzo had thought there was any danger, he would have hunted the kid down and killed him. It wasn't mercy that spared the boy's life, but cocksureness. Ouzo never made mistakes.

He checked to make sure nothing had been left in his room, hefted his overnight bag, and walked down the stairs to the front lobby in the slightly dragging gait of a weary, arthritic woman. He even gave a nod to the elderly nun who appeared from nowhere to open the door for him.

Beyond the iron gates of the convent, the street was clear. At night it would be a different story: every stoop and porch crowded with people escaping the heat inside. Radios blaring, teens necking in the shadows and flaunting themselves on the street.

By then Ouzo would be far away. Even if the murder got out and some smart cop tied it up to Luke's trail, there was no way to connect it with Ouzo. He smiled as he made his way into the dim coolness of St. Anthony's. He was pleased with himself.

Zebulon Williams leaned on the buzzer that would eventually bring a nun to the door. When the neighborhood had been middle-class Irish and Italian, the door had opened at the slightest touch and the caller could wait in a vestibule furnished with comfortable chairs. Now the vestibule was bare, and the doors that led from it were kept locked.

Zeb danced with impatience. He had just run from his third-floor apartment down the street, where he had watched the gun-toting old lady head downhill to St. Anthony's. He had waited until she was gone before coming to tell Mother Mary Dominic his story. She'd know what to do. She always did.

The door was opened by sister Vincent. Zeb didn't like her. Sister Vincent had joined the Daughters of Elias in the palmy days when a single family owned an entire house now converted to six apartments and all the neighbors were white. Nuns were considered a spiritual luxury then, a jewel in the crown of the parish, for the Daughters of Elias were not teaching nuns. They were spiritual directors. The convent was a house of prayer for all who felt the need.

In those days, people who requested spiritual favors came laden with welcome gifts. Delicacies the nuns never purchased for themselves appeared to brighten feast days. Fine linens, warm sweaters, expensive chocolates, imported liqueurs—all were accepted gratefully, for when God moved hearts to generosity, it would be churlish not to accept with joy.

But as urban blight took over, the fine old houses with their molded ceilings and paneled rooms housed the refuse of the city. The fall from middle to lower class to racially-mixed impoverished happened in a decade. Now the only white faces to be seen were within the convent walls.

Seldom now was the plain convent fare broken with delicacies. The neighbors rarely asked for prayers. They wanted help with landlords who shut off the heat, with children dealing drugs, with intemperate or disappearing spouses.

Sister Vincent found the change most contrary to her idea of the calling of a Daughter of Elias. Mary Dominic, on the other hand, thrived on it. She knew all the neighbors by name. They held her in reverence, not knowing how she managed to get faulty plumbing fixed and exorbitant rents reduced; where she found scholarships for students who would otherwise have to leave school. Some said when Mary Dominic spoke, the very demons of hell jumped to obey.

Zebulon looked up at the imposing height and scowling face of Sister Vincent and grimaced. "I want Sister Mary Dominic, please."

"She is busy," Sister Vincent said loftily. She considered it a scandal that Mary Dominic allowed everyone such easy access to her office.

"But we are not a cloistered community," Mary Dominic explained patiently to Vincent. "We embody the ideals of the contemplative *and* the active life. Would Our Lord have turned His back on the need of these people? He is our model. Our life has no meaning if it is not patterned on His."

Sister Vincent was silenced but not convinced. In her opinion, a reasonable community would have followed their supporters to the suburbs and not let the inner city surround them; but having made the initial mistake of staying, they might at least hold themselves separate from the riffraff around them.

"It's important," Zeb said urgently.

"I will be the judge of that." Vincent's tone was frosty. "What do you wish to tell her, young man?"

Zebulon considered. He could always scale the convent wall and hide in the garden until Mary Dominic appeared for her evening exercise. Meantime he would leave his message.

"One of the old ladies who was in here has a gun," Zebulon said. "She shot one of the sisters."

"Yes, of course she did," Vincent sniffed. "Run along now. I'll see that your message is delivered."

"Yes'm. Only when Sister Mary Dominic sees me, she gives me a chocolate chip cookie."

"Indeed." Vincent's voice conveyed her disapproval. She closed the door, her sense of righteousness strengthened. One of the retreatants shooting a nun, indeed! What a tale! Obviously the result of too much television. How people as poor as these could afford TV—and color at that—was just one indication of how wrong things were in the world.

In Vincent's day, the poor were decently humble. They

didn't spend their meager resources on TV and cigarettes. Altogether, the world was far better in the old days.

Sister Vincent went back to mopping floors. She would convey Zebulon's message as she had promised, but at a suitable time—recreation, when the whole community could enjoy the the tale.

Sharon felt too ill for lunch. "I think it's flu," she told Sister Angela, mistress of novices. "If I could lie down—"

"Of course," Angela, a sweet-faced, kind-tempered woman, agreed promptly. "Don't try to come to choir or evening prayer. I'll look in on you a bit later to see how you are."

Sharon thanked her. She felt very odd. She had always been strong physically. Even the flu rarely laid her low for more than a day or two. Perhaps she was coming down with one of the new strains; her legs and arms felt heavy and her head was swimming. Had Mary Dominic read her letter yet? she wondered. At any rate, the nuns wouldn't be able to put her out sick. She'd have a little longer with them, at least.

Mary Dominic remained in the chapel after Night Prayer, interceding for the well-being of the community. Tonight she was especially concerned about Sharon. Mary Dominic had doubted her fitness for the religious life from the beginning; but as the months passed, Sharon had shown an astonishing progress in prayer and understanding of what it meant to live in community. She had a sweet, complaisant nature that became more evident as the months went on, yet she was stubborn when injustice showed itself. Like Mary Dominic herself, she seemed to have a deeper appreciation of the needs of the neighborhood than some of the nuns who felt prayer was everything, older nuns with little use for the more recent trust of the church towards social justice.

The community had voted to accept Sharon, and Mary Dominic had agreed, but she sensed difficulties ahead.

She was interrupted by Sister Angela. "Mother, please come. It's Sharon." Sister Angela was pale.

Mary Dominic rose at once and followed Angela down the long corridor to the novices' wing. It had been built for twenty girls; now there was only Sharon, and three of the older nuns, including Gabriela, who found the stairs to the upper cells difficult.

Sharon seemed to be sleeping peacefully under the single blanket on her straw mattress. On her face was a look of utter peace, as if she were experiencing a splendidly consoling dream. Her hair, not yet cropped, spread thick and dark around her, a rich halo.

"She didn't feel well at lunch-time," Angela said. "I gave her permission to rest in her cell. I looked in on her before going to bed. She doesn't seem to be breathing."

Mary Dominic laid her hand on Sharon's forehead. It was cool.

"I tried to wake her before I came to you," Angela said. Her eyes met Mary Dominic's. Death was no intruder in their lives but only the final earthly tryst of the soul with God. "Send for Dr. Richards and for Father Lowell," Mary Dominic said. "I can't understand it. Sharon seemed like such a healthy girl."

"Perhaps her heart," Sister Angela suggested. "She seemed overcome when we told her she had been accepted. So much excitement. So much joy."

After doctor and priest fulfilled their offices, the community would gather at the bedside with lighted candles and invoke the angels to lead Sharon's soul to paradise. "Shall I call the others now?" Angela asked.

Some instinct prompted Mary Dominic to say, "Not just yet, sister. We'll wait for the doctor."

Dr. Richards was a distant cousin of Mary Dominic's, a distinguished physician with well-to-do patients. He made himself available to the nuns out of kindness and the strong sense of kinship that had always united the family. When he left Sharon's cell, his face was as gray as his hair.

"I'm afraid this is a police matter," he told his cousin. "There has to be an autopsy." And as Mary Dominic stared at him, uncomprehending, he added gently, "There's a bullet graze beneath the left ear."

"Police?" Only years of searching every event for the will of God kept Mary Dominic's voice under control. She was thinking of the nuns. Vincent would be difficult. Gabriela and some of the older nuns would be frightened into fits. "Are you saying a shot killed her? Sharon was murdered here, in a house of prayer?"

"It may have been an accident," Richards said. "One of the neighborhood kids trying target practice from the wall. Would you prefer to call the police yourself, or would you like me to do it for you?"

"You, please," Mary Dominic said. She wasn't sure she would be coherent if she phoned.

Police calls were common in the neighborhood, but never before at the convent of the Daughters of Elias. Medical examiner, photographer, technicians, investigators—a nightmare. The nuns must be questioned and the retreatants as well, according to Sergeant Mike Maguire.

"I would like to protect the community as much as possible," Mary Dominic said in her most charming manner. "Some of the nuns are quite elderly—"

She didn't expect to be rounded on like a common criminal by that redheaded upstart of a sergeant. "I know who you are, Mary Dominic Hughes. I know your father was ambassador to France. Your uncle is a congressman. One of your brothers is married to a Hollywood superstar and one of your sisters to a European prince. None of it matters to me. I'm here to find a killer and I won't let you charm me or bribe me out of it."

Mary Dominic wasn't often taken aback, but Mike Maguire had managed it. "Surely you don't think one of us is a murderer."

"I keep an open mind until all the evidence is in," Mike said like a defiant schoolboy. "One of you may have seen or heard something we should know."

The nuns tried hard to remain serene and cooperative, but as Mary Dominic had feared, the older ones were terribly upset, and Clare Francis, the cook, asked if she might do some extra baking to calm her nerves. "I can't settle, Mother," she complained, "and I know I won't sleep. I might as well be useful."

They might have managed without difficulty if there had been only one questioning, but Mike Maguire's parting words were "I'll be back."

It was midnight when Mary Dominic climbed the staircase to her third floor cell and found Sharon's letter. Often newly accepted members found themselves overwhelmed with feelings of unworthiness, or a terrible longing to return to the world, and shared this in imprudent letters that Mary Dominic later returned after long discussions. She expected Sharon's to be of that kind and would have waited to read it until morning except for the circumstances of her death.

She read quickly. Then she folded the letter and put it back in the envelope. Mike Maguire should be told, she knew, but she didn't want him using Sharon's history to intimidate the community. Whatever the girl had been, during her months with the Daughters of Elias God had touched her heart. She had behaved well, in defiance of her past. She had been loved. Mary Dominic could imagine Mike Maguire using Sharon's history as a bludgeon to assault everything the community believed in. She was determined to prevent it. And she knew more than Mike Maguire— she knew the motive.

"It's absurd to think one of us harmed Sister Sharon," she told the community early the next day, choosing her words to jog their memories without alarming them. "It's almost as absurd to think one of our retreatants could have acted so wrongfully. But people do make enemies, and it's possible that someone who disliked Sister Sharon or bore her a grudge could have come here pretending to be a retreatant. I think it would be wise for us to consider everything that happened yesterday. If any of you recall something out of the ordinary, no matter how small or how remote it may seem, I wish to be told."

She had hardly left for her office than Sister Vincent hurried after her. "Mother," she gasped. "I forgot to give you Zebulon's message." And Vincent poured out her tale. "It sounded so farfetched, I was sure he'd seen it on television. A woman shooting one of the nuns, indeed!"

A woman? From Sharon's letter, Mary Dominic would have expected a man.

And then she remembered Gabriela's shaving woman.

"Sister Vincent, ask the community to pray for a speedy conclusion to this matter," she said. "Please ask Sister Gabriela to come to my office, and tell Zebulon I'd like to see him this afternoon."

When Gabriela arrived at the office, her radiant smile once more in evidence despite the upset of having the police in and out, Mary Dominic asked, "That woman you spoke of to me yesterday, Mrs. Prestavolta. Did you see her face clearly?"

Gabriela's smile dimmed. "Oh, yes, Mother. I noticed her when she registered—such a terrible face. So empty. There was no peace in that face, Mother. No joy. And I saw her clearly while she was shaving. Her back was to me but her face was reflected in the mirror. Fortunately I was standing out of range of the mirror or she would have noticed me." Gabriela's smile faded entirely. "I felt bad that she left without wanting any spiritual direction."

"Could you draw her face, do you think?"

"Yes, of course, Mother."

"I would like you to do so. And also draw the face of our foundress from her portrait in the upper hallway. And one other, of your own choosing. Then I would like you to draw the same faces, but with men's haircuts. And then once again, with men's haircuts and beards. Could you have the drawings ready by lunchtime?"

"Yes, Mother, if I don't labor over them."

"They needn't be finished to perfection," Mary Dominic said, "as long as the features are recognizable."

Gabriela nodded and left at once to execute her task. There was something to be said for pre-Vatican II training, Mary Dominic thought. No question, no argument, no hesitation— just a simple "Yes." Gabriela probably didn't even wonder why she had been asked to make the drawings. If she did wonder, she would most likely assume it was a kind of penance for her "sin" of the day before.

Mary Dominic had the drawings when Mike Maguire showed up that afternoon. She greeted him with a beautiful smile. "Before we call the community for questioning, something has been brought to my attention that I think you should share."

"I'm not in the mood for games, sister," Mike said, glowering at her from his six foot four height. "Once upon a time I might have agreed that all nuns were angels. Now I know better. They're just people, and people are capable of surprising things."

"Once upon a time," Mary Dominic echoed softly. "Does that mean you no longer believe in God?"

Mike glared. "That has nothing to do with this investigation."

"I see." Mary Dominic made a mental note to put Mike Maguire on the prayer list. "Mr. Maguire, one of the sisters came to me with a fantastic tale. One of the neighborhood children apparently saw the shooting. He's waiting in the parlor. I haven't heard his story yet. I thought you'd like to be present." She swept out with great dignity, leaving Mike to follow.

Zebulon was waiting in a rose-colored Queen Anne chair, a platter of chocolate chip cookies and a pitcher of lemonade at his side and a beatific expression on his face. He rose when Mary Dominic entered and cast a curious look at Mike. "Is he police?" he asked Mary Dominic.

"Yes, Zebulon. This is Sergeant Mike Maguire. Sergeant, meet Zebulon, one of our friends. Now if you'll tell me what you told Sister Vincent, Zeb—"

Zebulon enjoyed telling his tale. He had seen it all; the grayhaired woman checking her surroundings, aiming and firing the gun, hiding it afterwards in her purse.

"She didn't see me. I was in a tree up high," Zeb confided. "When I saw her aim the gun, I scooted down. She saw me after she put the gun away, but I ran." He frowned. "That was a funny kind of lady."

"Most ladies don't shoot people," Mary Dominic agreed.

"Different funny," Zebulon persisted. "If I could take some of these cookies home with me, I might remember more."

"You may take all of them," Mary Dominic agreed. "What was funny about the lady?"

"The pocketbook. She held it funny. Like she wasn't used to having one."

Mike Maguire was letting Mary Dominic run the show. "Zebulon, I have some pictures here I'd like you to look at. "She unfolded the drawings of women. Gabriela had included St. Therese as her choice. Mary Dominic held back a chuckle. It was probably the first time the saint had been included in a rogues' gallery.

Zebulon stabbed Mrs. Prestavolta's picture instantly. "That's her! That's the lady with the gun."

"Thank you, Zeb. Now, Mr. Maguire, if you'd care to look at these—" and Mary Dominic showed him the men's pictures, three clean-shaven, three bearded. He passed over St. Therese and the foundress. The drawings of "Mrs. Prestavolta" held his attention.

"You know him," Mary Dominic guessed.

He looked as if he'd like to swear. Instead he said, "Everyone knows him. Frank 'Ouzo' Ferrante. A dozen aliases. Suspected of numerous crimes. I don't think we can nail him. He's slippery."

"Zebulon, please show the sergeant Mrs. Prestavolta's picture."

Zeb was pleased to do so, and even more pleased to be dismissed with the bulging bag of cookies clutched safely in his hand.

"Prestavolta-Ouzo shot Sister Sharon, it seems." Mary Dominic handed Maguire Sharon's letter. "And this explains why."

"The bullet itself didn't kill her," Mike said. "She was poisoned by it. It was treated with nicotine. A single drop of the pure stuff is lethal." He thrust his fingers through his hair, standing it up like a peacock's tail. "Where did you get the drawings?"

"Our Sister Gabriela is a talented artist. She doesn't know her Mrs. Prestavolta is a man. Perhaps now you might not need to question the whole community again today? And the retreatants might be allowed to leave?"

Mike knew when he was licked. "I'll want to see this Sister Gabriela and Sister Vincent. That should do it."

"We've been asking God to provide a speedy solution," Mary Dominic said. She had remembered Mike Maguire when he ruffled his hair. He had been altar boy at her father's funeral twenty years before.

"In my book, a real God would blast that scum off the face of the earth," he said.

"'Let the wheat and tares grow up together until the harvest,'" Mary Dominic reminded him, "'lest in pulling up the tares, the young wheat come, too.'"

The second questioning went far more graciously then the first. Mike Maguire and Mary Dominic parted on sufficiently friendly terms for him to call her several weeks later.

"I guess there's some kind of justice in the world after all," he said. "Ouzo was killed in a freak accident. A bridge he was traveling on alone collapsed under him. No one else was hurt."

"Indeed," Mary Dominic murmured. Mike cleared his throat.

"I was wondering if you nuns had been praying about it."

Mary Dominic smiled. "We always pray for God's mercy," she said.

THE STRIPPER

Anthony Boucher

He was called Jack the Stripper because the only witness who had seen him and lived (J.F. Flugelbach, 1463 N. Edgemont) had described the glint of moonlight on bare skin. The nickname was inevitable.

Mr. Flugelbach had stumbled upon the fourth of the murders, the one in the grounds of City College. He had not seen enough to be of any help to the police; but at least he had furnished a name for the killer heretofore known by such routine cognomens as "butcher," "werewolf," and "vampire."

The murders in themselves were enough to make a newspaper's fortune. They were frequent, bloody, and pointless,

"Anthony Boucher" was the pseudonym of William Anthony Parker White (1911–1968), a remarkable writer, editor, and critic who was equally at home in the mystery and science fiction fields, as well as in the world of opera. It's to be hoped that one day his two novels and three short stories about Sister Ursula will be collected in a single volume. "The Stripper" is the best of the short stories, with an ecclesiastic clue to the killer's identity. Boucher was a committed Catholic and a lay reader at Sunday Mass during the years before his death. His science fiction writing also reflected his deeply felt Catholicism, especially in one of his best stories, "The Quest for St. Aquin."

since neither theft nor rape was attempted. The murderer was no specialist, like the original Jack, but rather an eclectic, like Kürten the Düsseldorf Monster, who struck when the mood was on him and disregarded age and sex. This indiscriminate taste made better copy; the menace threatened not merely a certain class of unfortunates but every reader.

It was the nudity, however, and the nickname evolved from it, that made the cause truly celebrated. Feature writers dug up all the legends of naked murderers—Courvoisier of London, Durrant of San Francisco, Wallace of Liverpool, Borden of Fall River—and printed them as sober fact, explaining at length the advantages of avoiding the evidence of bloodstains.

When he read this explanation, he always smiled. It was plausible, but irrelevant. The real reason for nakedness was simply that it felt better that way. When the color of things began to change, his first impulse was to get rid of his clothing. He supposed that psychoanalysts could find some atavistic reason for that.

He felt the cold air on his naked body. He had never noticed that before. Noiselessly he pushed the door open and tiptoed into the study. His hand did not waver as he raised the knife.

The Stripper case was Lieutenant Marshall's baby, and he was going nuts. His condition was not helped by the constant allusions of his colleagues to the fact that his wife had once been a stripper of a more pleasurable variety. Six murders in three months, without a single profitable lead, had reduced him to a state where a lesser man might have gibbered, and sometimes he thought it would be simpler to be a lesser man.

He barked into phones nowadays. He hardly apologized when he realized that his caller was Sister Ursula, that surprising nun who had once planned to be a policewoman and who had extricated him from several extraordinary cases. But that was just it; those had been extraordinary, freak locked-room problems, while this was the horrible epitome of ordinary, clueless, plotless murder. There was no room in the Stripper case for the talents of Sister Ursula.

He was in a hurry and her sentences hardly penetrated his mind until he caught the word "Stripper." Then he said sharply, "So? Backtrack please, Sister. I'm afraid I wasn't listening."

"He says," her quiet voice repeated, "that he thinks he knows who the Stripper is, but he hasn't enough proof. He'd like to talk to the police about it; and since he knows I know you, he asked me to arrange it, so that you wouldn't think him just a crank."

"Which," said Marshall, "he probably is. But to please you, Sister . . . What did you say his name is?"

"Flecker. Harvey Flecker. Professor of Latin at the University."

Marshall caught his breath. "Coincidence," he said flatly. "I'm on my way to see him now."

"Oh. Then he did get in touch with you himself?"

"Not with me," said Marshall. "With the Stripper."

"God rest his soul . . ." Sister Ursula murmured.

"So. I'm on my way now. If you could meet me there and bring this letter—"

"Lieutenant, I know our order is a singularly liberal one, but still I doubt if Reverend Mother—"

"You're a material witness," Marshall said authoritatively. "I'll send a car for you. And don't forget the letter."

Sister Ursula hung up and sighed. She had liked Professor Flecker, both for his scholarly wit and for his quiet kindliness. He was the only man who could hold his agnostic own with Father Pearson in disputatious sophistry, and he was also the man who had helped keep the Order's soup-kitchen open at the depth of the depression.

She took up her breviary and began to read the office for the dead while she waited for the car.

"It is obvious," Professor Lowe enunciated, "that the Stripper is one of the three of us."

Hugo Ellis said, "Speak for yourself." His voice cracked a little, and he seemed even younger than he looked.

Professor de' Cassis said nothing. His huge hunchbacked body crouched in the corner and he mourned his friend.

"So?" said Lieutenant Marshall. "Go on, Professor."

"It was by pure chance," Professor Lowe continued, his lean face alight with logical satisfaction, "that the back door was latched last night. We have been leaving it unfastened for Mrs. Carey since she lost her key; but Flecker must have forgotten that fact and inadvertently reverted to habit. Ingress by the front door was impossible, since it was not only secured by a spring lock but also bolted from within. None of the windows shows any sign of external tampering. The murderer presumably counted upon the back door to make plausible the entrance of an intruder; but Flecker had accidentally secured it, and that accident," he concluded impressively, "will strap the Tripper."

Hugo Ellis laughed, and then looked ashamed of himself.

Marshall laughed too. "Setting aside the Spoonerism, Professor, your statement of the conditions is flawless. This house was locked tight as a drum. Yes, the Stripper is one of the three of you." It wasn't amusing when Marshall said it.

Professor de' Cassis raised his despondent head. "But why?" His voice was guttural. "Why?"

Hugo Ellis said, "Why? With a madman?"

Professor Lowe lifted one finger as though emphasizing a point in a lecture. "Ah, but is this a madman's crime? There is the point. When the Stripper kills a stranger, yes, he is mad. When he kills a man with whom he lives . . . may he not be applying the technique of his madness to the purpose of his sanity?"

"It's an idea," Marshall admitted. "I can see where there's going to be some advantage in having a psychologist among the witnesses. But there's another witness I'm even more anxious to—" His face lit up as Sergeant Raglan came in. "She's here, Rags?"

"Yeah," said Raglan. "It's the sister. Holy smoke, Loot, does this mean this is gonna be another screwy one?"

Marshall had said *she* and Raglan had said *the sister*. These facts may serve as sufficient characterization of Sister Felicitas, who had accompanied her. They were always a pair, yet always spoken of in the singular. Now Sister Felicitas dozed in the corner where the hunchback had crouched, and Marshall read and reread the letter which seemed like the posthumous utterance of the Stripper's latest victim:

My dear Sister:

I have reason to fear that someone close to me is Jack the Stripper.

You know me, I trust, too well to think me a sensationalist striving to be a star witness. I have grounds for what I say. This individual, whom I shall for the moment call "Quasimodo" for reasons that might particularly appeal to you, first betrayed himself when I noticed a fleck of blood behind his ear—a trifle, but suggestive. Since then I have religiously observed his comings and goings, and found curious coincidences between the absence of Quasimodo and the presence elsewhere of the Stripper.

I have not a conclusive body of evidence, but I believe that I do have sufficient to bring to the attention of the authorities. I have heard you mention a Lieutenant Marshall who is a close friend of yours. If you will recommend me to him as a man whose word is to be taken seriously, I shall be deeply obliged.

I may, of course, be making a fool of myself with my suspicions of Quasimodo, which is why I refrain from giving you his real name. But every man must do what is possible to rid this city *a negotio perambulante in tenebris.*

Yours respectfully,

Harvey Flecker

"He didn't have much to go on, did he?" Marshall observed. "But he was right, God help him. And he may have known more than he cared to trust to a letter. He must have slipped somehow and let Quasimodo see his suspicions. . . . What does that last phrase mean?"

"Lieutenant! And you an Oxford man!" exclaimed Sister Ursula.

"I can translate it. But what's its connotation?"

"It's from St. Jerome's Vulgate of the ninetieth psalm. The Douay version translates it literally: *of the business that walketh about in the dark;* but that doesn't convey the full horror of that nameless prowling *negotium.* It's one of the most terrible phrases I know, and perfect for the Stripper."

"Flecker was a Catholic?"

"No, he was a resolute agnostic, though I have always had hopes that Thomist philosophy would lead him into the Church. I almost think he refrained because his conversion would have left nothing to argue with Father Pearson about. But he was an excellent Church Latinist and knew the liturgy better than most Catholics."

"Do you understand what he means by Quasimodo?"

"I don't know. Allusiveness was typical of Professor Flecker; he delighted in British crossword puzzles, if you see what I mean. But I think I could guess more readily if he had not said that it might particularly appeal to me . . ."

"So? I can see at least two possibilities—"

"But before we try to decode the Professor's message, Lieutenant, tell me what you have learned here. All I know is that the poor man is dead, may he rest in ⌐eace."

Marshall told her. Four university teachers lived in this ancient (for Southern California) two-story house near the Campus. Mrs. Carey came in every day to clean for them and prepare dinner. When she arrived this morning at nine, Lowe and de' Cassis were eating breakfast and Hugo Ellis, the youngest of the group, was out mowing the lawn. They were not concerned over Flecker's absence. He often worked in the study till all hours and sometimes fell asleep there.

Mrs. Carey went about her work. Today was Tuesday, the day for changing the beds and getting the laundry ready. When she had finished that task, she dusted the living room and went on to the study.

The police did not yet have her story of the discovery. Her

scream had summoned the others, who had at once called the police and, sensibly, canceled their classes and waited. When the police arrived, Mrs. Carey was still hysterical. The doctor had quieted her with a hypodermic, from which she had not yet revived.

Professor Flecker had had his throat cut and (Marshall skipped over this hastily) suffered certain other butcheries characteristic of the Stripper. The knife, an ordinary kitchen-knife, had been left by the body as usual. He had died instantly, at approximately one in the morning, when each of the other three men claimed to be asleep.

More evidence than that of the locked doors proved that the Stripper was an inmate of the house. He had kept his feet clear of the blood which bespattered the study, but he had still left a trail of small drops which revealed themselves to the minute police inspection—blood which had bathed his body and dripped off as he left his crime.

This trail led upstairs and into the bathroom, where it stopped. There were traces of watered blood in the bathtub and on one of the towels—Flecker's own.

"Towel?" said Sister Ursula. "But you said Mrs. Carey had made up the laundry bundle."

"She sends out only sheets and such—does the towels herself."

"Oh." The nun sounded disappointed.

"I know how you feel, Sister. You'd welcome a discrepancy anywhere, even in the laundry list. But that's the sum of our evidence. Three suspects, all with opportunity, none with an alibi. Absolutely even distribution of suspicion, and our only guidepost is the word Quasimodo. Do you know any of these three men?"

"I have never met them, Lieutenant, but I feel as though I know them rather well from Professor Flecker's descriptions."

"Good. Let's see what you can reconstruct. First, Ruggiero de' Cassis, professor of mathematics, formerly of the University of Turin, voluntary exile since the early days of Fascism."

Sister Ursula said slowly, "He admired de' Cassis, not only

for his first-rate mind, but because he seemed to have adjusted himself so satisfactorily to life despite his deformity. I remember he said once, 'De' Cassis has never known a woman, yet every day he looks on Beauty bare.'"

"On Beauty . . . ? Oh yes. Millay. *Euclid alone* . . . All right. Now Marvin Lowe, professor of psychology, native of Ohio, and from what I've seen of him a prime pedant. According to Flecker . . . ?"

"I think Professor Lowe amused him. He used to tell us the latest Spoonerisms; he swore that flocks of students graduated from the University believing that modern psychology rested on the researches of two men named Frung and Jeud. Once Lowe said that his favorite book was Max Beerbohm's *Happy Hypocrite*; Professor Flecker insisted that was because it was the only one he could be sure of pronouncing correctly."

"But as a man?"

"He never said much about Lowe personally; I don't think they were intimate. But I do recall his saying, 'Lowe, like all psychologists, is the physician of Greek proverb.'"

"Who was told to heal himself? Makes sense. That speech mannerism certainly points to something a psychiatrist could have fun with. All right. How about Hugo Ellis, instructor in mathematics, native of Los Angeles?"

"Mr. Ellis was a child prodigy, you know. Extraordinary mathematical feats. But he outgrew them, I almost think deliberately. He made himself into a normal young man. Now he is, I gather, a reasonably good young instructor—just run of the mill. An adult with the brilliance which he had as a child might be a great man. Professor Flecker turned the French proverb around to fit him: 'If youth could, if age knew . . .'"

"So. There they are. And which," Marshall asked, "is Quasimodo?"

"Quasimodo . . ." Sister Ursula repeated the word, and other words seemed to follow it automatically. "*Quasimodo geniti infantes* . . ." She paused and shuddered.

"What's the matter?"

"I think," she said softly, "I know. But like Professor

Flecker, I fear making a fool of myself—and worse, I fear
damning an innocent man. . . . Lieutenant, may I look
through this house with you?"

*He sat there staring at the other two and at the policeman watching
them. The body was no longer in the next room, but the blood was. He
had never before revisited the scene of the crime; that notion was the
nonsense of legend. For that matter he had never known his victim.*

*He let his mind go back to last night. Only recently had he been
willing to do this. At first it was something that must be kept apart,
divided from his normal personality. But he was intelligent enough to
realize the danger of that. It could produce a seriously schizoid
personality. He might go mad. Better to attain complete integration,
and that could be accomplished only by frank self-recognition.*

It must be terrible to be mad.

"Well, where to first?" asked Marshall.

"I want to see the bedrooms," said Sister Ursula. "I want to
see if Mrs. Carey changed the sheets."

"You doubt her story? But she's completely out of the—all
right. Come on."

Lieutenant Marshall identified each room for her as they
entered it. Harvey Flecker's bedroom by no means consorted
with the neatness of his mind. It was a welter of papers and
notes and hefty German works on Latin philology and puzzle
books by Torquemada and Caliban and early missals and
codices from the University library. The bed had been changed
and the clean upper sheet was turned back. Harvey Flecker
would never soil it.

Professor de' Cassis's room was in sharp contrast—a chaste
monastic cubicle. His books—chiefly professional works, with a
sampling of Leopardi and Carducci and other Italian poets and
an Italian translation of Thomas à Kempis—were neatly stacked
in a case, and his papers were out of sight. The only ornaments
in the room were a crucifix and a framed picture of a family
group, in clothes of 1920.

Hugo Ellis's room was defiantly, almost parodistically the

room of a normal, healthy college man, even to the University banner over the bed. He had carefully avoided both Flecker's chaos and de' Cassis's austerity; there was a precisely calculated normal litter of pipes and letters and pulp magazines. The pin-up girls seemed to be carrying normality too far, and Sister Ursula averted her eyes.

Each room had a clean upper sheet.

Professor Lowe's room would have seemed as normal as Ellis's, if less spectacularly so, if it were not for the inordinate quantity of books. Shelves covered all wall space that was not taken by door, window, or bed. Psychology, psychiatry, and criminology predominated; but there was a selection of poetry, humor, fiction for any mood.

Marshall took down William Roughead's *Twelve Scots Trials* and said, "Lucky devil! I've never so much as seen a copy of this before." He smiled at the argumentative pencilings in the margins. Then as he went to replace it, he saw through the gap that there was a second row of books behind. Paperbacks. He took one out and put it back hastily. "You wouldn't want to see that, Sister. But it might fit into that case we were proposing about repressions and word-distortions."

Sister Ursula seemed not to heed him. She was standing by the bed and said, "Come here."

Marshal came and looked at the freshly made bed.

Sister Ursula passed her hand over the mended but clean lower sheet. "Do you see?"

"See what?"

"The answer," she said.

Marshall frowned. "Look, Sister—"

"Lieutenant, your wife is one of the most efficient house-keepers I've ever known. I thought she had, to some extent, indoctrinated you. Think. Try to think with Leona's mind."

Marshall thought. Then his eyes narrowed and he said, "So . . ."

"It is fortunate," Sister Ursula said, "that the Order of Martha of Bethany specializes in housework."

Marshall went out and called downstairs. "Raglan! See if the laundry's been picked up from the back porch."

The Sergeant's voice came back. "It's gone, Loot. I thought there wasn't no harm—"

"Then get on the phone quick and tell them to hold it."

"But what laundry, Loot?"

Marshal muttered. Then he turned to Sister Ursula. "The men won't know of course, but we'll find a bill somewhere. Anyway, we won't need that till the preliminary hearing. We've got enough now to settle Quasimodo."

He heard the Lieutenant's question and repressed a startled gesture. He had not thought of that. But even if they traced the laundry, it would be valueless as evidence without Mrs. Carey's testimony . . .

He saw at once what had to be done.

They had taken Mrs. Carey to the guest room, that small downstairs bedroom near the kitchen which must have been a maid's room when this was a large family house. There were still police posted outside the house, but only Raglan and the lieutenant inside.

It was so simple. His mind, he told himself, had never been functioning more clearly. No nonsense about stripping this time; it was not for pleasure. Just be careful to avoid those crimson jets. . . .

The Sergeant wanted to know where he thought he was going. He told him.

Raglan grinned. "You should've raised your hand. A teacher like you ought to know that."

He went to the back porch toilet, opened and closed its door without going in. Then he went to the kitchen and took the second best knife. The best had been used last night.

It would not take a minute. Then he would be safe and later when the body was found what could they prove? The others had been out of the room too.

But as he touched the knife it began to happen. Something came from the blade up his arm and into his head. He was in a hurry, there was no time—but holding the knife, the color of things began to change. . . .

He was half naked when Marshall found him.

Sister Ursula leaned against the jamb of the kitchen door. She felt sick. Marshall and Raglan were both strong men, but they needed help to subdue him. His face was contorted into an unrecognizable mask like a demon from a Japanese tragedy. She clutched the crucifix of the rosary that hung at her waist and murmured a prayer to the Archangel Michael. For it was not the physical strength of the man that frightened her, not the glint of his knife, but the pure quality of incarnate evil that radiated from him and made the doctrine of possession a real terror.

As she finished her prayer, Marshall's fist connected with his jaw and he crumpled. So did Sister Ursula.

"I don't know what you think of me," Sister Ursula said as Marshall drove her home. (Sister Felicitas was dozing in the back seat.) "I'm afraid I couldn't ever have been a policewoman after all."

"You'll do," Marshall said. "And if you feel better now, I'd like to run over it with you. I've got to get my brilliant deductions straight for the press."

"The fresh air feels good. Go ahead."

"I've got the sheet business down pat, I think. In ordinary middle-class households you don't change both sheets every week; Leona never does, I remembered. You put on a clean upper sheet, and the old upper sheet becomes the lower. The other three bedrooms each had one clean sheet—the upper. His had two—upper and lower; therefore his upper sheet had been stained in some unusual way and had to be changed. The hasty bath, probably in the dark, had been careless, and there was some blood left to stain the sheet. Mrs. Carey wouldn't have thought anything of it at the time because she hadn't found the body yet. Right?"

"Perfect, Lieutenant."

"So. But now about Quasimodo . . . I still don't get it. He's the one it *couldn't* apply to. Either of the others—"

"Yes?"

"Well, who is Quasimodo? He's the Hunchback of Notre Dame. So it could mean the deformed de' Cassis. Who wrote Quasimodo? Victor Hugo. So it could be Hugo Ellis. But it wasn't either; and how in heaven's name could it mean Professor Lowe?"

"Remember, Lieutenant: Professor Flecker said this was an allusion that might particularly appeal to me. Now I am hardly noted for my devotion to the anticlerical prejudices of Hugo's *Notre-Dame de Paris*. What is the common meeting-ground of my interests and Professor Flecker's?"

"Church liturgy?" Marshall ventured.

"And why was your Quasimodo so named? Because he was born—or found or christened, I forget which—on the Sunday after Easter. Many Sundays, as you may know, are often referred to by the first work of their introits, the beginning of the proper of the Mass. As the fourth Sunday in Lent is called *Laetare* Sunday, or the third in Advent *Gaudete* Sunday. So the Sunday after Easter is known as *Quasimodo* Sunday, from its introit *Quasimodo geniti infantes* . . . 'As newborn babes.'"

"But I still don't see— "

"The Sunday after Easter," said Sister Ursula, "is more usually referred to as *Low* Sunday."

"Oh," said Marshall. After a moment he added reflectively, "*The Happy Hypocrite* . . ."

"You see that too? Beerbohm's story is about a man who assumes a mask of virtue to conceal his depravity. A schizoid allegory. I wonder if Professor Lowe dreamed that he might find the same happy ending."

Marshall drove on a bit in silence. Then he said, "He said a strange thing while you were out."

"I feel as though he were already dead," said Sister Ursula. "I want to say, 'God rest his soul.' We should have a special office for the souls of the mad."

"That cues into my story. The boys were taking him away

and I said to Rags, 'Well, this is once the insanity plea justifies itself. He'll never see the gas chamber.' And he turned on me—he'd quieted down by then—and said, 'Nonsense, sir! Do you think I would cast doubt on my sanity merely to save my life?'"

"Mercy," said Sister Ursula. At first Marshall thought it was just an exclamation. Then he looked at her face and saw that she was not talking to him.

THE ORACLE
OF THE DOG

G. K. Chesterton

🐾 "Yes," said Father Brown, "I always like a
dog so long as he isn't spelt backwards."

Those who are quick in talking are not always quick in
listening. Sometimes even their brilliancy produces a sort of
stupidity. Father Brown's friend and companion was a young
man with a stream of ideas and stories, an enthusiastic young
man named Fiennes, with eager blue eyes and blond hair that
seemed to be brushed back, not merely with a hairbrush, but
with the wind of the world as he rushed through it. But he
stopped in the torrent of his talk in a momentary bewilderment
before he saw the priest's very simple meaning.

Though he did not formally join the Catholic Church until eleven years
after the first Father Brown book appeared, it could be truly said that
G. K. Chesterton (1874-1936) was a Catholic writer all his life. I am not
alone in considering "The Oracle of the Dog" from *The Incredulity of
Father Brown* to be the best of the Father Brown tales, although some
earlier stories also have their supporters. Here Chesterton presents us
with both an impossible murder and the seemingly supernatural
behavior of a dog, with a cleverly constructed solution in which one
explains the other. In a way it is also one of his most religious stories,
with a blending of paradox and puzzle that is uniquely Chestertonian.

"You mean that people make too much of them?" he said. "Well, I don't know. They're marvellous creatures. Sometimes I think they know a lot more than we do."

Father Brown said nothing, but continued to stroke the head of the big retriever in a half-abstracted but apparently soothing fashion.

"Why," said Fiennes, warming again to his monologue, "there was a dog in the case I've come to see you about; what they call the 'Invisible Murder Case,' you know. It's a strange story, but from my point of view the dog is about the strangest thing in it. Of course, there's the mystery of the crime itself, and how old Druce can have been killed by somebody else when he was all alone in the summer house—"

The hand stroking the dog stopped for a moment in its rhythmic movement; and Father Brown said calmly, "Oh, it was a summer house, was it?"

"I thought you'd read all about it in the papers," answered Fiennes. "Stop a minute; I believe I've got a cutting that will give you all the particulars." He produced a strip of newspaper from his pocket and handed it to the priest, who began to read it, holding it close to his blinking eyes with one hand while the other continued its half-conscious caress of the dog. It looked like the parable of a man not letting his right hand know what his left hand did.

Many mystery stories, about men murdered behind locked doors and windows, and murderers escaping without means of entrance and exit, have come true in the course of the extraordinary events at Cranston on the coast of Yorkshire, where Colonel Druce was found stabbed from behind by a dagger that has entirely disappeared from the scene, and apparently even from the neighbourhood.

The summer house in which he died was indeed accessible at one entrance, the ordinary doorway which looked down the central walk of the garden towards the house. But by a combination of events almost to be called a coincidence, it appears that both the path and the entrance were watched during the crucial time, and there is a chain of witnesses who confirm each other. The summer house stands at the extreme end of the garden, where there is no exit or entrance of any kind. The central garden path is a lane between two ranks of tall delphiniums, planted so close that any stray step off the path would leave its traces; and both path and plants run right up to the very mouth of the summer house, so that no straying from the straight path could fail to be observed, and no other mode of entrance can be imagined.

Patrick Floyd, secretary of the murdered man, testified that he had been in a position to overlook the whole garden from the time when Colonel Druce last appeared alive in the doorway to the time when he was found dead; as he, Floyd, had been on the top of a stepladder clipping the garden hedge. Janet Druce, the dead man's daughter, confirmed this, saying that she had sat on the terrace of the house throughout that time and had seen Floyd at his work. Touching some part of the time, this is again supported by Donald Druce, her brother, who overlooked the garden standing at his bedroom window in his dressing gown, for he had risen late. Lastly the account is consistent with that given by Dr. Valentine, a neighbour, who called for a time to talk with Miss Druce on the terrace, and by the colonel's solicitor, Mr. Aubrey Traill, who was apparently the last to see the murdered man alive—presumably with the exception of the murderer.

All are agreed that the course of events was as follows: about half past three in the afternoon, Miss Druce went down the path to ask her father when he would like tea; but he said he did not want any and was waiting to see Traill, his lawyer, who was to be sent to him in the summer house. The girl then came away and met Traill coming down the path; she directed him to her father and he went in as directed. About half an hour afterwards he came out again, the colonel coming with him to the door and showing himself to all appearance in health and even high spirits. He had been somewhat annoyed earlier in the day by his son's irregular hours, but seemed to recover his temper in a perfectly normal fashion, and had been rather markedly genial in receiving other visitors, including two of his nephews who came over for the day. But as these were out walking during the whole period of the tragedy, they had no evidence to give. It is said, indeed, that the colonel was not on very good terms with Dr. Valentine, but that gentleman only had a brief interview with the daughter of the house, to whom he is supposed to be paying serious attentions.

Traill, the solicitor, says he left the colonel entirely alone in the summer house, and this is confirmed by Floyd's bird's-eye view of the garden, which showed nobody else passing the only entrance. Ten minutes later Miss Druce again went down the garden and had not reached the end of the path when she saw her father, who was conspicuous by his white linen coat, lying in a heap on the floor. She uttered a scream which brought others to the spot, and on entering the place they found the colonel lying dead beside his basket-chair, which was also upset. Dr. Valentine, who was still in the immediate neighbourhood, testified that the wound was made by some sort of stiletto, entering under the shoulder blade and piercing the heart. The police have searched the neighbourhood for such a weapon, but no trace of it can be found.

"So Colonel Druce wore a white coat, did he?" said Father Brown as he put down the paper.

"Trick he learnt in the tropics," replied Fiennes with some wonder. "He'd had some queer adventures there, by his own account; and I fancy his dislike of Valentine was connected with the doctor coming from the tropics too. But it's all an infernal puzzle. The account there is pretty accurate; I didn't see the tragedy, in the sense of the discovery; I was out walking with the young nephews and the dog—the dog I wanted to tell you about. But I saw the stage set for it as described: the straight lane between the blue flowers right up to the dark entrance, and the lawyer going down it in his blacks and his silk hat, and the red head of the secretary showing high above the green hedge as he worked on it with his shears. Nobody could have mistaken that red head at any distance; and if people say they saw it there all the time, you may be sure they did. This red-haired secretary Floyd is quite a character: breathless, bounding sort of fellow, always doing everybody's work as he was doing the gardener's. I think he is an American; he's certainly got the American way of life; what they call the viewpoint, bless 'em."

"What about the lawyer?" asked Father Brown.

There was a silence and then Fiennes spoke quite slowly for him. "Traill struck me as a singular man. In his fine black clothes he was almost foppish, yet you can hardly call him fashionable. For he wore a pair of long, luxuriant black whiskers such as haven't been seen since Victorian times. He had rather a fine grave face and a fine grave manner, but every now and then he seemed to remember to smile. And when he showed his white teeth he seemed to lose a little of his dignity and there was something faintly fawning about him. It may have been only embarrassment, for he would also fidget with his cravat and his tiepin, which were at once handsome and unusual, like himself. If I could think of anybody—but what's the good, when the whole thing's impossible? Nobody knows who did it. Nobody knows how it could be done. At least there's only one exception I'd make, and that's why I really mentioned the whole thing. The dog knows."

Father Brown sighed and then said absently, "You were there as a friend of young Donald, weren't you? He didn't go on your walk with you?"

"No," replied Fiennes, smiling. "The young scoundrel had gone to bed that morning and got up that afternoon. I went with his cousins, two young officers from India, and our conversation was trivial enough. I remember the elder, whose name I think is

Herbert Druce and who is an authority on horse breeding, talked about nothing but a mare he had bought and the moral character of the man who sold her; while his brother Harry seemed to be brooding on his bad luck at Monte Carlo. I only mention it to show you, in the light of what happened on our walk, that there was nothing psychic about us. The dog was the only mystic in our company."

"What sort of a dog was he?" asked the priest.

"Same breed as that one," answered Fiennes. "That's what started me off on the story, your saying you didn't believe in believing in a dog. He's a big black retriever named Nox, and a suggestive name too; for I think what he did a darker mystery than the murder. You know Druce's house and garden are by the sea; we walked about a mile from it along the sands and then turned back, going the other way. We passed a rather curious rock called the Rock of Fortune, famous in the neighbourhood because it's one of those examples of one stone barely balanced on another, so that a touch would knock it over. It is not really very high, but the hanging outline of it makes it look a little wild and sinister; at least it made it look so to me, for I don't imagine my jolly young companions were afflicted with the picturesque. But it may be that I was beginning to feel an atmosphere; for just then the question arose of whether it was time to go back to tea, and even then I think I had a premonition that time counted for a good deal in the business. Neither Herbert Druce nor I had a watch, so we called out to his brother, who was some paces behind, having stopped to light his pipe under the hedge. Hence it happened that he shouted out the hour, which was twenty past four, in his big voice through the growing twilight; and somehow the loudness of it made it sound like the proclamation of something tremendous. His unconsciousness seemed to make it all the more so; but that was always the way with omens; and particular ticks of the clock were really very ominous things that afternoon. According to Dr. Valentine's testimony, poor Druce had actually died just about half past four.

"Well, they said we needn't go home for ten minutes and we walked a little farther along the sands, doing nothing in particular—throwing stones for the dog and throwing sticks into the sea for him to swim after. But to me the twilight seemed to grow oddly oppressive and the very shadow of the top-heavy Rock of Fortune lay on me like a load. And then the curious thing happened. Nox had just brought back Herbert's walking stick out of the sea and his brother had thrown his in also. The dog swam out again, but just about what must have been the stroke of the half hour, he stopped swimming. He came back again on to the shore and stood in front of us. Then he suddenly threw up his head and sent up a howl or wail of woe, if ever I heard one in the world.

"What the devil's the matter with the dog?" asked Herbert; but none of us could answer. There was a long silence after the brute's wailing and whining died away on the desolate shore; and then the silence was broken. As I live, it was broken by a faint and far-off shriek, like the shriek of a woman from beyond the hedges inland. We didn't know what it was then; but we knew afterwards. It was the cry the girl gave when she first saw the body of her father."

"You went back, I suppose," said Father Brown patiently. "What happened then?"

"I'll tell you what happened then," said Fiennes with a grim emphasis. "When we got back into that garden the first thing we saw was Traill the lawyer; I can see him now with his black hat and black whiskers relieved against the perspective of the blue flowers stretching down to the summer house, with the sunset and the strange outline of the Rock of Fortune in the distance. His face and figure were in shadow against the sunset; but I swear the white teeth were showing in his head and he was smiling.

"The moment Nox saw that man, the dog dashed forward and stood in the middle of the path barking at him madly, murderously, volleying out curses that were almost verbal in their dreadful distinctness of hatred. And the man doubled up and fled along the path between the flowers."

Father Brown sprang to his feet with a startling impatience.

"So the dog denounced him, did he?" he cried. "The oracle

of the dog condemned him. Did you see what birds were flying, and are you sure whether they were on the right hand or the left? Did you consult the augers about the sacrifices? Surely you didn't omit to cut open the dog and examine his entrails. That is the sort of scientific test you heathen humanitarians seem to trust, when you are thinking of taking away the life and honour of a man."

Fiennes sat gaping for an instant before he found breath to say, "Why, what's the matter with you? What have I done now?"

A sort of anxiety came back into the priest's eyes—the anxiety of a man who has run against a post in the dark and wonders for a moment whether he has hurt it.

"I'm most awfully sorry," he said with sincere distress. "I beg your pardon for being so rude; pray forgive me."

Fiennes looked at him curiously. "I sometimes think you are more of a mystery than any of the mysteries," he said. "But anyhow, if you don't believe in the mystery of the dog, at least you can't get over the mystery of the man. You can't deny that at the very moment when the beast came back from the sea and bellowed, his master's soul was driven out of his body by the blow of some unseen power that no mortal man can trace or even imagine. And as for the lawyer, I don't go only by the dog; there are other curious details too. He struck me as a smooth, smiling, equivocal sort of person; and one of his tricks seemed like a sort of hint. You know the doctor and the police were on the spot very quickly; Valentine was brought back when walking away from the house, and he telephoned instantly. That, with the secluded house, small numbers, and enclosed space, made it pretty possible to search everybody who could have been near; and everybody was thoroughly searched—for a weapon. The whole house, garden, and shore were combed for a weapon. The disappearance of the dagger is almost as crazy as the disappearance of the man."

"The disappearance of the dagger," said Father Brown, nodding. He seemed to have become suddenly attentive.

"Well," continued Fiennes, "I told you that man Traill had

a trick of fidgeting with his tie and tiepin— especially his tiepin. His pin, like himself, was at once showy and old-fashioned. It had one of those stones with concentric coloured rings that look like an eye; and his own concentration on it got on my nerves, as if he had been a Cyclops with one eye in the middle of his body. But the pin was not only large but long; and it occurred to me that his anxiety about its adjustment was because it was even longer than it looked; as long as a stiletto in fact."

Father Brown nodded thoughtfully. "Was any other instrument ever suggested?" he asked.

"There was another suggestion," answered Fiennes, "from one of the young Druces—the cousins, I mean. Neither Herbert nor Harry Druce would have struck one at first as likely to be of assistance in scientific detection; but while Herbert was really the traditional type of heavy dragoon, caring for nothing but horses and being an ornament to the Horse Guards, his younger brother Harry had been in the Indian Police and knew something about such things. Indeed in his own way he was quite clever; and I rather fancy he had been too clever; I mean he had left the police through breaking some red-tape regulations and taking some sort of risk and responsibility of his own. Anyhow, he was in some sense a detective out of work, and threw himself in this business with more than the ardour of an amateur. And it was with him that I had an argument about the weapon—an argument that led to something new. It began by his countering my description of the dog barking at Traill; and he said that a dog at his worst didn't bark, but growled."

"He was quite right there," observed the priest.

"This young fellow went on to say that, if it came to that, he'd heard Nox growling at other people before then; and among others at Floyd the secretary. I retorted that his own argument answered itself; for the crime couldn't be brought home to two or three people, and least of all to Floyd, who was as innocent as a harum-scarum schoolboy, and had been seen by everybody all the time perched above the garden hedge with his fan of red hair as conspicuous as a scarlet cockatoo. 'I know there's difficulties anyhow,' said my colleague, 'but I wish you'd come with me down the garden a minute. I want to show you something I don't think anyone else has seen.' This was on the very day of the discovery, and the garden was just as it had been: the stepladder was still standing by the hedge, and just under the hedge my guide stooped and disentangled something from the deep grass. It was the shears used for clipping the hedge, and on the point of one of them was a smear of blood."

There was a short silence, and then Father Brown said suddenly, "What was the lawyer there for?"

"He told us the colonel sent for him to alter his will," answered Fiennes. "And, by the way, there was another thing about the business of the will that I ought to mention. You see, the will wasn't actually signed in the summer house that afternoon."

"I suppose not," said Father Brown; "there would have to be two witnesses."

"The lawyer actually came down the day before and it was signed then; but he was sent for again next day because the old man had a doubt about one of the witnesses and had to be reassured."

"Who were the witnesses?" asked Father Brown.

"That's just the point," replied his informant eagerly, "the witnesses were Floyd the secretary and this Dr. Valentine, the foreign sort of surgeon or whatever he is; and the two had a quarrel. Now I'm bound to say that the secretary is something of a busybody. He's one of those hot and headlong people whose warmth of temperament has unfortunately turned mostly to pugnacity and bristling suspicion; to distrusting people instead of to trusting them. That sort of red-haired red-hot fellow is always either universally credulous or universally incredulous; and sometimes both. He was not only a jack-of-all-trades, but he knew better than all tradesmen. He not only knew everything, but he warned everybody against everybody. All that must be taken into account in his suspicions about Valentine; but in that particular case there seems to have been something behind it. He said the name of Valentine was not really Valentine. He said he had seen him elsewhere known by the name of De Villon. He said it would invalidate the will; of course he was kind enough to explain to the lawyer what the law was on that point. They were both in a frightful wax."

Father Brown laughed. "People often are when they are to witness a will," he said. "For one thing it means that they can't have any legacy under it. But what did Dr. Valentine say? No doubt the universal secretary knew more about the doctor's name than the doctor did. But even the doctor might have some information about his own name."

Fiennes paused a moment before he replied.

"Dr. Valentine took it in a curious way. Dr. Valentine is a curious man. His appearance is rather striking but very foreign. He is young but wears a beard cut square; and his face is very pale and dreadfully serious. His eyes have a sort of ache in them, as if he ought to wear glasses or had given himself a headache thinking; but he is quite handsome and always very formally dressed, with a top hat and dark coat and a little red rosette. His manner is rather cold and haughty, and he has a way of staring at you which is very disconcerting. When thus charged with having changed his name, he merely stared like a sphinx and then said with a little laugh that he supposed Americans had no names to change. At that I think the colonel also got into a fuss and said all sorts of angry things to the doctor; all the more angry because of the doctor's pretensions to a future place in his family. But I shouldn't have thought much of that but for a few words that I happened to hear later, early in the afternoon of the tragedy. I don't want to make a lot of them, for they weren't the sort of words on which one would like, in the ordinary way, to play the eavesdropper. As I was passing out towards the front gate with my two companions and the dog, I heard voices which told me that Dr. Valentine and Miss Druce had withdrawn for a moment into the shadow of the house, in an angle behind a row of flowering plants, and were talking to each other in passionate whisperings—sometimes almost like hissings; for it was something of a lovers' quarrel as well as a lovers' tryst. Nobody repeats the sorts of things they said for the most part; but in an unfortunate business like this

I'm bound to say that there was repeated more than once a phrase about killing somebody. In fact, the girl seemed to be begging him not to kill somebody, or saying that no provocation could justify killing anybody; which seems an unusual sort of talk to address to a gentleman who has dropped in to tea."

"Do you know," asked the priest, "whether Dr. Valentine seemed to be very angry after the scene with the secretary and the colonel—I mean about witnessing the will?"

"By all accounts," replied the other, "he wasn't half so angry as the secretary was. It was the secretary who went away raging after witnessing the will."

"And now," said Father Brown, "what about the will itself?"

"The colonel was a very wealthy man, and his will was important. Traill wouldn't tell us the alternation at that stage, but I have since heard, only this morning in fact, that most of the money was transferred from the son to the daughter. I told you that Druce was wild with my friend Donald over his dissipated hours."

"The question of motive has been rather overshadowed by the question of method," observed Father Brown thoughtfully. "At that moment, apparently, Miss Druce was the immediate gainer by the death."

"Good God! What a cold-blooded way of talking," cried Fiennes, staring at him. "You don't really mean to hint that she—"

"Is she going to marry that Dr. Valentine?" asked the other.

"Some people are against it," answered his friend. "But he is liked and respected in the place and is a skilled and devoted surgeon."

"So devoted a surgeon," said Father Brown, "that he had surgical instruments with him when he went to call on the young lady at teatime. For he must have used a lancet or something, and he never seems to have gone home."

Fiennes sprang to his feet and looked at him in a heat of inquiry. "You suggest he might have used the very same lancet—"

Father Brown shook his head. "All these suggestions are fancies just now," he said. "The problem is not who did it or what did it, but how it was done. We might find many men and even many tools—pins and shears and lancets. But how did a man get into the room? How did even a pin get into it?"

He was staring reflectively at the ceiling as he spoke, but as he said the last words his eye cocked in an alert fashion as if he had suddenly seen a curious fly on the ceiling.

"Well, what would you do about it?" asked the young man. "You have a lot of experience; what would you advise now?"

"I'm afraid I'm not much use," said Father Brown with a sigh. "I can't suggest very much without having ever been near the place or the people. For the moment you can only go on with local inquiries. I gather that your friend from the Indian Police is more or less in charge of your inquiry down there. I should run down and see how he is getting on. See what he's been doing in the way of amateur detection. There may be news already."

As his guests, the biped and the quadruped, disappeared, Father Brown took up his pen and went back to his interrupted occupation of planning a course of lectures on the encyclical *Rerum Novarum*. The subject was a large one and he had to recast it more than once, so that he was somewhat similarly employed some two days later when the big black dog again came bounding into the room and sprawled all over him with enthusiasm and excitement. The master who followed the dog shared the excitement if not the enthusiasm. He had been excited in a less pleasant fashion, for his blue eyes seemed to start from his head and his eager face was even a little pale.

"You told me," he said abruptly and without preface, "to find out what Harry Druce was doing. Do you know what he's done?"

The priest did not reply, and the young man went on in jerky tones: "I'll tell you what's he's done. He's killed himself."

Father Brown's lips moved only faintly, and there was nothing practical about what he was saying—nothing that has anything to do with this story or this world.

"You give me the creeps sometimes," said Fiennes. "Did you—expect this?"

"I thought it possible," said Father Brown; "that was why I asked you to go and see what he was doing. I hoped you might not be too late."

"It was I who found him," said Fiennes rather huskily. "It was the ugliest and most uncanny thing I ever knew. I went down that old garden again and I knew there was something new and unnatural about it besides the murder. The flowers still tossed about in blue masses on each side of the black entrance into the old grey summer house; but to me the blue flowers looked like devils dancing before some dark cavern of the underworld. I looked all round; everything seemed to be in its ordinary place. But the queer notion grew on me that there was something wrong with the very shape of the sky. And then I saw what it was. The Rock of Fortune always rose in the background beyond the garden hedge and against the sea. And the Rock of Fortune was gone."

Father Brown had lifted his head and was listening intently.

"It was as if a mountain had walked away out of a landscape or a moon fallen from the sky; though I knew, of course, that a touch at any time would have tipped the thing over. Something possessed me and I rushed down that garden path like the wind and went crashing through that hedge as if it were a spider's web. It was a thin hedge really, though its undisturbed trimness had made it serve all the purposes of a wall. On the shore I found the loose rock fallen from its pedestal; and poor Harry Druce lay like a wreck underneath it. One arm was thrown round it in a sort of embrace as if he had pulled it down on himself; and on the broad brown sands beside it, in large crazy lettering, he had sprawled the words 'The Rock of Fortune falls on the Fool.'"

"It was the Colonel's will that did that," observed Father Brown. "The young man had staked everything on profiting himself by Donald's disgrace, especially when his uncle sent for him on the same day as the lawyer, and welcomed him with so much warmth. Otherwise he was done; he'd lost his police job;

he was beggared at Monte Carlo. And he killed himself when he found he'd killed his kinsman for nothing."

"Here, stop a minute!" cried the staring Fiennes. "You're going too fast for me."

"Talking about the will, by the way," continued Father Brown calmly, "before I forget it, or we go on to bigger things, there was a simple explanation, I think, of all that business about the doctor's name. I rather fancy I have heard both names before somewhere. The doctor is really a French nobleman with the title of the Marquis de Villon. But he is also an ardent Republican and has abandoned his title and fallen back on the forgotten family surname. 'With your Citizen Requetti you have puzzled Europe for ten days.'"

"What is that?" asked the young man blankly.

"Never mind," said the priest. "Nine times out of ten it is a rascally thing to change one's name; but this was a piece of fine fanaticism. That's the point of his sarcasm about Americans having no names—that is, no titles. Now in England the Marquis of Hartington is never called Mr. Hartington; but in France the Marquis de Villon is called Monsieur de Villon. So it might well look like a change of names. As for the talk about killing, I fancy that also was a point of French etiquette. The doctor was talking about challenging Floyd to a duel, and the girl was trying to dissuade him."

"Oh, I *see*," cried Fiennes slowly. "Now I understand what she meant."

"And what is that about?" asked his companion, smiling.

"Well," said the young man, "it was something that happened to me just before I found that poor fellow's body; only the catastrophe drove it out of my head. I suppose it's hard to remember a little romantic idyll when you've just come on top of a tragedy. But as I went down the lanes leading to the colonel's old place, I met his daughter walking with Dr. Valentine. She was in mourning of course, and he always wore black as if he were going to a funeral; but I can't say that their faces were very funereal. Never have I seen two people looking in their way more respectably radiant and cheerful. They stopped and saluted me and then she told me they were married and living in a little house on the outskirts of the town, where the doctor was continuing his practice. This rather surprised me, because I knew that her old father's will had left her his property; and I hinted at it delicately by saying I was going along to her father's old place and had half expected to meet her there. But she only laughed and said, 'Oh, we've given up all that. My husband doesn't like heiresses.' And I discovered with some astonishment that they really had insisted on restoring the property to poor Donald; so I hope he's had a healthy shock and will treat it sensibly. There was never much really the matter with him; he was very young and his father was not very wise. But it was in connection with that that she said something I didn't understand at the time; but now I'm sure it must be as you say. She said with a sort of sudden and splendid arrogance that was entirely altruistic, "I hope it'll stop that red-haired fool from fussing any more about the will. Does he think my husband, who has given up a crest and a coronet as old as the Crusades for his principles, would kill an old man in a summer house for a legacy like that?' Then she laughed again and said, 'My husband isn't killing anybody except in the way of business. Why, he didn't even ask his friends to call on the secretary.' Now, of course, I see what she meant."

"I see part of what she meant, of course," said Father Brown. "What did she mean exactly by the secretary fussing about the will?"

Fiennes smiled as he answered, "I wish you knew the secretary, Father Brown. It would be a joy to you to watch him make things hum, as he calls it. He made the house of mourning hum. He filled the funeral with all the snap and zip of the brightest sporting event. There was no holding him, after something had really happened. I've told you how he used to oversee the gardener as he did the garden, and how he instructed the lawyer in the law. Needless to say, he also instructed the surgeon in the practice of surgery; and as the surgeon was Dr. Valentine, you may be sure it ended in accusing him of something worse than bad surgery. The secretary got it fixed in his red head that the doctor had committed the crime; and when the police arrived he was perfectly sublime. Need I say that he became on the spot the greatest of all amateur detectives? Sherlock Holmes never towered over Scotland Yard with more titanic intellectual pride and scorn than Colonel Druce's private secretary over the police investigating Colonel Druce's death. I tell you it was a joy to see him. He strode about with an abstracted air, tossing his scarlet crest of hair and giving curt impatient replies. Of course it was his demeanour during these days that made Druce's daughter so wild with him. Of course he had a theory. It's just the sort of theory a man would have in a book; and Floyd is the sort of man who ought to be in a book. He'd be better fun and less bother in a book."

"What was his theory?" asked the other.

"Oh, it was full of pep," replied Fiennes gloomily. "It would have been glorious copy if it could have held together for ten minutes longer. He said the colonel was still alive when they found him in the summer house and the doctor killed him with the surgical instrument on pretence of cutting the clothes."

"I see," said the priest. "I suppose he was lying flat on his face on the mud floor as a form of siesta."

"It's wonderful what hustle will do," continued his informant. "I believe Floyd would have got his great theory into the papers at any rate, and perhaps had the doctor arrested, when all these things were blown sky high as if by dynamite by the discovery of that dead body lying under the Rock of Fortune. And that's what we come back to after all. I suppose the suicide is almost a confession. But nobody will ever know the whole story."

There was a silence, and then the priest said modestly, "I rather think I know the whole story."

Fiennes stared. "But look here," he cried, "How do you come to know the whole story, or to be sure it's the true story? You've been sitting here a hundred miles away writing a sermon; do you mean to tell me you really know what happened already? If you've really come to the end, where in the world do you begin? What started you off with your own story?"

Father Brown jumped up with a very unusual excitement and his first exclamation was like an explosion.

"The dog!" he cried. "The dog, of course! You had the whole story in your hands in the business of the dog on the beach, if you'd only noticed the dog properly."

Fiennes stared still more. "But you told me just now that my feelings about the dog were all nonsense, and the dog had nothing to do with it."

"The dog had everything to do with it," said Father Brown, "as you'd have found out, if you'd only treated the dog as a dog and not as God Almighty, judging the souls of men."

He paused in an embarrassed way for a moment, and then said, with a rather pathetic air of apology:

"The truth is, I happen to be awfully fond of dogs. And it seemed to me that in all this lurid halo of dog superstitions nobody was really thinking about the poor dog at all. To begin with a small point, about barking at the lawyer or growling at the secretary. You asked how I guess things a hundred miles away; but honestly it's mostly to your credit, for you described people so well that I know the types. A man like Traill who frowns usually and smiles suddenly, a man who fiddles with things, especially at his throat, is a nervous, easily embarrassed man. I shouldn't wonder if Floyd, the efficient secretary, is nervy and jumpy too; those Yankee hustlers often are. Otherwise he wouldn't have cut his fingers on the shears and dropped them when he heard Janet Druce scream.

"Now dogs hate nervous people. I don't know whether they make the dog nervous too; or whether, being after all a brute, he is a bit of a bully; or whether his canine vanity (which is colossal) is simply offended at not being liked. But anyhow there was nothing in poor Nox protesting against those people except that he disliked them for being afraid of him. Now I know you're awfully clever, and nobody of sense sneers at cleverness. But I sometimes fancy, for instance, that you are too clever to understand animals. Sometimes you are too clever to understand men, especially when they act almost as simply as animals. Animals are very literal; they live in a world of truisms.

Take this case; a dog barks at a man and a man runs away from a dog. Now you do not seem to be quite simple enough to see the fact; that the dog barked because he disliked the man and the man fled because he was frightened of the dog. They had no other motives and they needed none. But you must read psychological mysteries into it and suppose the dog had super-normal vision, and was a mysterious mouthpiece of doom. You must suppose the man was running away, not from the dog, but from the hangman. And yet, if you come to think of it, all this deeper psychology is exceedingly improbable. If the dog really could completely and consciously realize the murderer of his master, he wouldn't stand yapping as he might at a curate at a tea party; he's much more likely to fly at his throat. And on the other hand, do you really think a man who had hardened his heart to murder an old friend and then walk about smiling at the old friend's family, under the eyes of his old friend's daughter and post mortem doctor—do you think a man like that could be doubled up by mere remorse because a dog barked? He might feel the tragic irony of it; it might shake his soul, like any other tragic trifle. But he wouldn't rush madly the length of a garden to escape from the only witness whom he knew to be unable to talk. People have a panic like that when they are frightened, not of tragic ironies, but of teeth. The whole thing is simpler than you can understand. But when we come to that business by the seashore, things are much more interesting. As you stated them, they were much more puzzling. I didn't understand that tale of the dog going in and out of the water; it didn't seem to me a doggy thing to do. If Nox had been very much upset about something else, he might possibly have refused to go after the stick at all. He'd probably go off nosing in whatever direction he suspected the mischief. But when once a dog is actually chasing a thing, a stone or a stick or a rabbit, my experience is that he won't stop for anything but the most peremptory command, and not always for that. That he should turn because his mood changed seems to me unthinkable."

"But he did turn round," insisted Fiennes, "and came back without the stick."

"He came back without the stick for the best reason in the world," replied the priest. "He came back because he couldn't find it. He whined because he couldn't find it. That's the sort of thing a dog really does whine about. A dog is a devil of a ritualist. He is as particular about the precise routine of a game as a child about the precise repetition of a fairy tale. In this case something had gone wrong with the game. He came back to complain seriously of the conduct of the stick. Never had such a thing happened before. Never had an eminent and distinguished dog been so treated by a rotten old walking stick."

"Why, what had the walking stick done?" inquired the young man.

"It had sunk," said Father Brown.

Fiennes said nothing, but continued to stare, and it was the priest who continued:

"It had sunk because it was not really a stick, but a rod of steel with a very thin shell of cane and a sharp point. In other words, it was a sword stick. I suppose a murderer never got rid of a bloody weapon so oddly and yet so naturally as by throwing it into the sea for a retriever."

"I begin to see what you mean," admitted Fiennes; "but even if a sword stick was used, I have no guess of how it was used."

"I had a sort of guess," said Father Brown, "right at the beginning when you said the words 'summer house.' And another when you said that Druce wore a white coat. As long as everybody was looking for a short dagger, nobody thought of it; but if we admit a rather long blade like a rapier, it's not so impossible."

He was leaning back, looking at the ceiling , and began like one going back to his own first thoughts and fundamentals.

"All that discussion about detective stories like the Yellow Room, about a man found dead in sealed chambers which no one could enter, does not apply to the present case, because it is a summer house. When we talk of a Yellow Room, or any room, we imply walls that are really homogeneous and impenetrable. But a summer house is not made like that; it is often made, as it was in this case, of closely interlaced but still separate boughs and strips of wood, in which there are chinks here and there. There was one of them just behind Druce's back as he sat in his chair up against the wall. But just as the room was a summer house, so the chair was a basketchair. That also was a lattice of loopholes. Lastly, the summer house was close up under the hedge; and you have just told me that it was really a thin hedge. A man standing outside it could easily see, amid a network of twigs and branches and canes, one white spot of the colonel's coat as plain as the white of a target.

"Now, you left the geography a little vague; but it was possible to put two and two together. You said the Rock of Fortune was not really high; but you said it could be seen dominating the garden like a mountain peak. In other words, it was very near the end of the garden, though your walk had taken you a long way round to it. Also, it isn't likely the young lady really howled so as to be heard half a mile. She gave an ordinary involuntary cry and yet you heard it on the shore. And among other interesting things that you told me, may I remind you that you said Harry Druce had fallen behind to light his pipe under a hedge."

Fiennes shuddered slightly. "You mean he drew his blade there and sent it through the hedge at the white spot. But surely it was a very odd chance and a very sudden choice. Besides, he couldn't be certain the old man's money had passed to him, and as a fact it hadn't."

Father Brown's face animated.

"You misunderstand the man's character," he said, as if he himself had known the man all his life. "A curious but not unknown type of character. If he had really *known* the money would come to him, I seriously believe he wouldn't have done it. He would have seen it as the dirty thing it was."

"Isn't that rather paradoxical?" asked the other.

"This man was a gambler," said the priest, "and a man in disgrace for having taken risks and anticipated orders. It was probably for something pretty unscrupulous, for every imperial police is more like a Russian secret police than we like to think.

But he had gone beyond the line and failed. Now, the temptation of that type of man is to do a mad thing precisely because
the risk will be wonderful in retrospect. He wants to say,
'Nobody but I could have seized that chance or seen that it was
then or never. What a wild and wonderful guess it was, when I
put all those things together: Donald in disgrace; and the lawyer
being sent for; and Herbert and I sent for at the same time—and
then nothing more but the way the old man grinned at me and
shook hands. Anybody would say I was mad to risk it; but that
is how fortunes are made, by the man mad enough to have a
little foresight.' In short, it is the vanity of guessing. It is the
megalomania of the gambler. The more incongruous the coincidence, the more instantaneous the decision, the more likely he
is to snatch the chance. The accident, the very triviality, of the
white speck and the hole in the hedge intoxicated him like a
vision of the world's desire. Nobody clever enough to see such
a combination of accidents could be cowardly enough not to use
them! That is how the devil talks to the gambler. But the devil
himself would hardly have induced that unhappy man to go
down in a dull, deliberate way and kill an old uncle from whom
he'd always had expectations. It would be too respectable."

He paused a moment; and then went on with a certain quiet
emphasis.

"And now try to call up the scene, even as you saw it
yourself. As he stood there, dizzy with his diabolical opportunity, he looked up and saw that strange outline that might have
been the image of his own tottering soul—the one great crag
poised perilously on the other like a pyramid on its point—and
remembered that it was called the Rock of Fortune. Can you
guess how such a man at such a moment would read such a
signal? I think it strung him up to action and even to vigilance.
He who would be a tower must not fear to be a toppling tower.
Anyhow he acted; his next difficulty was to cover his tracks. To
be found with a sword stick, let alone a blood-stained sword
stick, would be fatal in the search that was certain to follow. If he
left it anywhere, it would be found and probably traced. Even if
he threw it into the sea the action might be noticed, and thought

noticeable—unless indeed he could think of some more natural way of covering the action. As you know, he did think of one, and a very good one. Being the only one of you with a watch, he told you it was not yet time to return, strolled a little farther, and started the game of throwing in sticks for the retriever. But how his eyes must have rolled darkly over all that desolate seashore before they alighted on the dog!"

Fiennes nodded, gazing thoughtfully into space. His mind seemed to have drifted back to a less practical part of the narrative.

"It's queer," he said, "that the dog really was in the story after all."

"The dog could almost have told you the story, if he could talk," said the priest. "All I complain of is that because he couldn't talk, you made up his story for him, and made him talk with the tongues of men and angels. It's part of something I've noticed more and more in the modern world, appearing in all sorts of newspaper rumours and conversational catchwords; something that's arbitrary without being authoritative. People readily swallow the untested claims of this, that, or the other. It's drowning all your old rationalism and scepticism, it's coming in like a sea; and the name of it is superstition." He stood up abruptly, his face heavy with a sort of frown, and went on talking almost as if he were alone. "It's the first effect of not believing in God that you lose your common sense, and can't see things as they are. Anything that anybody talks about, and says there's a good deal in it, extends itself indefinitely like a vista in a nightmare. And a dog is an omen and a cat is a mystery and a pig is a mascot and a beetle is a scarab, calling up all the menagerie of polytheism from Egypt and old India; Dog Anubis and great green-eyed Pasht and all the holy howling Bulls of Bashan; reeling back to the bestial gods of the beginning, escaping into elephants and snakes and crocodiles; and all because you are frightened of four words: 'He was made Man.'"

The young man got up with a little embarrassment, almost as if he had overheard a soliloquy. He called to the dog and left the room with vague but breezy farewells. But he had to call the dog twice, for the dog had remained behind quite motionless for a moment, looking up steadily at Father Brown as the wolf looked at Saint Francis.

THE DEVIL AND HIS DUE

Dorothy Salisbury Davis

    Thomas MacIntosh Gordon III was learning a great deal about the devil, especially for someone about to turn fifteen. He had chosen as his subject for a Religious Studies term paper, "The Devil and All His Works." The reason he chose the devil—as opposed to such possibilities as St. Frances of Assisi (at least four of his classmates chose St. Francis), the Augustinian Hermits, the Spanish Inquisition, Savonarola, or John Knox, was the premonition of boredom as he pondered them. His religious instructor sanctioned his choice for the same reason: there was no more disruptive influence at St. Christopher's Preparatory School in east Manhattan than Thomas MacIntosh Grodon III when he was bored.

Dorothy Salisbury Davis, novelist, short story writer, and recipient of the Grand Master award from Mystery Writers of America, has published two memorable mystery novels about quite different priests—Father Duffy in *A Gentle Murderer* and Father Joseph McMahon in *Where the Dark Streets Go*. Neither reappears in her own novels or short stories, but the story that follows, about a teen-age student at a Catholic prep school and his adventure in a Fifth Avenue bookstore, gives some idea of the depth of her characterizations and the sheer readability of her prose.

Thomas had to have special letters from both the school and his parents in order to gain access to the rare books he wished to see at the New York Public Library and the Morgan Library. The permissions having been granted at the top, the staffs extended him the privileges of a scholar. He accepted gravely and concentrated with all his might. But sometimes, to ease the feeling of gravity, he would stop off at one or another of the Fifth Avenue bookstores to search out more modern literature giving the devil his due. Most of it couldn't hold a candle to the ancients, but one day, at Glasgow's, he discovered something that quite enchanted him—an exquisitely illustrated new edition of Flaubert's *The Temptation of St. Anthony.*

There remained until this time, which was not so very long ago, a cozy, old-world atmosphere to Glasgow's. Customers and non-customers alike browsed undisturbed by the sales personnel. A few were disconcerted now and then by the cold eye of Frank O'Reilly, the store detective. He retired last year and uniformed security guards took over, putting an end to an era as well as to a man's career.

Frank was not popular on the floor. To him every browser was a potential thief, and according to Miss Murray, whose seniority equaled Frank's, he had scared off more buyers over the years than thieves. His eyes glowing, his breath a mixture of whiskey and cloves, he pushed among the customers like a pouter pigeon, bumping them out of his way rather than lose sight of a subject under surveillance. Many an order was abandoned on the way to the cash register because of Frank, and the story is told of the time Miss Murray turned on him after one such abortion and flung every book in the order at his head. Frank stood his ground stoutly, merely removing his bowler hat to protect it under his arm.

There were not many customers in the store when Frank first noticed Thomas. The boy caught his attention by glancing slyly around to see if anyone was watching him. Frank dropped his eyes before Thomas' reached them. When Thomas went back to the book, Frank sized him up: a well-dressed, sassy-looking lad, small for his age, no doubt, given to reading in corners when he should have been on the football field; cunning too, Frank decided; he wore a private-school blazer and a cap. He'd have money in his pocket which would only reinforce his larcenous impulses. He put Frank in mind of the youngsters old Mr. Glasgow had used to hire when he was running the store; he required only that they came of good family and had passed their sixteenth birthday, and he wouldn't have cared about that except for the law. The union shop put an end to the practice.

Frank sidled down the aisle and surreptitiously glimpsed the book the youngster was into—drawings of nude women and the horny heads of animals among them. For a respectable bookstore Glasgow's had some of the damnedest things right out where any school child could feast his greedy little eyes on them. There'd be a hot time in the locker room if he popped something like that out of his duffelbag, and if he could boast of having snitched it—what an example that to his chums! It would be far better for the boy in the long run to be caught in the theft of it. And not bad for Frank O'Reilly to whom a little thief was better than none. He retreated to the Sports and Wildlife section and took up his vigil, rather like a hunter in the blind.

Bradford Pope observed the scene from the balcony where he was waiting for old Mr. Glasgow to come with the key. Pope had the look of the diplomatic service about him—a European cut to his clothes, a school tie you felt you ought to recognize, and shoes polished to a gloss. He wore his graying hair in a crest to camouflage a barren stretch of scalp. His hand dangled languorously over the railing, and his dark eyes, while quick, were limpid.

When the boy looked up at him he smiled, meaning to convey a knowing sympathy. What he wanted was the boy to stay where he was and to continue to hold the security man's attention, something the boy seemed quite unaware of. The youngster blushed guiltily and averted his eyes. Pope was delighted; he had been about the boy's age himself when he stole his first book.

Mr. Glasgow came along in that brisk, gingerly step of the aging wherein they resemble tightrope walkers which, indeed, they are. He no longer owned any part of Glasgow's, but he had been allowed to stay on and write his memoirs while presiding over what was left of the once-famous Old and Rare Department. He knew very well that he and Old and Rare would go out of Glasgow's together.

"I knew you'd be back, Mr. Bishop," he said. "Matter of fact, I had my secretary make out the authentication when you left me Friday."

"Pope, Bradford Pope, Mr. Glasgow."

"Yes, of course, as in Alexander." Mr. Glasgow selected his key from a ring chained to his belt. "I don't suppose you'd be interested in an 1866 copy of *Satires and Epistles?*"

Pope shook his head regretfully.

"Pity." The old man proceeded to one of the finely crafted glass-doored cases with which the balcony was lined at the turn of the century when Glasgow's moved uptown from lower Broadway.

Pope hung back until the case was opened. "Mr. Glasgow?" He beckoned him to the balcony rail and pointed out Thomas MacIntosh Gordon. "I may be wrong, but I suspect that lad is about to steal a book."

Mr. Glasgow leaned over the rail and scouted the floor until he spotted Frank O'Reilly. "Hadn't better," he said. Then, with an appraising look at Thomas: "Bright-looking chap, isn't he? In my day we put his sort to work. Didn't stop their thieving, but we got something in return."

Pope had thought he'd have more time. He regretted the banality of the next ploy and delayed it by a second or two, saying, "But isn't it reassuring in these times that someone his age cares enough about a book to want to steal it?"

Mr. Glasgow gave a dry grunt of assent.

"Excuse me, sir, but your shoelace is untied." Pope dropped to one knee at the old man's feet and pulled the lace loose before Mr. Glasfow realized what he was about. "Get up from there! I'm not so feeble that I can't tie my own laces."

Pope retreated toward the open case. "No offense, Mr. Glasgow," he said almost obsequiously.

"None taken." But the old face, still handsome despite the sagging, quivering jowls, was flushed. He lifted his foot, straining to conceal the effort, and planted it on the rail. He tied a double knot while he was about it.

Pope, knowing exactly where the book he wanted was, deftly plucked it from the shelf and slipped it into a pouch at his waist. It was a slender volume containing Richard Hooker's life of Izaak Walton, an extraordinary find, published within fifty years of Hooker's own lifetime. It would bring him thousands if he waited a bit. Or took sufficient care in making up a provenance. He leaped forward and caught the old gentlemen's elbow when he teetered, off balance. Mr. Glasgow shrugged off his assistance, returned to the bookcase, and got out the Leyden edition of an Eighteenth Century medical handbook; it was the time they had discussed and bargained over on Pope's last visit.

"I've often wondered," Pope said the while, "why the Pilgrims pulled out of Leyden when they did. It's a mystery that's never been satisfactorily solved, you know."

"Won't find out here." The old man chortled and waved the medical handbook.

The moment Pope had smiled at him, Thomas knew the man was up to no good. He half expected to be sneakily beckoned up the stairs and hustled into some secret passage behind the bookshelves. Which was why he had looked away so quickly. He had been thoroughly instructed in how to repulse such an overture. But when the old man also came to the railing and Thomas felt himself the object of both their attentions, he wondered if Pope might not be a truant officer. People were always asking Thomas why he wasn't in school. He had composed several answers: "Don't you know it's St. Crispin's Day?" Or "Madam, I've been expelled for promiscuity." None of which he had ever used.

He returned to paging *The Temptation of St. Anthony.* The fact was, he was having trouble with his project: the devil had too many works. It occurred to Thomas he might more easily contain his subject if he approached the devil from the viewpoint of St. Anthony.

Miss Murray wandered down the aisle and rearranged a stack of books across the table from Thomas. She had in mind to discourage this youngster if he intended mischief which, plainly, Frank O'Reilly anticipated. Frank shook his fist at her when she threw him a hypocritical smile. A customer, waiting at the cash register, asked if someone in the store wouldn't mind taking his money. Miss Murray hastened back to her station.

Thomas opened the briefcase at his feet and took out pen and notebook. He carefully wrote down the title and the author of the book that he might add it to his references. He also noted dates of publication and copyright, the text dated 1910. That set him to wondering just how Flaubert came to know what happened to St. Anthony who had lived in the fourth century. Flaubert had made it up, of course, which set Thomas to further thought on whether it might not be a sin to make up such things about a saint. He'd thought before about the viewpoint of St. Anthony. Flaubert, he decided, was a hypocrite, pretending to write about St. Anthony, when what he really wanted to write about was the devil. Thomas jumped when the phone rang on the post behind him.

The woman clerk came and identified herself as Miss Murray. "Yes, Mr. Glasgow," she said. "I'll be waiting for him."

Thomas followed her eyes to the top of the balcony stairs. There stood the man he had suspected of flirting with him. Very shortly he was joined by the old gentleman.

Mr. Glasgow had brought the Leyden book and its authentication along with the bill of sale which Miss Murray would process when Pope got downstairs. The two men shook hands. Pope had with him a certified check for $1512; it had all but cleaned him out. He ran down the steps, paused there and saluted the old gentleman watching at the top. As soon as Miss Murray took over, Mr. Glasgow retreated to his nook among the executive offices.

Pope, to expand his air of casualness, pretended, in passing, an interest in the book which so absorbed Thomas. Thomas looked up at him icily. "Why aren't you in school?" Pope asked.

"Because I have the mumps," Thomas said.

Pope pulled in his neck, as it were.

Miss Murray, seeing the figure of Pope's purchase which, no matter how Bookkeeping dealt with it eventually, would appear with her initials on that day's register tape, began to hum to conceal her excitement. She made a mistake in punching the first digit and had to correct it.

"Miss Murray," Pope said, "hold on a moment, will you?"

Miss Murray remained crouched over the electronic keys, her fingers poised.

Pope moistened his lips. He was about to violate one of his basic rules: Don't get greedy. But the setup was irresistible. The youngster was putting something in his briefcase and the security officer, unnoticed by the boy, was so intent on him that he was actually on tiptoe, ready to take off after the youngster when he headed for the exit.

"I'm frightfully sorry if it's an inconvenience," Pope said, affecting a British accent which usually ingratiated him with elderly salesladies, "but you know, I'd like another day to consider. I'm sure Mr. Glasgow will understand."

"I'm sure he will," Miss Murray said, shooting her teeth at him. The following day was her day off. She cleared her register, then locked it, tucked the invoice and the documentation within the book's cover, and left the floor to take the book back to Mr. Glasgow.

Thomas hadn't missed a step. He had already decided to follow the man out of the store on the chance of his committing himself to something not yet defined in Thomas' imagination. Thomas only knew that the man was wicked, a conviction best accounted for by his recent studies.

Pope waited until Miss Murray was almost up the stairs, then ambled into the Sculpture Department. It was a direct line from there to the Fifth Avenue exit. He gradually accelerated his pace.

Thomas grabbed his briefcase and ran after him, at which point every customer in the store, most of them in the Fifth Avenue wing, became aware that something was happening.

Frank O'Reilly was momentarily off balance, shocked at Miss Murray's leaving the floor without a word or a sign to him. He was sure that it was pure cantankerousness, her trying to prove that, left on his honor, the little savage would turn noble. The little savage, having dropped something into his briefcase, was galloping through Sculpture with it. Frank took a short cut behind the stairs. Up front, a woman screamed, "Stop thief!"

There was one in every crowd, Frank thought, someone doing his work for him. He could not make an arrest until the suspect got beyond the store premises.

As soon as Thomas heard the cry, "Stop thief!" he put things together approximately right, dead right in the conclusion that the man was on his way out of the store with a book he had stolen from the Old and Rare Department. Thomas paused long enough to call out to a clerk, "Call a cop, a policeman!"

"The store detective's right behind you, sonny."

"Thanks," O'Reilly said bitterly. There wasn't a clerk in the store who wasn't his enemy.

Thomas sprinted ahead. He caught up with Pope in the revolving door, hitting the door with enough force to send the unready thief reeling past the exit. O'Reilly, in the compartment behind Thomas, held the door back at that point, hoping to flush the boy outdoors: all he had to do was go, he was in the open. But Thomas had no intention of letting the thief get out of his sight. Pope was hung up like a bird in a glass cage.

Finally Pope braced himself, his back up to the panel next to Thomas, and pushed. O'Reilly, surmising what he had in mind, yielded and the door slipped back a few inches; Pope was able to slither outdoors. He immediately collared Thomas and pulled him into the street where he delivered him into the detective's arms. He then intended to lose himself in the crowd that was gathering as though drawn by a magnet.

Thomas was not to be held. He wheeled his briefcase over

his head and brought it up full force into O'Reilly's midriff. Frank let go of him and Thomas threw a flying tackle at Pope. He got him by the knees and brought him down. He hung on until Frank plucked him off and gave him over to the temporary custody of two willing by-standers. Frank helped Pope to his feet. Pope was swearing he would sue Glasgow's for the youngster's assault.

"You're as fine as new," Frank said heartily and brushed the dust of the street from Pope's suit. Thus did his hand come in contact with something that was unmistakably a book and in a place no man would ordinarily abide anything foreign to his person. Frank knew instantly he had caught a thief in spite of himself. When he saw Mr. Glasgow and Miss Murray conveying one another through the revolving door he caught onto the fact that the book must belong to Old and Rare. He clapped his hand on Pope's shoulder and pronounced a solemn arrest.

"Well done, Frank!" Mr. Glasgow cried. He had discovered the Richard Hooker missing when he returned the medical handbook to the shelf.

Pope surrendered the book. His one consolation was that he still had the certified check—at least he could post bail.

Mr. Glasgow noticed Thomas and remembered Pope's using him as a cunning decoy. "And the little ruffian—you got him too!"

"Me?" Thomas said, a squeak.

His captors took a tighter hold.

Pope, knowing to whom he owed his captivity, said in his best Cockney, "'Is name is Oliver," and bared his teeth at Thomas in a sardonic grin.

"My name is Thomas MacIntosh Gordon, Third," Thomas declared loudly so that several people in the crowd whistled mockingly.

"Best let the boy go," Frank whispered to the man he still considered his employer. "We don't have much on him."

"I knew his grandfather," Mr. Glasgow said. "Or was it his great-grandfather? Shipbuilders. Started in the Clipper days, the *Mary Ellen,* if I'm not mistaken."

At a sign from O'Reilly, Thomas' captors set him free. He gathered his briefcase and his cap and said with haughty scorn, "You will hear from my lawyers."

Thomas never doubted that the devil had had a hand in what happened to him that day at Glasgow's. He was therefore the more determined to get on with his term paper, and certainly not to yield to the all but overwhelming temptation to switch subjects. He considered it a moral victory the day he turned the paper in. But that term Thomas, to whom straight A's were a commonplace, got the first C-minus of his academic career. In Religious Studies.

FINAL MARKS
FINAL SECRETS

Brendon DuBois

It started again, a month after I married my wife, Annie. We were in our new apartment in a small North Shore town outside of Boston, and we were playing a game newlyweds probably think up all the time. It was Annie's idea and though I smiled and played along with her, it felt like a cold ice cube was being run up and down my back.

The game was called "Secrets," and we went back and forth, telling each other past secrets we had kept from our families and our friends, but not from ourselves. No, not that, at least. We were in the living room and the sliding glass door to the deck was open, and I saw fireflies dance and blink over the

Brendon DuBois, a New Hampshire resident, is the newest mystery writer to be included in these pages. Since taking time out from his job with a private investigation agency to write and publish his first story in the February 1986 issue of *Ellery Queen's Mystery Magazine*, he has appeared regularly in both *EQMM* and *Alfred Hitchcock's Mystery Magazine*. During 1987, his second year as a professional writer, the prolific DuBois published eleven stories in all, the second-most of any writer in the mystery field. He is currently at work on his first novel. No one who reads the deeply emotional story which follows will doubt that its author attended a Catholic school.

Bellamy River as we played. I looked away, suddenly not liking the door being so open. Strawberry daiquiris in hand and candles on an oak dining table, we talked the night away. Annie had just told me of a time when she was seventeen and had spent the night in Boston, partying, when she was supposed to be with a high school friend. And before that, I had told her about my first and only shoplifting offense, when I was twelve and stole a *Playboy* just for a chance to see what was hidden behind those glossy covers.

I took a leisurely sip from my frozen strawberry drink, which was in a delicate and long glass, one of the countless wedding gifts from nameless aunts or uncles that cluttered our apartment. I wondered how long it would take before "Uncle Ray's table" became our table, and I wondered how long before the game was over. But in the candlelight Annie's blue eyes were laughing at me.

"C'mon, Lew, it's your turn for a secret," she said. "You know secrets aren't healthy for a modern marriage."

The flickering light made her blonde hair sparkle and looking at her I had a warm feeling that everything, at long last, was right. I had met the right woman, I had made the right choices, and things were going to be perfect. Annie was a layout artist for an advertising company in Boston, while I was a wire editor for one of the city's two largest newspapers. I had gone many miles to get here, and I hoped I was happy.

"Sorry," I said. "My life isn't that sordid. I'm squeaky clean; even your parents think so."

She stuck out her tongue. "Maybe, Lew, but your parents told me a few secrets. Especially your mother."

The ice cube was back. "My mother?"

"Right." Annie picked up her matching glass and took a long swallow, and put her drink down. A breeze from the river made the candles flicker. She gave me an arch look with her eyebrows. "Your mother. About the time you were at the Catholic high school and forged your report card."

I tried to smile but I failed. I picked up my glass and there was a sharp *crack* and my hand felt suddenly cold and then warm. Annie screamed and I looked down, and part of the shattered glass was still in my hand. The dull pink of frozen strawberry was dripping down my wrist, joined by the shockingly bright red of something else. Good God, I thought. He's come back.

Lewis Callaghan was fourteen years old and was certain of one thing—by tomorrow, Saturday, he would be dead.

He slouched low in his classroom seat, trying to be as inconspicuous as possible, though it felt like a spotlight was trained on him. Like every other male in St. Mary's High School in North Manchester, he wore black shoes, black pants, a white shirt, and a blue necktie with S.M.H.S. in gold thread in the center. The windows were open for the first time that year, promising spring with a warm breeze and the smell of wet earth, but he could only concentrate on one thing—what he held in his sweaty hands.

It was a folded piece of white cardboard, with the school seal on the outside and his handwritten name and "Grade 9" underneath it. Inside were columns listing school subjects and inside the report card was his death warrant.

He sank lower in his seat.

A few hours ago he had watched Sister Juanita, sitting behind her large wooden desk in her flowing black and white habit, as she reached into a side drawer and came up with the blank report cards for that semester. She had slowly transfered the marks for each student from a leather-bound ledger on her desk to the blank cards, and once she had looked up at him and glared at Lewis with those cold blue eyes of hers. At that look his heart felt like stone. He was dead.

Lewis opened the report card just a bit, ashamed of what was in there, not wanting anyone else to see the scarlet mark. History, B+. Geography, B. English, A. Religion, A. French, B. And Algebra, F.

F.

His hands felt dirty. God, he had never gotten a D in his life, never mind an F. His parents were away visiting his aunt and uncle in Rhode Island and were due back tomorrow, and that was the day he was going to die. He was sure of it. Up on the pale green wall, over the clock that said he had ten minutes left of the school day, was a crucifix. He said a Hail Mary, remembering the miracles he had read about in religion class. Please God, just this once.

He opened the card again. It still said F.

Around him the other students—the boys dressed like him, the girls in their plaid skirts and blazers—doodled in notebooks or read. He heard someone whisper at the back of the class and Sister Juanita looked up as the whispering stopped. He felt like shaking his head as he looked at his classmates. He wasn't really close to any of them. They seemed so . . . silly, though that really wasn't a good word. It was just that Lewis had it all planned, knew exactly where he was going, and these kids were satisfied with what they had, happy at the thought of living in North Manchester the rest of their lives.

But not Lewis, he thought. As long as he could remember he had always gotten A's in English and he was counting on that to take him places after high school and college. He wanted to be a newspaper reporter, talk to governors and astronauts, presidents and criminals, and see his name on the front page of a big newspaper. This summer one of his cousins in Rhode Island had gotten him a job as a copy boy at the Providence *Journal*. Mom hadn't been so crazy about the idea of his spending a summer away from home, but Dad thought it was great. A summer working at a real newspaper, watching the giant presses roll out newspapers still damp with ink, and knowing the people who put those words on paper. It seemed like a dream.

The final bell rang and he mechanically put the report card in the center of his history book and went out to the hallway, picking up his corduroy coat along the way. Yep, a dream all right. F, F, F. Once his parents saw that, so long summer job. And who knew if Cousin Paul would be able to arrange that copy boy job again.

His hands felt grimy from handling the report card so he

went to the basement, where the lavatories were. The boys' bathroom was empty and he washed his hands in one of the large, dirty porcelain sinks. Over the sinks were large windows cranked open with a hand wheel, and the center one was open. In spite of it all he smiled at the sight. Poor Mr. Flaherty still hadn't gotten that window fixed, despite how many complaints from Sister Alicia, the principal.

The basement of the school held storage rooms, the nurse's office, a jumble of old desks and chairs, and the boiler room, where Mr. Flaherty held court. Lewis stopped outside the boiler room, jacket slung over one arm. The door was open and along a short bricklined hallway was a row of trashcans. One of the prized chores in school was dumping the classroom wastebaskets because it meant a trip to the boiler room and a chance to talk to Mr. Flaherty. And if he was in a good mood, he'd let you dump trash right into the incinerator, which was at the end of the brick hallway. That door was also open and Lewis watched the roaring of the flames and the red and orange glow of the coals. That must be what Hell looks like, he thought. Spending forever there, with the coals against your skin, burning and burning.

Mr. Flaherty stepped out from his workroom, which led off from the hallway. He wore dark green chino workpants and shirt, and his hands were browned and permanently stained with grease. He was almost completely bald and his black-rimmed glasses were held together with masking tape.

Before he spoke Lewis could smell him, smell the thick odor of mouthwash. "You need something?" he demanded.

Mr. Flaherty was not in a good mood. Lewis thought quickly for a moment and said, "The window in the boy's bathroom still won't close."

The janitor snorted in distaste. "That nun principal send you down on that? Let me tell you, kiddo, bad enough I spent twelve years learning from the likes of her, now I have to work for her, too. Now you run along, 'fore I take a hand to you."

He ran along.

* * *

At home his older brother Earl had left a note, saying he would be out with friends that night. Drinking, no doubt. Lewis didn't care. Their parents wouldn't be back until tomorrow.

He rambled through the empty house and in the kitchen he ate some chocolate chip cookies and drank a glass of milk. He sat on a high wooden stool and through the kitchen window he watched the sun set out beyond the dull brown hills that ringed North Manchester. Occasionally he glanced over at the small wall clock and checked the time. Five P.M. Six thirty P.M. The minutes were sliding away. He looked over at the counter where Mom made her Italian dinners and pizza or fish every Friday night. The dull white report card sat in the middle of the counter, mocking him.

Maybe, he thought, maybe we could tell Mom and Dad we lost the report card. Or the nuns couldn't find it and would give him a new one on Monday. It might work.

He slapped his hands with disgust on the counter and walked out the back door to the rear lawn. Sure. It'd work. But only for a couple of days. And what would those be like? Skulking around the house, wondering if his parents believed him, wondering if maybe they'd call up the convent to complain or double-check. And then it would be worse, much worse, if they found out that deceit.

Lewis sat down on the stone steps and drew up his knees to his chin. He felt like he was six. He was panicking, his chin was trembling, and his eyes were teary. And over what? An ink mark on a piece of cardboard. That was all. He took a deep, shuddering breath, and thought, yeah, that's all. He imagined Mom and Dad coming home tomorrow. Looking at the report card. The tense looks. The yelling. Maybe even a slap or two across the face. Then the phone calls. One to the school, demanding to know how he screwed up. And one to Cousin Paul, canceling the summer job. All because of one lousy mark.

The night air was still warm, strange for March. Stars were starting to appear against the dark sky and the color reminded him of Sister Juanita's habit. He recalled how she reached into her bottom desk drawer, pulling out the blank report cards and filling in those marks and he remembered wondering, which one of those will be mine. Which one of those will bear that damnable F. He shook his head and tightened his grip on his knees, and the smell of the school soap on his hands made him think of something, of something in the boy's bathroom, and in a very few minutes he had locked the house and was walking back into town.

This sure is crazy, he thought, huddled against the cold brick of St. Mary's High School. And all because of algebra. Something about it never clicked with him. He could understand numbers all right, multiplication and division and fractions. But letters instead of numbers? X's and Y's? It was like part of his brain was dead, that it couldn't even begin to grasp the meaning or basic function of algebra. So he had gone from a B to a C and now, that blasted F.

The wind picked up, stirring dust and dead leaves from last year around his feet. He was at the rear of the school, in the fenced-in asphalt lot where gym and recess were held. In front of him were three windows, and the middle one moved easily enough in his hands. All he had to do was swing himself in, put his feet on the bathroom sink, and he'd be in. Clipped to his belt was an old Boy Scout flashlight. And then . . .

He turned around again. God, can I do this? Will I go to Hell? Not only are we we trespassing, we're stealing and lying. Because inside the school was Sister Juanita's desk, and it would be easy enough, yes, so easy, to steal a blank one and forge a new card. One with a C in algebra instead of an F. Forge it and give it to his parents tomorrow, apologize for not doing better. Get some good-natured kidding from Dad, and on Sunday, forge Dad's signature on the real card, pass it in, and start working like the Devil himself to do better next semester.

Against the brick wall his hands were trembling. It was very dark and there had been hardly any traffic on the short walk to the school. Up and over. That's all it would take. Or face parents tomorrow with the real thing, and spend a summer here instead of Rhode Island. He tried deep breathing to calm the trembling but instead it made his head dizzy. Such a small town. It only took a few minutes to walk from one end to another, and it wasn't for him. He imagined living in a big city, bigger than Manchester or Boston, where it was hard to sleep at night because of the traffic and the music. He wanted that so bad it was almost something he could grab. He closed his eyes and tried to imagine Hell again, the burning coals and fire, but all he saw was the red mark. F.

He flipped down the window and clambered inside, reaching out with his feet to the sink. His feet flailed in the empty air and he started sliding on his stomach on the window, banging his chin in the process, and he bit his tongue. He almost cried out, imagining falling to the cement floor and breaking a leg, but one foot touched the sink and in a few seconds he was there.

The bathroom was dark and there was a sharp odor of chemicals. Mr. Flaherty must've cleaned it before leaving. He touched the flashlight on his belt and rubbed his chin. A scratch was there, one that stung, and he looked up at the window. Could he make it back up there when he was done? He touched the cold porcelain of the sink. He'd have to. There was nothing else left. In the lavatory another sink was dripping, the loud noise sounding like a series of gunshots.

He stood at the doorway, wondering why his legs were shaking so. This is stupid, he thought. We've been down here dozens of times, hell, *hundreds* of times before. Why the shaking of legs? Why the dry mouth which wouldn't go away? Why did his hands itch, as if they wanted a gun or a club to hold? To his right were the stairs and to the left were the piles of furniture, storage rooms, and the boiler room. God, I'm so scared, and it was because of the time and place. During the day when there was light and hundreds of other kids here, the school seemed to be alive. Now it was so dark it almost hurt his eyes to squint, and the only sounds were from dripping water and the occasional creak or groan from the pipes.

Can a school be haunted?

Lewis started up the stairs, a hand gliding along the cold

metal of the bannister. He noticed the dusty smell of the school—the dirt, the chalk dust, the sweat from all the kids roaming around during the day. The stairs were gritty from dirt and he was halfway up the first flight when the noise made him freeze and grab onto the bannister with both hands.

Below him a door had slammed.

He forced himself to look. Below and at the other end of the basement a red glowing light was coming out of an open door, and the bannister was sweaty in his hands as he tried to imagine what was there. A fire? The Devil? Some footsteps echoed out and the door closed, and he heard muttered cursing as Mr. Flaherty stepped out and slowly walked up the other stairs. Oh Lord, Lewis thought Mr. Flaherty's still here and he's drunk. And he had heard whispered stories out in the playground about Mr. Flaherty's temper when he was drunk. He tried not to move but his arms were shaking as he watched Mr. Flaherty ascend the other stairs, his way lit by streetlights from outside. Lewis let out a breath of air when he heard another slam. The door outside. Mr. Flaherty must be outside. That's all.

The lavatory was still there, with the open window that led out. And out there was a real report card, with a real failing grade. He started back up the stairs.

At the first corridor he saw he didn't need his flashlight. The outside streetlights lit up enough of the interior but when he started up the hallway, hugging close to the wall, something struck his face and he stopped, listening to a clattering noise that seemed to go on forever. He reached up and touched a swinging coat hanger which his head had struck. Idiot, he thought. Let's make some more noise. He waited a few more minutes and then kept on going down the hallway, but this time he stayed in the middle. His heart was pounding so hard he couldn't make out the individual beats. The sound was one giant roar that filled his ears.

The door to Sister Juanita's classroom was partially opened and he slowly opened it farther, the creaking of the hinges echoing in the room. The room and the rows of desks seemed smaller in the nighttime, less real, like it was all a bad dream.

Sister Juanita's desk was in the far corner, the American flag next to it, and the blackboards seemed like polished stone in the faint light. His chest felt as if it was going to burst and he licked his dry lips as he walked across the classroom floor. At every step a floorboard creaked.

At the desk he wondered what Sister Juanita might do if she found him there. If she came in right now, habit swishing and flowing, the rosary beads clicking, switching on the overhead lights. What would she do? Grab him by the hair, no doubt, and hit him a few times. Call home and maybe speak to his older brother Earl, or even demand the phone number of his aunt and uncle in Rhode Island. He wiped his hands on his jacket and leaned forward, not quite believing he was actually gong to go through Sister Juanita's desk. It was stealing.

But his hand moved forward anyway, touching the polished wood of the lower desk handle. He tugged at it and the drawer wouldn't budge. He tugged again, harder, and then knelt down and used both hands.

Damn! He sank forward on his knees. The drawer was locked. He jerked at it a a few times, his hands finally slipping off the handle in the effort. It was locked, and he had done all of this for nothing. Tomorrow he was still going to be dead. This time he sat down against the desk and drew up his knees and cried into his hands, muffling the tears with his coatsleeve, the musty smell no comfort at all.

In a while he was done, his face dried, his eyes watery and aching from the sharp sting of tears. He was about to get up and slink downstairs when he tried to remember one thing, what Sister Juanita did every morning. She would sweep into class and nod at the kids, her books and ledger in her gnarled hands, and then she'd sit down, open the center desk drawer, and then . . .

Still on his knees, he moved over to the center drawer, pushing her swivel chair out of the way. He tugged at the center drawer and it slid easily out, and from inside the desk there was a click, as a mechanism of some sort was released. He tried again with the lower drawer and it came out with no problem at all.

The flashlight was in his hands and the strong light made him blink. Inside the drawer were pencils, pens, an ink pad, two blackboard erasers, a pile of envelopes, and there, almost at the bottom and bound with an elastic band, the blank report cards. His prize. He gently pulled one free and replaced everything in the drawer, and then closed both drawers shut, also moving the swivel chair back. He put the blank report card down his shirt, and even though it was cold and scratchy on his skin, it felt wonderful. He was going to make it.

And he was halfway out of the classroom when the voice came. "Hey, you! Stop that!"

He closed his eyes. Caught. He couldn't move, waiting for the hand on his shoulder, the slap on the face, the fingers tugging at his ear. The failure and now all of this. He should have stayed home, for what could he ever do now? He started praying but instead of the formal Hail Mary or Our Father, he just said, Oh Lord, over and over.

The voice came again, louder. "Stop that, now!" He opened his eyes. He was still alone in the room. The voice was coming from outside. Without knowing why he was doing so, he walked over to the row of windows, just above the bright gray of the radiator. One window was still open and he looked down through the screen, at the fenced-in yard where he had been a hundred hours ago. The corner streetlight cast an odd glow over the asphalt and Mr. Flaherty was there, a bottle in one hand, his other hand raised. He wasn't alone. Two young men were in front of him, laughing and poking at him with their hands. They had long hair and both wore dungaree jackets. Lewis held his breath. No one could see them from the street. Only Lewis was watching. Mr. Flaherty tried to stumble away and the men were with him.

One said, "C'mon, Curt, grab the bum's wallet and let's screw."

Mr. Flaherty turned. "No, you won't," and he brought the bottle down on Curt's shoulder. The young man yelped and cursed and Lewis bit his lip, trying not to scream, trying not to cry out. Suddenly Mr. Flaherty was sitting on the asphalt, his legs splayed out, both hands clasped to his chest.

"Here," the young man said, reaching out with a hand, the streetlight glittering sharply on what was there, and he punched Mr. Flaherty twice in the chest again. He coughed and in an instant the two men were running away, heading for the street. They both turned in unison, as if they were brothers, and looked back at Mr. Flaherty, self-satisfied grins on their young faces.

Lewis held onto the wooden windowsill with both hands, not moving. Below him Mr. Flaherty sat on the asphalt, stock still, hands at his chest. Then Mr. Flaherty started weaving slightly, from side to side, and he slowly rolled over to the hard surface of the asphalt, as if he was suddenly exhausted. A leg twitched, and then he was still.

Out on the deck later that night I sat and looked out at the stars, and I tried not to look at the back yard, which fell towards the slow moving Bellamy River. I tried to keep my gaze up at the stars, trying to remember the constellations, but like so many things I failed at it. My right hand throbbed with a dull ache where an emergency room doctor had cleaned and stitched my wound. There was a taste of dead ashes in my mouth, despite the half-drunk bottle of beer in my hand. What Annie had said brought it all back.

I never mentioned it to anyone, not even the police. How could I explain what I was doing in school at that time of the night? The forgery had gone on, I had gotten the summer job and others, and I had gotten here, to where I wanted to go so bad. But it never had been like I planned. At some points in my life, like my high school and college graduations, at my first newspaper job and the time I won a journalism award two years ago, I could never quite enjoy what I had achieved. It was always spoiled by the thought of how I had gotten there, over the corpse of Mr. Flaherty. At those times when I was supposed to be happy, and when I had a little too much to drink, I always imagined I saw someone just stepping out of a door, or ducking behind a group of people. And this someone would always be wearing faded green chinos.

Annie came out, sitting next to me, a soft hand on my shoulder. "You okay?"

"Not bad," I said, trying to keep my tone light. "We ought to call your Aunt Mary and complain about those glasses."

"Maybe so," she said, and her voice was low.

We sat there for some minutes, until I couldn't stand it any more, and I said, "What did Mom say about my report card? She's never mentioned it to me, not ever."

Annie shrugged her shoulders. "She told me at my bridal shower that you were her best-behaved son, except for that report card your freshman year. Some nun had talked to her at a school function, congratulating her on making you work harder. I guess you went from an F to a B in one semester."

Which was true. "That's right."

"And that was the first time she had ever heard about it, but by that time you were in Rhode Island and she never bothered to bring it up. Your mom gave me the idea she thought it was kinda funny."

My throat was dry, despite the beer. Kinda funny. "Oh."

She touched my shoulder again, a soft flicker. "What happened, back then? It really bothered you, didn't it?"

I looked over at Annie and thought, well, maybe it's time to tell someone what happened back then. Maybe it was time to stop the lies. In her eyes I saw a look of love and concern, and I knew it was for a man she thought she knew everything about. And what would my wife then think, if she knew how I stood there and watched a man bleed to death, for a report card mark? I had wanted a wife like Annie all my days, but some secrets would always have to stay secrets.

"What's wrong?" she softly asked him.

The night air seemed cooler and my hand still ached.

"Nothing," I said, lying for the first time as a married man. I took a drink from my beer and looked down at the bushes and the yard out beyond the deck, and in the darkness I thought I saw someone move.

JEMIMA SHORE'S
FIRST CASE

Antonia Fraser

At the sound of the first scream, the girl in bed merely stirred and turned over. The second scream was much louder and the girl sat up abruptly, pushing back the meagre bedclothes. She was wearing a high-necked white cotton nightdress with long sleeves which was too big for her. The girl was thin, almost skinny, with long straight pale-red hair and oddly shaped slanting eyes in a narrow face.

Her name was Jemima Shore and she was fifteen years old.

The screams came again: by now they sounded quite blood-curdling to the girl alone in the small room—or was it that they were getting nearer? It was quite dark. Jemima Shore clambered out of bed and went to the window. She was tall, with long legs sticking out from below the billowing white cotton of the nightie, legs which like the rest of her body were

Antonia Fraser, one of Britain's leading historians and the author of *Mary Queen of Scots*, enriched the mystery field when she began writing her novels and stories about investigative reporter Jemima Shore in 1977. Both the author's and Jemima's close ties to the Catholic church were obvious in that first novel, *Quiet as a Nun*, and in the tale which follows, the title story from her 1987 collection.

too thin for beauty. Jemima pulled back the curtain which was made of some unlined flowered stuff. Between the curtain and the glass was an iron grille. She could not get out. Or, to put it another way, whatever was outside in the thick darkness, could not get in.

It was the sight of the iron grille which brought Jemima properly to her senses. She remembered at last exactly where she was: sleeping in a ground-floor room at a boarding-school in Sussex called the Convent of the Blessed Eleanor. Normally Jemima was a day-girl at the Catholic boarding-school, an unusual situation which had developed when her mother came to live next door to Blessed Eleanor's in her father's absence abroad. The situation was unusual not only because Jemima was the only day-girl at Blessed Eleanor's but also because Jemima was theoretically at least a Protestant: not that Mrs. Shore's vague ideas of religious upbringing really justified such a positive description.

Now Mrs. Shore had been called abroad to nurse her husband who was recovering from a bad attack of jaundice, and Reverend Mother Ancilla, headmistress of the convent, had agreed to take Jemima as a temporary boarder. Hence the little ground-floor room—all that was free to house her—and hence for that matter the voluminous nightdress, Mrs. Shore's ideas of nightclothes for her teenage daughter hardly according with the regulations at Blessed Eleanor's. To Jemima, still staring uncomprehendingly out into the darkness which lay beyond the grille and the glass, as though she might perceive the answer, none of this explained why she should now suddenly be awakened in the middle of the night by sounds which suggested someone was being murdered or at least badly beaten up: the last sounds you would expect to hear coming out of the tranquil silence which generally fell upon the Blessed Eleanor's after nine o'clock at night.

What *was* the time? It occurred to Jemima that her mother had left behind her own smart little travelling-clock as a solace in the long conventual nights. Squinting at its luminous hands—somehow she did not like to turn on the light and make herself visible through the flimsy curtains to whatever was outside in the night world—Jemima saw it was three o'clock. Jemima was not generally fearful either of solitude or the dark (perhaps because she was an only child) but the total indifference with which the whole convent appeared to be greeting the screams struck her as even more alarming than the noise itself. The big red-brick building, built in the twenties, housed not only a girls' boarding-school but the community of nuns who looked after them; the two areas were divided by the chapel.

The chapel! All of a sudden Jemima realized not only that the screams were coming from that direction but also—another sinister thought—she might conceivably be the only person within earshot. The so-called "girls' guest-room" (generally old girls) was at the very edge of the lay part of the building. Although Jemima had naturally never visited the nuns' quarters on the other side, she had had the tiny windows of their cells pointed out by her best friend Rosabelle Powerstock, an authority on the whole fascinating subject of nuns. The windows were high up, far away from the chapel.

Was it from a sense of duty, or was it simply due to that ineradicable curiosity in her nature to which the nuns periodically drew grim attention suggesting it might be part of her unfortunate Protestant heritage . . . at all events, Jemima felt impelled to open her door a crack. She did so gingerly. There was a small night-light burning in the long corridor before the tall statue of the Foundress of the Order of the Tower of Ivory—Blessed Eleanor, dressed in the black habit the nuns still wore. The statue's arms were outstretched.

Jemima moved warily in the direction of the chapel. The screams had ceased but she did hear some other sound, much fainter, possibly the noise of crying. The night-light cast a dim illumination and once Jemima passed the statue with its long welcoming arms—welcoming, that is, in daylight; they now seemed to be trying to entrap her—Jemima found herself in virtual darkness.

As Jemima cautiously made her way in to the chapel, the lingering smell of incense began to fill her nostrils, lingering from that night's service of benediction, that morning's mass, and fifty other years of masses said to incense in the same place. She entered the chapel itself—the door was open—and perceived a few candles burning in front of a statue to her left. The incense smell was stronger. The little red sanctuary lamp seemed far away. Then Jemima stumbled over something soft and shapeless on the floor of the central aisle.

Jemima gave a sharp cry and at the same time the bundle moved, gave its own anguished shriek and said something which sounded like: "Zeeazmoof, Zeeazmoof." Then the bundle sat up and revealed itself to be not so much a bundle as an Italian girl in Jemima's own form called Sybilla.

At this point Jemima understood that what Sybilla was actually saying between sobs was: "She 'as moved, she 'as moved," in her characteristic strong Italian accent. There was a total contrast between this sobbing creature and the daytime Sybilla, a plump and rather jolly dark-haired girl, who jangled in illicit gold chains and bracelets, and wore more than a hint of equally illicit make-up. Jemima did not know Sybilla particularly well despite sharing classes with her. She pretended to herself that this was because Sybilla (unlike Jemima and her friends) had no interest in art, literature, history or indeed anything very much except Sybilla herself; pleasure, parties and the sort of people you met at parties, principally male. Sybilla was also old for her form—seventeen already—whereas Jemima was young for it, so that there was a considerable age gap between them. But the truth was that Jemima avoided Sybilla because she was a princess (albeit an Italian one, not a genuine British Royal) and Jemima, being middle class and proud of it, had no wish to be accused of snobbery.

The discovery of Sybilla—Princess Maria Sybilla Magdalena Graffo di Santo Stefano to give her her full title—in the chapel only deepened the whole mystery. Knowing Sybilla, religious mania, a sudden insane desire to pray alone in the chapel at night, to make a novena for example, simply could not be the answer to her presence. Sybilla was unashamedly lazy where religion was concerned, having to be dragged out of bed to go to mass even when it was obligatory on Sundays and feast days, protesting plaintively, like a big black cat ejected from the fireside. She regarded the religious fervour of certain other girls, such as Jemima's friend Rosabelle Powerstock, with good-natured amazement.

"So boring" she was once overheard to say about the Feast of the Immaculate Conception (a holiday of obligation). "Why do we have this thing? I think we don't have this thing in Italy." It was fortunate that Sybilla's theological reflections on this occasion had never come to the ears of Reverend Mother Ancilla who would have quickly set to rights this unworthy descendant of a great Roman family (and even, delicious rumour said, of a Pope or two).

Yes, all in all, religious mania in Princess Sybilla could definitely be ruled out.

"Sybilla," said Jemima, touching her shoulder, "don't cry—"

At that moment came at last the sound for which Jemima had been subconsciously waiting since she first awoke: the characteristic swoosh of a nun in full habit advancing at high speed, rosary at her belt clicking, rubber heels twinkling down the marble corridor.

"Sybilla, *Jemima*?" The rising note of surprise on the last name was evident in the sharp but controlled voice of Sister Veronica, the Infirmarian. Then authority took over and within minutes nun-like phrases such as "To bed at once both of you" and "No more talking till you see Reverend Mother in the morning" had calmed Sybilla's convulsive sobs. The instinctive reaction of nuns in a crisis, Jemima had noted, was to treat teenage girls as children; or perhaps they always mentally treated them as children, it just came to the surface in a crisis. Sybilla after all was nearly grown-up, certainly if her physical appearance was any guide. Jemima sighed; was she to be hustled to bed with her curiosity, now quite rampant, unsatisfied?

It was fortunate for Jemima that before dispatching her charges, Sister Veronica did at least make a quick inspection of the chapel—as though to see what other delinquent pupils might be lurking there in the middle of the night.

"What happened, Sybilla?" Jemima took the opportunity to whisper. "What frightened you? I thought you were being murdered—"

Sybilla extended one smooth brown arm (unlike most of the girls at Blessed Eleanor's, she was perpetually sun-tanned, and unlike Jemima, she had somehow avoided wearing the regulation white nightdress).

"Oh, my God, Jemima!" It came out as "Omigod, Geemima! I am telling you. She 'as moved!"

"Who moved, Sybilla?"

"The statue. You know, the one they call the Holy Nelly. She moved her arms towards me. She 'as touched me, Jemima. It was *miraculo*. How do you say? A mir-a-cul."

Then sister Veronica returned and imposed silence, silence on the whole subject.

But of course it was not to be like that. The next morning at assembly the whole upper school, Jemima realized, was buzzing with excitement in which words like "miracle", "Sybilla's miracle" and "there was a miracle, did you hear" could be easily made out. Compared to the news of Sybilla's miracle—or the Blessed Eleanor's miracle depending on your point of view—the explanation of Sybilla's presence near the chapel in the middle of the night passed almost unnoticed: except by Jemima Shore that is, who definitely did not believe in miracles and was therefore still more avid to hear about Sybilla's experiences than she had been the night before. Jemima decided to tackle her just after Sister Hilary's maths lesson, an experience calculated to leave Sybilla unusually demoralized.

Sybilla smiled at Jemima, showing those dimples in her pinkish-olive cheeks which were her most attractive feature. (Come to think of it, was that pinkish glow due to a discreet application of blush-on? But Jemima, no nun, had other things on her mind.)

"Eet's ridiculous," murmured Sybilla with a heavy sigh; there was a clank as her gold charm bracelet hit the desk; it struck Jemima that the nuns' rosaries and Sybilla's jewellery made roughly the same sound and served the same purpose, to advertise their presence. "But you know these nuns, they won't let me write to my father. So boring. Oh yes, they will let me *write*, but it seems they must read the letter. Mamma made them do that, or maybe they did it, I don't know which. Mamma is so holy, Omigod, she's like a nun . . . Papa"—Sybilla showed her dimples again— "Papa, he is—how do you say—a bit of a bad dog."

"A gay dog," suggested Jemima helpfully. Sybilla ignored the interruption. She was busy speaking affectionately even yearningly of Prince Graffo di Santo Stefano's bad (or gay) dog-like tendencies which seemed to include pleasure in many forms. (The Princess being apparently in contrast a model of austere piety, Jemima realized that Sybilla was very much her father's daughter.) The Prince's activities included racing in famous motor cars and escorting famously beautiful women and skiing down famous slopes and holidaying on famous yachts, and other things, amusing things. "Papa he 'ates to be bored, he 'ates it!" These innocuous pursuits had according to Sybilla led the killjoy Princess to forbid her husband access to his daughter: this being Italy there could of course be no divorce either by the laws of the country or for that matter by the laws of Mother Church to which the Princess at least strictly adhered.

"But it's true, Papa, he doesn't want a divorce either," admitted Sybilla. "Then he might have to marry—I don't know who but he might have to marry this woman or that woman. That would be terrible for Papa. So boring. No, he just want some money, poor papa, he has no money, Mama has all the money, I think it's not fair that, she should *give* him the money, *si*, he is her *marito*, her 'usband, she should give it to him. What do you think, Jemima?"

Jemima, feeling the first stirrings of primitive feminism in her breast at this description of the Santo Stefano family circumstances, remained politely silent on that subject.

Instead: "And the statue, Sybilla?" she probed gently.

"Ah." Sybilla paused. "Well, you see how it is, Jemima. I

write to him. I write anything, amusing things. And I put them in a letter but I don't like the nuns to read these things so—" she paused again. "So I am making an arrangement with Gregory," ended Sybilla with a slight but noticeable air of defiance.

"Yes, Gregory," she repeated. "That man. The gardener, the chauffeur, the odd-things man, whatever he is, the taxi-man."

Jemima stared at her. She knew Gregory, the convent's new odd-job man, a surprisingly young fellow to be trusted in this all-female establishment, but all the same—

"And I am placing these letters under the statue of the Holy Nelly in the night," continued Sybilla with more confidence. "To wake up? Omigod, no problem. To go to sleep early, *that* is the problem. They make us go to bed like children here. And he, Gregory, is collecting them when he brings the post in the morning. Later he will leave me an answer which he takes from the post office. That day there will be one red flower in that big vase under the statue. And so we come to the night when I am having my *miraculo*," she announced triumphantly.

But Jemima who did not believe in miracles, fell silent once more at what followed: Sybilla's vivid description of the statue's waving arms, warm touch just as she was about to hide the letter (which she then retrieved) and so forth and so on—an account which Jemima had a feeling was rapidly growing even as she told it.

"So you see I am flinging myself into the chapel," concluded Sybilla. "And sc-r-r-reaming and sc-r-r-reaming. Till you, Jemima *cara*, have found me. Because you only are near me!"

Well, that at least was true, thought Jemima: because she had formed the strong impression that Sybilla for all her warmth and confiding charm was not telling her the truth; or not the whole truth. Just as Jemima's reason would not let her believe in miracles, her instinct would not let her believe in Sybilla's story, at any rate not all of it.

Then both Jemima and Sybilla were swirled up in the sheer drama of Sister Elizabeth's lesson on her favourite Wordsworth ("Oh, the lovely man!").

"Once did she hold the gorgeous East in fee," intoned Sister Liz in a sonorous voice before adding rather plaintively: "Sybilla, do wake up; this is *your* Venice after all, as well as dear Wordsworth's." Sybilla raised her head reluctantly from her desk where it had sunk as though under the weight of the thick dark hair, unconfined by any of the bands prescribed by convent rules. It was clear that her thoughts were very far from Venice, "hers" or anyone else's, and even further from Wordsworth.

Another person who did not believe in miracles or at any rate did not believe in this particular miracle was Reverend Mother Ancilla. Whether or not she was convinced by Sybilla's explanation of sleep-walking—"since a child I am doing it"— Mother Ancilla dismissed the mere idea of a moving statue.

"Nonsense child, you were asleep at the time. You've just said so. You dreamt the whole thing. No more talk of miracles please, Sybilla; the ways of Our Lord and indeed of the Blessed Eleanor may be mysterious but they are not as mysterious as *that*," announced Mother Ancilla firmly with the air of one to whom they were not in fact at all that mysterious in the first place. "Early nights for the next fourteen days—no, Sybilla, that is what I said, you need proper rest for your mind which is clearly, contrary to the impression given by your report, over-active . . ."

Even Sybilla dared do no more than look sulky-faced with Mother Ancilla in such a mood. The school as a whole was compelled to take its cue from Sybilla: with no further grist to add to the mill of gossip, gradually talk of Sybilla's miracle died away to be replaced by scandals such as the non-election of the Clitheroe twins Annie and Pettie (short for Annunziata and Perpetua) as Children of Mary. This was on the highly unfair grounds that they had appeared in a glossy magazine in a series called "Cloistered Moppets" wearing some Mary Quantish version of a nun's habit.

Jemima Shore did sometimes wonder whether Sybilla's illicit correspondence still continued. She also gazed from time to time at Gregory as he went about his tasks, all those tasks which could not be performed by the nuns themselves (surprisingly few of them as a matter of fact, picking up and delivering the post being one of them). Gregory was a solid-looking individual in his thirties with nice thick curly hair cut quite short, but otherwise in no way striking; were he not the only man around the convent grounds (with the exception of visiting priests in the morning and evening and parents at weekends) Jemima doubted whether she would have remembered his face. But he was a perfectly pleasant person, if not disposed to chat, not to Jemima Shore at least. The real wonder was, thought Jemima, that Sybilla had managed to corrupt him in the first place.

It was Jemima's turn to sigh. She had better face facts. Sybilla was rich—that much was obvious from her appearance—and she was also voluptuous. Another sigh from Jemima at the thought of Sybilla's figure, so much more like that of an Italian film star—if one fed on dollops of spaghetti—than anything Jemima could achieve. No doubt both factors, money and figure, had played their part in enabling Sybilla to capture Gregory. It was time to concentrate on other things—winning the English Prize for example (which meant beating Rosabelle) or securing the part of Hamlet in the school play (which meant beating everybody).

When Sybilla appeared at benediction on Saturday escorted by a middle-aged woman, and a couple of men in camel-haired coats, one very tall and dark, the other merely dark, Jemima did spare some further thought for the Santo Stefano family. Were these relations? The convent rules were strict enough for it to be unlikely they were mere friends, especially when Mamma Principessa was keeping such a strict eye on access to her daughter. Besides, the woman did bear a certain resemblance to Sybilla, her heavily busted figure suggesting how Sybilla's voluptuous curves might develop in middle age.

Jemima's curiosity was satisfied with unexpected speed: immediately after benediction Sybilla waved in her direction, and with wreathed smiles and much display of dimple, introduced her cousin Tancredi, her Aunt Cristiana and her Uncle Umberto.

"Ah now, Jemima, you come with us, you come with us for dinner? Yes, I insist. You have saved me. *Si, si,* it was her"—to her relations. To Jemima she confided: "What a surprise, they are here. I am not expecting them. They come to spy on the naughty Sybilla," dimples again. "But listen, Tancredi, he is very much like my Papa, now you know what Papa looks like, 'andsome, yes? And Papa, he like Tancredi very much, so you come?"

"I don't have a Permission—" began Jemima rather desperately. One look at Tancredi had already told her that he approximated only too wonderfully to her latest ideal of masculine attraction, derived partly from the portrait of Lord Byron at the front of her O-level text, and partly from a character in a Georgette Heyer novel called *Devil's Cub*. (Like many would-be intellectuals, Jemima had a secret passion for Georgette Heyer. Jemima, with Rosabelle, Annie, Pettie and the rest of her coterie, were relieved when from time to time some older indisputably intellectual female would announce publicly in print, tribute perhaps to her own youth, that Georgette Heyer was an important if neglected literary phenomenon.)

Alas, Jemima felt in no way ready to encounter Tancredi, the man of her dreams, at this precise juncture: she was aware that her hair, her best feature, hung lankly, there having been no particular reason in recent days to wash it. Her "home clothes" in which she would be allowed to emerge from the convent, belonged to a much shorter girl (the girl Mrs. Shore had in fact bought the clothes for, twelve months previously), nor could they be passed off as mini-skirted because they were too unfashionable.

One way and another, Jemima was torn between excitement and apprehension when Sybilla, in her most wayward mood, somehow overrode these very real difficulties ("But it's charming, the long English legs; Tancredi has seen you, *ma che bella*! Yes, yes, I am telling you . . .") and also, even more surprisingly, convinced Mother Ancilla to grant permission.

"An unusual friendship, dear Jemima," commented the Reverend Mother drily, before adding: "But perhaps you and

Sybilla have both something to learn from each other." Her bright shrewd little eyes beneath the white wimple moved down Jemima's blouse and that short distance covered by her skirt.

"Is that a mini-skirt?" asked Mother Ancilla sharply. "No, no, I see it is not. And your dear mother away . . ." Mother Ancilla's thoughts were clearly clicking rapidly like the beads of her rosary. "What will the Marchesa think? Now, child, go immediately to Sister Baptist in the sewing-room, I have a feeling that Cecilia Clitheroe"—she mentioned the name of a recent postulant, some relation to Annie and Pettie—"is about your size." Marvelling, not for the first time at the sheer practical worldliness of so-called unworldly nuns, Jemima found herself wearing not so much a drooping blouse and outmoded skirt as a black suit trimmed in beige braid which looked as if it had come from Chanel or thereabouts.

Without the suit, would Jemima really have captured Tancredi in quite the way she did at the dinner which followed? For undoubtedly, as Jemima related it to Rosabelle afterwards, Tancredi *was* captured and Rosabelle, summing up all the evidence agreed that it must have been so. Otherwise why the slow burning looks from those dark eyes, the wine glass held in her direction, even on one occasion a gentle pressure of a knee elegantly clad in a silk suit of a particular shade of blue just a little too bright to be English? As for Tancredi himself, was he not well worth capturing, the muscular figure beneath the dandyish suit, nothing effeminate about Tancredi, the atmosphere he carried with him of international sophistication—or was it just the delicious smell of *Eau Sauvage?* (Jemima knew it was *Eau Sauvage* because on Rosabelle's recommendation she had given some to her father for Christmas; not that she had smelt it on him subsequently beyond one glorious whiff at Christmas dinner itself.)

As for Sybilla's uncle and aunt, the Marchesa spoke very little but when she did so it was in careful English, delivered, whether intentionally or not, in a reproachful tone as though Jemima's presence at dinner demanded constant explanation if not apology. Jemima's answers to the Marchesa's enquiries about her background and previous education seemed to disgust her particularly; at one point, hearing that Jemima's father was serving in the British army, the Marchesa simply stared at her. Jemima hoped that the stare was due to national prejudice based on wartime memories, but feared it was due to simple snobbery.

Uncle Umberto was even quieter, a short pock-marked Italian who would have been plausible as a waiter, had he not been an Italian nobleman. Both uncle and aunt, after the first unfortunate interrogation, spoke mainly in Italian to their niece: family business, Jemima assumed, leaving Tancredi free for his pursuit of Jemima while their attention was distracted.

The next day: "You 'ave made a conquest, Jemima" related Sybilla proudly. "Tancredi finds you so int-ell-igent"—she drawled out the word—"and he asks if all English girls are so int-ell-igent, but I say that you are famous for being clever, so clever that you must find him so stu-pid!"

"I'm not all *that* clever, Sybilla." Jemima despite herself was nettled; for once she had hoped her attraction lay elsewhere than in her famous intelligence. That might win her the English Prize (she had just defeated Rosabelle) but intelligent was not quite how she wished to be regarded in those sophisticated international circles in which in her secret daydreams she was now dwelling . . .

Tancredi's letter, when it came, did not however dwell upon Jemima's intelligence but more of her particular brand of English beauty, her strawberries-and-cream complexion (Sybilla's blush-on had been liberally applied), her hair the colour of Italian sunshine and so forth and so on in a way that Jemima had to admit could scarcely be bettered even in daydream. The method by which the letter arrived was less satisfactory: the hand of Sybilla, who said that it had been enclosed in a letter from Tancredi's sister Maria Gloria (letters from accredited female relations were not generally opened). Had Sybilla read the letter which arrived sealed with sellotape? If she had,

Jemima was torn between embarrassment and pride at the nature of the contents.

Several more letters followed until one day—"He wants to see you again. Of course he wants to see you again!" exclaimed Sybilla. "He loves you. Doesn't he say so always?" Jemima shot her a look: so Sybilla did know the letters' contents. To her surprise Jemima found that she was not exactly eager to see Tancredi again, despite the fact that his smuggled letters had become the centre of her emotional existence. Tancredi's passion for Jemima had something of the miraculous about it— Jemima smiled to herself wryly, she who did not believe in miracles—and she couldn't help being worried that the miracle might not happen a second time . . . It was in the end more sheer curiosity than sheer romance which made Jemima continue to discuss Sybilla's daring idea for a rendezvous. This was to be in Jemima's own ground-floor room no less—Tancredi to be admitted through the grille left open for the occasion.

"The key!" cried Jemima "No, it's impossible. How would we ever get the key?"

"Oh Jemima, you who are so clever," purred Sybilla, looking more than ever like a fat black cat denied its bowl of cream. "Lovely Jemima . . . I know you will be thinking of something. Otherwise I am thinking that Tancredi goes to Italy and you are not seeing him. So boring. He has so many girls there."

"Like Papa?" Jemima could not resist asking. But Sybilla merely pouted.

"I could give such a long, long letter to Papa if you say yes," she sighed. "I'm frightened to speak to Gregory now, you know. Papa thinks—" She paused. "He's a bit frightened too. That moving statue." Sybilla shuddered.

"No, Sybilla," said Jemima.

Nevertheless in her languorously persistent way, Sybilla refused to let the subject of Tancredi's projected daring expedition to Blessed Eleanor's drop. Jemima for her part was torn between a conviction that it was quite impossible to secure the key to the grille in front of her ground-floor window and a pride

which made her reluctant to admit defeat, defeat at the hands of
the nuns. In the end pride won, as perhaps Jemima had known
all along that it would. She found by observing Sister Dympna,
who swept her room and was responsible for locking the grille
at darkness, that the grille was opened by a key, but snapped
shut of its own accord. From there it was a small step to trying
an experiment: a piece of blackened cardboard between grille
and jamb, and the attention of Sister Dympna distracted at the
exact moment the busy little nun was slamming the grille shut.

It worked. Jemima herself had to close the grille properly
after Sister Dympna left. That night Jemima lay awake, conscious of the outer darkness and the window through which
Tancredi would come if she wanted him to come. She began to
review the whole thrilling affair, beginning so unpropitiously as
it had seemed at the time, with Sybilla's screams in the night.
She remembered that night in the chapel with the terrified girl,
the smell of incense in her nostrils, and then switched her
thoughts to her first and so far her only encounter with Tancredi . . . Her own personal miracle. She heard Sybilla's voice:
"Miraculo."

But I don't believe in miracles, said the coldly reasonable
voice of Jemima enclosed in the darkness, away from the
seductive Mediterranean charm of Sybilla. And there's something else too: my instinct. I thought she was lying that first
night, didn't I? Why did the statue move? A further disquieting
thought struck Jemima. She got out of bed, switched on the
light, and gazed steadily at her reflection in the small mirror
over the basin.

"Saturday," said Jemima the next morning; she sounded
quite cold. "Maria Gloria had better pass the message." But
Sybilla, in her pleasure at having her own way, did not seem to
notice the coldness. "And Sybilla—" added Jemima.

"Cara?"

"Give me the letter for your father in good time because I've
got permission to go over to my own house to borrow some
decent dresses of my mother's, she's coming back, you know.

As I may not see you later, give me the letter before I go." Sybilla enfolded Jemima in a soft, warm, highly scented embrace.

By Saturday, Jemima found herself torn between two exactly contradictory feelings. Half of her longed for the night, for the rendezvous—whatever it might bring—and the other half wished that darkness would never come, that she could remain for the rest of her life, suspended, just waiting for Tancredi . . . Was this what being in love meant? For Jemima, apart from one or two holiday passions, for her father's young subalterns, considered that she had never been properly in love; although it was a matter much discussed between herself and Rosabelle (of her other friends the Clitheroe twins, Annie and Pettie being too merrily wanton and Bridget too strictly pious to join in these talks). Then there was another quite different side to her character, the cool and rational side, which simply said: I want to investigate, I want to find out what's going on, however painful the answer.

Jemima made her visit to her parents' home driven by the silent Gregory and chaperoned by Sister Veronica who was cross enough at the waste of time to agree with Jemima that the garden was in an awful state, and rush angrily at the neglected branches— "Come along, Jemima, we'll do it together." Jemima took a fork to the equally neglected beds and dug diligently out of range of Sister Veronica's conversation. (Gregory made no move to help but sat in the car.) Jemima herself was also extremely quiet on the way back, which with Gregory's enigmatic silence, meant that Sister Veronica could chatter on regarding the unkempt state of the Shore home ("Your poor dear mother . . . no gardener") to her heart's content. For the rest of the day and evening, Jemima had to keep the investigative side of her nature firmly to the fore. She found her emotional longings too painful.

Darkness fell on the convent. From the corner of her window—unbarred or rather with a crack left in the grille, so that only someone who knew it would open, would be able to detect it—Jemima could watch as the yellow lights in the high dormitories were gradually extinguished. Sybilla was sleeping somewhere up there in the room which she shared with a monkey-like French girl called Elaine, who even in the summer at Blessed Eleanor's was huddled against the cold: "She is too cold to wake up. She is like your little mouse who sleeps," Sybilla had told Jemima. But Sybilla now was certainly watched at night and could not move about freely as she had once done.

On the other side of the building were the nuns, except for those on duty in the dormitories or Sister Veronica in the infirmary. Jemima had no idea where Mother Ancilla slept—alone perhaps in the brief night allowed to nuns before the early morning mass? But Mother Ancilla was another subject about which Jemima preferred not to think; the nun was so famously percipient that it had required some mental daring for Jemima even to say goodnight to her. She feared that the dark shrewd eyes might see right through to her intentions.

In her room, Jemima decided not to change into her convent night gown; she snuggled under the covers in jeans (collected that afternoon from home—strictly not allowed at Blessed Eleanor's)—and a skimpy black polo-necked jersey. In spite of herself, convent habits inspired in her a surprising desire to pray.

Reflecting that to do so even by rationalist standards, could not exactly do any *harm*, Jemima said three Hail Marys.

Oddly enough it was not until Jemima heard the faint—very faint—sound of someone rapping on the window, which was her clue to wind back the grille, that it occurred to Jemima that what she was doing might not only be foolhardy but actively dangerous. By then of course it was too late. She had no course now but to pull back the grille as silently as possible—since Sybilla's escapade the nuns had taken to patrolling the outside corridor from time to time. She raised the window cautiously.

Over the sill, dressed as far as she could make out entirely in black, at any rate in black jersey (remarkably similar to her own) and black trousers, with black rubber-soled shoes, came Tancredi. The smell of *Eau Sauvage* filled the room: for one wild moment the sweetness of it made Jemima regret . . . then she allowed herself to be caught into Tancredi's arms. He kissed her, his rather thin lips forcing apart her own.

Then Tancredi stood back a little and patted her lightly on her denim-clad thigh, "What protection! You are certainly not anxious to seduce me, *cara*," he said softly. Jemima could sense him smiling in the darkness. "This is a little bit like a nun, yes?" He touched her breast in the tight black jersey. "This not so much."

"Tancredi, you mustn't, I mean—" What did she mean? She knew what she meant. She had it all planned, didn't she?

"Tancredi, listen, you've simply got to take Sybilla's packet, her letter that is, it's quite thick, the letter, you must take it and then go. You see, the nuns are very suspicious. I couldn't let you know, but I have a feeling someone suspects . . . Mother Ancilla, she's the headmistress, she's awfully beady." Jemima was conscious she was babbling on. "So you must take the letter and *go*."

"Yes, I will take the letter. In good time. Or now, *tesoro*, if you like. I don't want to make tr-r-rouble for you." Tancredi sounded puzzled. "But first, oh I'm so tired, all that walking through this park, it's enor—mous, let's sit down a moment on this ridiculous little bed. Now this is really for a nun, this bed."

"I think you should just collect the letter and go," replied Jemima, hoping that her voice did not quaver.

"Collect, you mean you don't have it" Tancredi was now a little brisker, more formal.

"I—I hid it. By the statue outside. You see we have inspection on Saturdays, drawer inspection, cupboard inspection, everything. I didn't dare keep it. So I used her place, Sybilla's place. Look, I'll explain where you go—"

To Jemima's relief, yes, it really was to her relief, she found Tancredi seemed to accept the necessity for speed, and even for a speedy departure. The embrace he gave her as he vanished into the ill-lit corridor was quite perfunctory, only the lingering smell of *Eau Sauvage* in her room reminded her of what a romantic tryst this might under other circumstances have turned out to be. Jemima sat down on the bed suddenly and waited for Tancredi's return. Then there would be one last embrace, perhaps perfunctory, perhaps a little longer, and he would vanish into the darkness from which he had come, out of her life.

She waited.

But things did not turn out quite as Jemima had planned. One moment Tancredi was standing at the door again, with a clear view of the big statue behind him; he had a pencil torch in his hand and a packet opened at one end. The next moment he had leapt towards her and caught her throat in the fingers of one strongly muscled hand.

"Where is it?" he was saying in a fierce whisper, "Where is it? Have you taken it? Who has taken it?" And then, with more indignation—"What is *this*?" He was looking at some white Kleenex which protruded from the packet, clearly addressed to the Principe Graffo di Santo Stefano in Sybilla's flowing hand. The fingers tightened on Jemima's throat so that she could hardly speak, even if she had some answer to the fierce questioning.

"Tancredi, I don't know what—" she began. Then beyond Tancredi, at the end of the corridor, to Jemima's horror she saw something which looked to her very much like the statue of the Blessed Eleanor moving. Jemima gave a scream, cut off by the pressure of Tancredi's fingers. After that a lot of things happened at once, so that later, sorting them out for Rosabelle (under very strict oath of secrecy—the Clitheroe twins and Bridget definitely not to be informed) Jemima found it difficult to get the exact order straight. At one moment the statue appeared to be moving in their direction, the next moment a big flashlight, of quite a different calibre from Tancredi's pencil torch, was shining directly on both of them. It must have been then that Jemima heard the voice of Gregory, except that Gregory was saying something like: Detective Inspector Michael Vann, Drugs Squad, and Michael Vann of Drugs Squad was, it seemed, in the process of arresting Tancredi.

Or rather he might have intended to be in the process, but an instant after Tancredi heard his voice and was bathed in the flashlight, he abandoned his hold on Jemima, dived in the direction of the window, pulled back the grille and vanished.

Then there were more voices, an extraordinary amount of voices for a tranquil convent at night, and phrases were heard like "Never mind, we'll get him", and words like "Ports, airports," all of which reverberated in the mind of Jemima without making a particularly intelligible pattern. Nothing seemed to be making much sense, not since the statue had begun to move, until she heard someone—Gregory—say:

"And after all that, he's managed to take the stuff with him."

"He hasn't," said Jemima Shore in a small but firm voice. "It's buried in the garden at home."

It was so typical of Mother Ancilla, observed Jemima to Rosabelle when the reverberations of that night had at long last begun to die away, so typical of her that the very first thing she should say was: "You're wearing jeans, Jemima."

"I suppose she had to start somewhere," commented Rosabelle. "Personally, I think it's a bit much having the Drugs Squad moseying round the convent even if it is the biggest haul etc. etc. and even if the Principe is a wicked drug pusher etc. etc. Thank goodness it's all over in time for the school play." Rosabelle had recently been cast as Hamlet (Jemima was cast as Laertes—"that dear misguided *reckless* young man, as Sister Elizabeth put it, with a meaning look in Jemima's direction). Rosabelle at least had the school play much on her mind. "Did Mother Ancilla give any proper explanation?" Rosabelle went on.

"You know Mother Ancilla," Jemima said ruefully, "She was really amazingly lofty about the whole thing. That is, until I remarked in a most innocent voice that the nuns obviously agreed with the Jesuits that the ends justify the means."

"Daring! Then what?"

"Then I was told to write an essay on the history of the Society of Jesus by Friday—you can't win with Mother Ancilla."

"Sybilla and Co. certainly didn't. Still, all things considered, you were quite lucky, Jem. You did save the cocaine. You didn't get struck down by Tancredi, and you didn't get ravished by him."

"Yes, I was lucky; wasn't I?" replied Jemima in a tone in which Rosabelle thought she detected just a hint of wistfulness.

The reverberations of that night had by this time included the precipitate departure of Sybilla from the convent, vast amounts of expensive green velvety luggage surrounding her weeping figure in the convent hall the next day. She refused to speak to Jemima beyond spitting at her briefly: "I 'ate you, Jemima, and Tancredi, he 'ates you too, he thinks you are *ugly*." Then Sybilla shook her black head furiously so that the long glittering earrings, which she now openly flaunted, jangled and glinted.

What would happen to Sybilla? The Drugs Squad were inclined to be lenient towards someone who was so evidently under the influence of a father who was both pleasure-loving and poverty-stricken (a bad combination). Besides, thanks to a tip-off, they had had her watched since her arrival in England, and the Prince's foolproof method of bringing drugs into the country via his daughter's school luggage—clearly labelled "Blessed Eleanor's Convent, Churne, Sussex"—had never in fact been as foolproof as he imagined. For that matter Gregory, the enigmatic gardener, had not been as subornable as Sybilla in her confident way and Jemima in her envious one, had imagined.

Gregory however, as an undercover operative, had not been absolutely perfect; it had been a mistake for example to let Sybilla glimpse him that night by the statue, provoking that fit of hysterics which had the effect of involving Jemima in the whole affair. Although it could be argued—and was by Jemima and Rosabelle—that it was Jemima's involvement which had flushed out Tancredi, the Prince's deputy, after Sybilla had become too frightened to contact Gregory. Then there was Jemima's valiant entrapment of Tancredi and her resourceful preservation of the cocaine.

All the same, Jemima Shore herself had not been absolutely

perfect in the handling of the whole matter, as Mother Ancilla pointed out very firmly, once the matter of the jeans had been dealt with. It was only after some very frank things had been said about girls who kept things to themselves, things best confided to authority, girls who contemplated late-night trysts with males (albeit with the highest motives as Mother Ancilla accepted) that Mother Ancilla put her bird's head on one side: "But, Jemima dear child, what made you—how did you guess?"

"I just never believed in the second miracle, Mother," confessed Jemima.

"The second miracle, dear child?"

"I didn't believe in the first miracle either, the miracle of Sybilla's waving statue. The second miracle was Tancredi, the cousin, falling in love with me. I looked in the mirror, and well . . ." Her voice trailed away. Mother Ancilla had the effect of making her confess things she would rather, with hindsight, have kept to herself.

Mother Ancilla regarded Jemima for a moment. Her gaze was quizzical but not unkind.

"Now Jemima, I am sure that when we have finished with you, you will make a wonder Ca– . . . a wonderful wife and mother"—she had clearly intended to say "Catholic wife and mother" before realizing who sat before her.

Jemima Shore saw her first and doubtless her last chance to score over Mother Ancilla.

"Oh, no, Reverend Mother," she answered boldly, "I'm not going to be a wife and mother. I'm going into television," and having already mentioned one of Mother Ancilla's pet banes, she was inspired to add another: "I'm going to be an investigative reporter."

THE SWEATING STATUE

Edward D. Hoch

It was the miracle at Father David Noone's aging inner-city parish that brought Monsignor Thomas Xavier to the city. He'd been sent by the Cardinal himself to investigate the miraculous event, and that impressed Father Noone, even though he might have wished for more run-of-the-mill parish problems now that he'd reached the age of fifty.

Monsignor Xavier was a white-haired man a few years older than Father Noone, with a jolly, outgoing manner that made him seem more like a fund-raiser than the Cardinal's trouble-shooter. He shook hands vigorously and said, "We met once years ago when you were at St. Monica's, Father. I accompanied the Cardinal."

"Of course," David Noone replied, bending the truth a little. The Cardinal's visit had been more than a decade earlier, and if he remembered the monsignor at all it was only vaguely.

I owe a debt to Graham Greene for more than one of my story ideas. The central incident in this mystery, the statue of the title, can be found in Greene's nonfiction account of Panama and its late leader, *Getting to Know the General*. This is the latest and best of a trio of stories I have written about Father David Noone.

"Holy Trinity isn't much like St. Monica's, is it?" Monsignor Xavier remarked as he followed David into the sitting room. "These inner-city parishes have changed a great deal."

"Well, we have to scrape a bit to get by. The Sunday collections don't bring in much money, but of course the diocese helps out." He poked his head into the rectory kitchen. "Mrs. Wilkins, could you bring us in some—what will it be, Monsignor, coffee or tea?"

"Tea is fine."

"Some tea, please."

Mrs. Wilkins, the parish housekeeper, turned from the freezer with a carton of ice cream in her hand. "Be right with you. Good of you to visit us, Monsignor."

When they'd settled down in the parlor, the white-haired monsignor asked, "Are you alone at Holy Trinity, Father?"

"I am at present. When I first took over as pastor five years ago I had an assistant, but there just aren't enough priests to go around. He was shifted to a suburban parish two years ago and I've been alone here with Mrs. Wilkins ever since."

Monsignor Xavier opened a briefcase and took out some papers. "The parish is mainly Hispanic now, I believe."

"Pretty much so, though in the past year we've had several Southeast Asian families settle here, mainly in the Market Street area. We're trying to help them as much as we can."

He nodded as if satisfied. "Now tell me about the statue."

Mrs. Wilkins arrived with tea, setting the cups before them and pouring with a steady hand. "I'll bring in a few little cookies too," she said. "You must be hungry after your journey, Monsignor."

"Oh, they gave us a snack on the plane. Don't worry about me."

"We'll have a nice dinner," she promised. "It's not often we have such a distinguished visitor."

When they were alone, Monsignor Xavier said, "You were going to tell me about the statue."

"Of course. That's what you've come about." David Noone took a sip of tea. "It began two weeks ago today. Our custodian,

Marcos, had unlocked the church doors for the seven A.M. Mass. There are always a few early arrivals and one of these, Celia Orlando, came up to light a candle before Mass began. She noticed that the wooden statue of the Virgin on the side altar seemed covered with sweat. When she called Marcos's attention to it, he wiped the statue dry with a cloth. But a few moments later the sweating began again."

He paused for some comment, but the monsignor only said, "Interesting. Please continue."

"Marcos showed it to me when I arrived to say the Mass. I didn't think too much of it at first. Perhaps the wood was exuding some sort of sap. In fact, I thought no more of the incident until later that day when Mrs. Wilkins reported that people were arriving to view the miracle. I went over to the church and found a half-dozen women, friends and neighbors of Celia Orlando."

"Tell me about the woman."

"Celia? Her parents moved here from Mexico City when she was a teenager. She's twenty-eight now, and deeply religious. Attends Mass every morning on her way to work at an insurance company."

A nod. "Go on with your story."

Father Noone shifted in his chair, feeling as if he was being questioned in a courtroom. "Well, I spoke to the women and tried to convince them there was no miracle. I thought things had settled down, but then the following morning the same thing happened. It kept happening, and each morning there's been a bigger crowd at morning Mass. After television covered it on the six o'clock news the church was jammed."

Monsignor Xavier finished the tea and rose to his feet. "Well, I think it's time I saw this remarkable statue."

Father Noone led the way through the rectory kitchen where Mrs. Wilkins was already at work on dinner. "It smells good," the monsignor commented, giving her a smile. They passed through a fire door into a corridor that connected the rectory with the rear of the church.

"It's handy in the winter," David Noone explained.

"Is the church kept locked at night?"

"Oh, yes, all the doors. It's a shame but we have to do it. And not just in the inner city, either. These days they're locked in the suburbs, too."

The two priests crossed in front of the main altar, genuflecting as they did so. The Blessed Virgin's altar was on the far side, and it was there that the wooden statue stood. "There are no people here now," Xavier commented.

"Since we've had all the publicity I've been forced to close the church in the afternoon too, just to get the people out of here. We open again at five for afternoon services."

Monsignor Xavier leaned over for a closer look at the statue. "There is moisture, certainly, but not as much as I'd expected."

"There's more in the morning."

He glanced curiously at Father Noone. "Is that so?"

The statue itself stood only about eighteen inches high and had been carefully carved by a parish craftsman many years before David Noone's arrival. It was a traditional representation of the Blessed Virgin, with the polished unpainted wood adding a certain warmth to the figure. Monsignor Xavier studied it from all angles, then put out a finger to intercept a drop of liquid which had started running down the side of the statue. He placed it to his tongue and said, "It seems to be water."

"That's what we think."

"No noticeable salty taste."

"Why should it be salty?"

"Like tears," the monsignor said. "I'm surprised no one has dubbed the liquid the Virgin's Tears or some such thing."

"That'll be next, I'm sure."

They were joined by a thin balding man who walked with stooped shoulders and wore a pair of faded overalls. David Noone introduced the monsignor to Marcos, the church's custodian. "That means janitor," the balding man said with a smile. "I know my place in the world."

"We'd be lost without you," David assured him, "Whatever you're called."

"You unlock the church doors every morning for the early Mass?" Monsignor Xavier asked.

"Sure."

"Ever find signs of robbery or forced entry?"

"No, not in years."

"When I first came here," David Noone explained, "it was customary to leave the side door facing the rectory unlocked all night. But someone stole one of our big gold candlesticks and that put an end to it. With the covered passageway from the rectory we don't really need any unlocked doors. On the rare occasion when someone needed to get into the church at night, they simply came to the rectory and Mrs. Wilkins or I took them over."

"What about this young woman, Celia Orlando?" the monsignor asked Marcos. "Do you know her?"

"Yes, her family has been in the parish many years. She is a good girl, very religious."

"Tell me, Marcos, what do you think causes the statue to sweat?"

The old man shifted his eyes to the wooden Virgin, then back to the monsignor. He seemed to be weighing his answer carefully. "A miracle, I suppose. Isn't that why you came here from the Cardinal?"

"Have you ever seen wood like that sweat before?"

"No."

"Could it be some sort of sap?"

"It has no taste. Sap would be sweet. And there would be no sap after all these years."

"So you think it is a miracle."

"I think whatever you want me to think. I am a good Catholic."

Monsignor Xavier turned away. "We'd best go see this young woman," he said to David Noone. "Celia Orlando."

In the car David tried to explain his people to Monsignor Xavier. "They are deeply religious. You are a stranger from another city, someone sent by the Cardinal himself. Naturally they do not want to offend you in any way."

"That old man does not believe in miracles, David. May I call you David? We might as well be informal about this. I'm Tom." He was relaxing a bit, feeling more at home with the situation, David thought. "Tell me a little about Marcos."

"There's not much to tell. His wife is dead and he lives alone. His children grew up and moved away. His son's a computer programmer."

"A story of our times, I suppose."

David Noone parked the car in front of the neat, freshly painted house where Celia Orlando lived with her brother Adolfo and his wife. It was almost dinner time, and Adolfo came to the door. "Hello, Father. Have you come to see my sister?"

"If she's home. Adolfo, this is Monsignor Thomas Xavier. The Cardinal sent him to look into our strange event."

"You mean the miracle." He ushered them into the living room.

Monsignor Xavier smiled. "That's what I'm here to determine. These things often have a natural explanation, you know."

Celia came into the room to greet them. She was still dressed for work, wearing a neat blue skirt and a white blouse. The presence of the monsignor seemed to impress her, and she hastened to explain that she deserved no special attention. "I attend Mass every morning, Monsignor, but I'm no Bernadette. I saw nothing the others did not see. I was merely the first to notice it."

"And you called it a miracle."

She brushed the black hair back from her wide dark eyes, and Father Noone realized that she was a very pretty young woman. He wondered why he'd never noticed it before. "An act of God," she responded. "That's a miracle isn't it?"

"We believe the wood of the statue is merely exuding moisture."

She shook her head in bewilderment. "Why is the church so

reluctant to accept a miracle? What the world needs now are more miracles, not less."

"We must be very careful in matters of this sort," Xavier explained. "Have you ever noticed anything strange about the statue before? Anything unusual?"

"No, nothing."

Her brother interrupted then. "What are you after, Monsignor?"

"Only the facts. I must return home tomorrow and report to the Cardinal."

"I have a boyfriend who thinks I'm crazy. He's not Catholic." The admission seemed to embarrass her. "He says the priests are twisting my mind. He should be here now to see me trying to convince you both of the miracle."

Father Noone glanced at his watch. "I have to get back for the afternoon Mass in fifteen minutes. I hadn't realized it was so late."

She saw them to the door. "Pray for me," she said.

"We should say the same to you," Monsignor Xavier told her.

On the drive back to the parish church he talked little. When he saw the crowds at the five-thirty Mass, filling the small church almost to capacity, he said nothing at all.

In the evening they sat in David Noone's small study, enjoying a bit of brandy. They were on a first-name basis now, and it was a time for confidences. "How do you do financially here?" Thomas Xavier asked.

"Poorly," David Noone admitted. "I have to go hat in hand to the bishop a couple of times a year. But he realizes the problems. He helps in every way he can."

"What does he think of the statue?"

"Strictly hands off, Tom. That's why he phoned the Cardinal. It's known as passing the buck."

"I know how he feels. If you think the church was crowded this afternoon, just wait till the national news gets hold of this. You'll have people coming here from all over the country."

"There was a call from the *New York Times* yesterday. They said they might send a reporter out this weekend."

"That's what I mean. We have to be very careful, David—"

He was interrupted by Mrs. Wilkins, who announced, "There's a young man to see you, Father Noone. He says it's very important."

David Noone sighed and got to his feet. "Excuse me, Tom. Duty calls."

He walked down the hall to the parlor where a sandy-haired man in his late twenties was waiting. "You're Father Noone?" the man asked, rising to meet him.

"Yes. What can I do for you?"

"My name is Kevin Frisk. Maybe Celia mentioned me."

"Celia Orlando? No, I don't believe so."

"I'm her boyfriend."

"Oh, yes. I think—"

"I want you to stay away from her."

David could see the anger in his eyes now. "I assure you—"

"You came this afternoon with another priest. She told me about it. I want you to leave her alone, stop filling her head with all these crazy notions of a miracle."

"Actually it's just the opposite. No one is more skeptical than a priest when there's talk of miracles."

"I want to marry her. I want to take her away from your influence."

"We have very little influence over Celia or anyone else. We only try to give a bit of comfort, and a few answers to the questions people ask. Do you work with Celia at the insurance office?"

"Yes. And I'm not Catholic." There was a challenge in his words.

"Celia told me that."

"If you think you can hypnotize me with your crazy notions—"

"Believe me, I'm not trying to hypnotize you or persuade you or convert you."

"Then stay away from Celia. Stop filling her head with

statues that sweat. If we're ever married it'll be far from here."

"Mr. Frisk—"

"That's all I have to say. Take it as a warning. The next time I might not be quite so civil."

David watched as he left the room and walked out the front door without looking back. He shook his head sadly and returned to the study where the monsignor was waiting.

"No special problem, I hope," Thomas Xavier said, putting down the magazine he'd been glancing through.

"Not really. It was a young man who's been dating Celia Orlando."

"Ah yes—the non-Catholic one. I caught that point when she made it."

"He thinks we're brainwashing her or something. He seemed a bit angry."

"The statue seems to be having a ripple effect on the lives of a great many people."

The meeting with Kevin Frisk had left David dissatisfied. He felt he'd given the wrong answers to questions that hadn't even been asked. "What will you tell the Cardinal when you go back tomorrow?"

"I want to have another look at our statue in the morning. That may help me decide."

It was Father Noone's habit to rise at six-thirty for the seven o'clock Mass, delaying breakfast until after the service. When the alarm woke him he dressed quickly and went downstairs, noting only that the door to the guest room where Monsignor Xavier slept was still closed. Passing through the kitchen he noted that Mrs. Wilkins was not yet up either. The brandy glasses from the previous night sat unwashed on the sideboard, and a carton of ice cream lay melting in the sink. The door to her room, at the rear of the main floor, was also closed.

Through the window he could see a parishioner trying the side door of the church, which was still locked. Had Marcos overslept too? David Noone hurried along the passageway and into the church, switching on lights as he went. It was already ten minutes to seven. He entered the sacristy and was about to open the cabinet where his vestments were hung when something drew him to the stairwell leading to the church basement. There was a light on down there, which seemed odd if Marcos was late arriving.

But Marcus was there, sprawled at the foot of the stairs. David knew before he reached him that the old man was dead.

David knelt by the body for a moment, saying a silent, personal prayer. Then he administered the last rites of the Church. He went back to the rectory and roused Monsignor Xavier, telling him what had happened. "Can you take the Mass for me while I call the police? There are people waiting."

"Certainly, David. Give me five minutes to dress."

He joined David Noone in three minutes and they returned to the church together. Staring down at the body, Thomas Xavier said a prayer of his own. "The poor man. It looks as if his neck was broken in the fall."

"He knew these stairs too well to fall on them," David said.

"You think he was pushed? But why, and by whom?"

"I don't know."

"Open the doors of your church. It's after seven and people are waiting. Tell them Mass will begin in a few moments."

"Where are you going now?"

"Just over to see the statue."

David Noone followed him across the sanctuary to the side altar. The Virgin's statue was sweating, perhaps more intensely than before. The monsignor reached out his right hand to touch it, then drew sharply back. "What is it?" David asked.

"The statue is cold, as if it's aware of the presence of death."

The Mass went on as the police arrived and went through their routine. A detective sergeant named Dominick was in charge. "Anything stolen, Father?" he wanted to know, peering over the rim of his glasses as he took notes.

"Nothing obvious. The chalices are all here. We don't keep any money in the church overnight, except what's in the poor box, and that hasn't been touched."

"Then foul play seems doubtful. He probably just missed his footing in the dark."

"The light was on," David reminded him.

"He was an old man, Father. We got enough crime these days without trying to find it where it doesn't exist."

When they returned to the rectory after Mass, Mrs. Wilkins was busy preparing breakfast. David told her what had happened and she started to cry softly. "He was a good man," she said. "He didn't deserve to die like that."

"The police are convinced it was an accident," David Noone said. "I'm not so sure."

She brought them their breakfast and Monsignor Xavier took a mouthful of scrambled egg. After a moment he said, "This is very good. I wish we had breakfast like this back home."

"What do you think about Marcos?" David Noone asked him.

He considered that for a moment. "I don't know. I did notice that Celia Orlando wasn't at Mass this morning. Didn't you say she comes every day?"

"Yes."

"Perhaps we should see why her routine changed today."

Father Noone had to make some calls at the hospital first, and he was surprised when the monsignor changed his return flight and arranged to stay over an extra day. He wondered what it meant. Then, just before noon, they called on Celia at the insurance office where she was employed.

She was startled to see them enter, and came up to the counter to greet them. "Is something wrong? It's not my brother is it?"

"No, no," Father Noone assured her. "It's just that you weren't at Mass and I wondered if you were ill."

She dropped her eyes. "Kevin—my boyfriend—doesn't want me to go there anymore. He says you're a bad influence on me."

"He certainly can't keep you from practicing your religion."

"He says I should go to another parish. All that business with the statue—"

At that moment one of the office doors opened and Kevin Frisk himself emerged. He hurried over to the counter and confronted the two priests. "Get out of here!" he ordered.

"You can't—"

"I can order you out when you're keeping employees from their jobs, and that's exactly what you're doing. Get out and don't let me see you here again."

David Noone turned to Celia as they departed. "Call me at the rectory. We need to talk."

"Stay away from her!" Frisk warned.

Outside, Monsignor Xavier shook his head. "A hotheaded young man. He could cause trouble."

"If he hasn't already. Maybe he broke into the church and Marcos caught him at it.

"There were no signs of forced entry, David. Perhaps that detective is right about looking for crime where none exists."

"I'm sorry, Tom. I just can't get that old man out of my mind."

As they walked back to the car they saw a headline on the noon edition of the newspaper: MAN FOUND DEAD AT "MIRACLE" CHURCH. Monsignor Xavier said, "I'm afraid this will bring you all the national publicity you've been trying to avoid. It's something more than a miracle now."

"Is that why you're staying over? Did you expect something like this?"

Thomas Xavier hesitated. "Not expect it, exactly. But in a large city we're more in tune with the way the press operates. They couldn't get the right angle on a sweating statue, but now there's a dead old man and they'll have a field day."

"What do you suggest I do?"

"We must have an answer ready when they ask the Church's position on the so-called miracle."

"And what is the Church's position? What will you report to the Cardinal?"

"The answer to that lies back at Holy Trinity."

There had been no Marcos to lock up the church during the early afternoon, and David Noone realized it had been left open as soon as he drove up to the rectory and saw the streams of people entering and leaving.

"I forgot to lock it," he said sadly.

"I doubt if there's any harm done."

They found Mrs. Wilkins just hanging up the telephone, almost frantic. "It's been like a circus here. Reporters calling from all over the country! The television stations have all been down, filming the statue for the evening news."

"Again? They did that last week."

"There are more people around now. And everyone wants to see where poor Marcos died. I was over there shooing them out of the sacristy myself."

The afternoon Mass was like a bad dream for David. People he'd never seen before filled the church, many with little interest in following the service. Instead they crowded around the side altar where the statue stood. The moisture was not as heavy as it had been that morning, but there was still some to be seen. In his sermon he said a few words about Marcos, then tried to make the point that the phenomenon of the statue was still unexplained. Following the services people lingered around the side altar until finally David had to ask them to leave so he could close the church.

"The only blessing to come out of all this," he told the monsignor over dinner, "is that the crowds, and the collections, have never been better. Still, I'm wondering if I should simply remove the statue temporarily and end all this fuss."

"That would surely bring complaints from some, though it's an option we must consider."

Mrs. Wilkins brought in their coffee. "Sorry there's no dessert tonight. What with all the commotion I didn't get to the store today."

"It'll do us both good," the monsignor assured her.

Later, they walked around the church in the darkness as David Noone checked all the doors to be sure they were locked. "I'll have to find a replacement for Marcos, of course, immediately after the funeral."

Monsignor Xavier stared up at the spire of Holy Trinity Church as it disappeared into the night sky. "I often wish I had a church like this. It would be just the right size for me. In the city, serving the Cardinal, I lose touch with things at times."

"With people?"

"With people, yes, and with their motives."

Later that night, just after eleven, as David was turning out the light and getting into bed, his door opened silently and Thomas Xavier slipped into the room. He held a finger to his lips. "Put on your robe and come with me," he said softly.

"What—"

"Just come, very quietly."

David took his robe and followed Thomas Xavier down the stairs. When they reached the main floor the monsignor headed for the kitchen, then paused as if listening.

"What—"

"Shh!"

He heard a noise from the passageway leading into the church, and then the kitchen door swung open.

It was Mrs. Wilkins, carrying the statue of the Virgin in her arms.

"Let me take that," Monsignor Xavier said with a kindly voice. "We don't want any more accidents, like what happened to poor old Marcos."

She gave him the statue, and then the will seemed to go out of her. For a long time she cried, and talked irrationally, and it was only the soft words of the monsignor that calmed her at last.

"We know all about it, Mrs. Wilkins. You carried the statue in here each evening, didn't you, and immersed it in water. Then you left it in the freezer overnight, carrying it back into the church each morning before Mass. Naturally as it thawed it seemed to sweat. That was why there was more moisture in the morning than later in the day, and why it was cold to my touch this morning. I remembered seeing the ice cream melting in the sink when I passed through the kitchen with Father Noone. You took it out of the freezer to make room for the statue, and then forgot to put it back, so there was no dessert for us tonight."

"I only did it so more people would come, so the collections would be bigger and we could help the poor souls in our parish. I never meant to do any harm!"

"Marcos caught you this morning, didn't he? If he was already suspicious, my presence might have prompted him to come in earlier than usual. He hid in the stairwell and turned on the light as you were returning the statue."

"Oh my God, the poor man! He startled me so; he tried to take the statue away and I pushed him. I didn't realize we were so close to the stairs. He just went down, and didn't move. I didn't mean to kill him." Her voice had softened until they could barely hear her.

"Of course you didn't," David Noone said, taking her hand.

"I read about it in a book, about putting the statue in the freezer. I thought it would help the parish. I never meant to hurt anybody."

Monsignor Xavier nodded. "There was something similar down in Nicaragua a few years back. I read about it too. When I saw the ice cream in the sink it reminded me. You see, David, if someone was tampering with the statue overnight it had to be either Marcos or Mrs. Wilkins. The church was locked, with the only entrance from the rectory here. It was locked this morning, when Marcos died. He had a key, and she didn't need one."

"What are they going to do with me?" she asked sadly.

"I don't know," David replied. "We'll have to phone the police. Then I'll go down there with you. I'll stay with you as long as I can. Don't worry."

In the morning Monsignor Xavier departed. He stood for a moment looking up at the church and then shook hands with David Noone. "You have a fine church here. Fine people. I'll tell the Cardinal that."

It was after the morning Mass, and as he watched the monsignor get into his taxi for the airport, Celia Orlando approached him. "The statue is gone, Father. Where is the statue?"

"I didn't expect to see you at Mass, Celia."

"He can't tell me how to pray. I said that to him. But where is the statue?"

"I'm keeping it in the rectory for a few days. It was all a hoax, I'm afraid. There was no miracle. You'll read about it in the papers."

She nodded, but he wondered if she really understood his words. "That's all right," she said. "I managed to wipe a bit of the sweat off one day with a piece of cotton. I carry it with me all the time. I'll never throw it away."

THE PATRON SAINT OF THE IMPOSSIBLE

Rufus King

The murder backdrop was the Florida room of the Hoffmann home in Halcyon, which is a small Florida town composed of the modestly retired, seasoned tourists, native crackers, horse-happy railbirds, amiable bookies, and glazed divorcées. It rests, this gentle haven, on the Atlantic seaboard between the gilt splendors of Miami Beach and the ormolu patina of Fort Lauderdale.

The Hoffmann house is one of the older and more pretentious of Halcyon's estates, being surrounded with lush masses of semitropical shrubbery and flowering trees that afford a screening of privacy from neighbors.

The hour when Monsignor Lavigny became involved in the crime (he lived directly to the east of the Hoffmanns) was eight o'clock on a Tuesday morning in April, during a tranquil moment in which the Monsignor was annoying several aphids

Rufus Kind (1893–1966) wrote more than two dozen mystery novels and short story collections during his lifetime. The novels ceased in 1951 and he turned increasingly to short stories like the following one for *Ellery Queen's Mystery Magazine*, set in the small Florida towns he knew so well.

118

on his Bella Romana camellias with a nicotine spray. Sunshine slanted gently onto his silver-crested head and distinguished appearance, which bore a nostalgic resemblance to the late Walter Hampden in his portrayal of Cardinal Richelieu.

The people involved in the tragedy he knew very well. They were Candice Hoffmann, the murdered man's teen-age niece-and-ward, and a black-browed athletic young ox with the romantic name of Raul Eusebio Fuentes, who was the Hoffmanns' neighbor to the west.

The youngsters were, of course, in love. It was the first and therefore the fiercest sort of blind emotion on Candice's part, but hardly the first on Raul's, whose reservoir of sentiment had begun operations in his birthplace in the Oriente province of Cuba at the tender age of twelve. This in no fashion diluted the young man's intensity, nor the passionate resentment he held toward Hoffmann (now a corpse) over Hoffmann's refusal to consent to his ward's marriage while she remained a minor and legally under his skeletal thumb.

Perhaps skeletal was a touch extreme, as Monsignor Lavigny believed that Hoffmann's air of fleshlessness, both physically and in the amenities, was basically due to the man's several ailments, among which was a rickety heart, and all of which combined to make him a decidedly acid character.

It was a character to be deplored even for its lesser sins of pride, conceit, and a miserly grip on possessions both human and material. So convinced was Hoffmann of his control over his body that he even refused to acknowledge the existence of physical pain. As for the parading of any bodily deficiency, that was out of the question. And yet, in spite of it all, Monsignor Lavigny had always looked upon Hoffmann as a soul to be enticed into the fold. Difficult, and now (thanks to a bashed skull) beyond further attempt.

The fourth member of the blood-tinged masque was Hoffmann's wife, Elise. She seemed a brave and handsome asset, much younger than her husband, and a woman whom Monsignor Lavigny considered to have been a bride of circumstance. Just what the circumstances were that introduced her into a marriage with Hoffmann he did not know, but he imagined they had lain within the periphery of economics, perhaps of loneliness, perhaps of some fortuitous avenue of escape. Gratitude also was a possible explanation—but never love.

The curtain rose at eight in the morning on the tooting of an automobile horn.

Monsignor Lavigny left the outraged aphids in a state of suspended peace, and responded with a wave to the gloved hand of Elise Hoffmann as she drove by in her foreign convertible, heading for home. The glimpse of her cotton-crisp freshness and gaily insolent excuse-for-a-hat blended pleasingly with the tone of the morning.

As he later told his young friend Stuff Driscoll, chief criminal investigator for the sheriff's department, not many minutes seemed to have passed before the Monsignor heard the scream. Even across the distance that separated the two houses, the scream came clearly through the fulling flora as one of shock mingled with horror.

The prelate cast dignity to the winds and broke into a lope that halted at the open jalousies of the Hoffmann Florida room, where the scene was appallingly similar to the final curtain of a Greek tragedy.

Elise Hoffmann, still hatted and gloved, stood stage center and had been turned, apparently, into a pillar of stone. At her feet, with his acid face flecked with blood, lay Hoffmann, flat as only the dead can lie flat. Then to complete the ghastly tableau, under an archway leading into a central hall, young Candice was stretched out on terrazzo tiling in a state of collapse.

The pillar of stone swayed as shock began to recede from Elise. Her clouded eyes seemed to clear as she focused them upon Monsignor Lavigny.

"He ran out," she said. "He struck Candice brutally—senselessly—"

"Who did, Elise?"

There was a flicker of irritation in her voice, as though the answer should be obvious.

"Why, Raul, of course."

* * *

"The thought is beyond belief," Monsignor Lavigny said to Stuff Driscoll as they sat in the Lavigny patio eating cashew nuts and drinking cooled Chablis.

"The evidence proves otherwise, Father." (The prelate preferred the usage of that title by his friends rather than Monsignor, with the latter's stiltedness and variety of mispronunciations.) "I am sorry about it, too, because I know you like the bum."

"Bum? No, never that. Patriot, if you wish. Raul is a youngster who is deeply, devotedly in love and hence unpredictable, but he is neither a killer nor a bum."

Stuff, whose mind and experience inclined him to the dogma that a fact was ruler-straight, could never accustom himself to Monsignor Lavigny's ability to throw a few curves across the plate. There had been that child-kidnapping case last year, the beach robbery of the Terressi diamonds the year before . . .

"What has patriotism got to do with it?" he asked skeptically, even while filing the thought for further consideration. "Raul Fuentes has been naturalized and living here for years."

"Perhaps it has everything to do with it. Or nothing. There is a parable—"

Stuff interrupted with a certain firmness, but still within the limits of respect. Monsignor Lavigny's parables were notoriously of interminable length. "Father, let me give you the picture as we are turning it over to the county prosecutor. I think you'll agree that the job was one of passion? Balked love, then murderous hate?"

"Yes, with some reservations."

"But what's left? Money? Profit? Neither motive figures. Whatever else he is, Fuentes is a rich kid, and Candice is a wealthy girl. Just happens she is under age. They could elope and get hitched by some J.P. up in Georgia but they're both sincerely religious, and surely such a marriage would not be acceptable in the eyes of the Church. Especially with her guardian forbidding it."

Monsignor Lavigny absently inclined his head.

"Actually," Stuff went on, "they had no alternative but to persuade Hoffmann to change his decision. Do you know his reasons for objecting to the match?"

"I did talk with him, and it is possible to understand his point of view."

"It makes good sense to me, too. Elise Hoffmann discussed it while you were staying over at the Sacred Heart with Candice." (This was the hospital where the young girl had been taken.) "Consider Raul's actions. He's in his early twenties and rich, but where does the money come from?"

"Why, from his paternal estate in Cuba, as I understand it."

"So he says. Then why within the past year did he set up a phony ranch in the boondocks west of Davie? Why does he keep a plane there which he pilots himself, and a camouflage stable of mixed-up plugs strictly out of old milk routes?"

Monsignor smiled blandly. "Hope springs eternal, especially on the race track."

"Now that's nonsense, Father, and you know it. If one of those antique platers even caught sight of a starting gate he'd collapse from fright. And what about Raul's habit of disappearing for a day, or a week, and then side-stepping questions as to where he was or why? According to Mrs. Hoffmann, even Candice can't dig it out of him."

"There are certain things that cannot be discussed except," Monsignor Lavigny murmured, "in the confessional. If I may refer to certain of the martyrs—"

"Fuentes? A martyr? In my book the guy's up to his neck in some sort of racket."

"My reference was oblique."

"Well, there was nothing oblique about the three-cornered row Elise Hoffmann overheard yesterday morning before she drove over to Pompano. She got a load of it while she was packing her bag in her bedroom. Hoffmann, Candice, and Fuentes were in the patio just outside her windows. Fuentes gave them *both* the works, the gist being that Hoffmann either change his mind, or Candice agree to forego the Church and elope, and then he tacked on the threadbare old cliché 'or else.'"

"The boy was overwrought. In his heart he did not mean it."

"Father, Father!" Stuff's tone was kindly with pity. "The evidence proves that Raul was sitting right at the table this morning while Hoffmann ate breakfast, and where he was killed."

"Did any of the servants—but they couldn't have. I remember that they are gone."

"Yes, the staff left yesterday to open up the Hoffmann summer place on Sea Island. The family were to drive up there today, which is why Elise Hoffmann made her early start back from Pompano." Stuff studied Monsignor Lavigny with a slight frown. "You have something on your mind, Father?"

"There is a definite contradiction. Please explain your conviction that Raul was seated at the breakfast table with Hoffmann."

"For one thing, you yourself were told by Mrs. Hoffmann that the man she saw escaping was Fuentes."

"The poor woman was in a state of shock."

"We'll have further confirmation when Candice recovers consciousness. But even if Candice didn't see who struck her, there is the circumstantial evidence of the drinking glass, and you can't get around it."

"What glass?"

"First, let's follow Elise Hoffmann's story. She waves hello to you as she drives by and you wave back. She puts her car in the garage, then carries her overnight bag into the house. She passes Candice's room and knows the girl is in it because through the closed door she hears Candice's portable TV set turned on. She leaves her bag in Hoffmann's and her suite, figures he's breakfasting in the Florida room, and goes there. You know what she found."

"A shocking, hideous thing!"

"She is stunned into senselessness. I will admit—in fact, she admits it herself—that her vision may have become blurred by the shock. She sees this figure who she thinks is Fuentes, and the drinking glass proves he *was* Fuentes, doing a quicksilver exit toward the archway where he bumps into Candice, bashes her with some sort of metal bar, and beats it as Mrs. Hoffmann gets back her vocal powers and starts to screech."

Monsignor Lavigny said patiently, "The glass?"

"Yes, the all-important glass. Now get this, Father. The breakfast table was laid for one, or Hoffmann. Candice had her own tray in her bedroom. Apart from other things like coffee and toast, there were a pitcher of orange juice and two glasses on the table. Both glasses had been used and each still contained some juice. One glass was beside Hoffmann's plate. The other was across the table where someone else had been sitting."

"Surely it was Candice, joining her uncle in a glass of orange juice after having prepared his breakfast?"

"No, Father—no on a couple of counts. Apart from the fact that she was probably in a huff over yesterday's row and therefore steering clear of Hoffmann, Elise Hoffmann tells me that Candice dislikes any citrus fruit or juice. All of which is purely academic, due to the fingerprints."

"On the second glass?"

"Yes. There are those of Fuentes where he held it while drinking. They have been identified by comparison with one found on objects in his bathroom and on silver toilet articles on his dresser. Now this is the clincher, Father. There are *also*—on that second glass, mind you—prints of the thumb and three fingers of Hoffmann's left hand, put there when he poured the orange juice into the glass and handed it to Fuentes."

Monsignor Lavigny's eyes were clouded. He said softly, "The contradictions increase."

"We think," Stuff continued, "that Fuentes stepped over to renew his demands of yesterday, or possibly to apologize and make peace with Candice. We think that somehow Hoffmann had discovered the nature of Fuentes's racket, the reason in back of his unexplained disappearances, and threatened exposure if the kid didn't agree to give Candice up. Well, you know Fuentes. You can imagine how his hot Spanish blood took over." Stuff felt sudden contrition at the expression on Monsignor Lavigny's kindly face. "Do not take it so hard, Father. Isn't it possible even for you to be mistaken in a man's character?"

"I am not mistaken, but I am a bewildered and a deeply disturbed old man."

"There's nothing to be bewildered about, Father."

Monsignor Lavigny disagreed, speaking with difficulty, as though he were trying to establish for himself a sounder belief in what he was saying. "At the Sacred Heart after several hours that I spent at Candice's bedside there was one moment, brief but perfectly sane and clear, when consciousness returned."

"She spoke? She recognized you?"

"She did. She said she had heard a crash as if someone had fallen—obviously her uncle when he was killed. It took a moment or two for the sound to register, then she ran out of her bedroom and got as far as the archway to the Florida room when she was struck on the head and knew nothing further."

"She didn't see who it was?"

Monsignor Lavigny spoke more hesitantly, as though reluctant to go on. "I must tell you that at this point her voice weakened in answer to my question as to whether her attacker might have been Raul. She said that that was impossible, that Raul was in New York City this morning, that—*she had seen him there*. Then her voice faltered and she relapsed into coma. She has been so ever since."

"Obviously it was delirium speaking, just a hallucination."

"Perhaps, and yet you have not found Raul out at his house, nor out at his ranch. And," Monsignor Lavigny added succinctly, "his plane is gone."

"Of course it is. When he fled from the Hoffmann's he would have driven directly out to the ranch and used the plane for escape."

Monsignor said with what, for him, held a quality of fierceness, "If it were only not for Elise Hoffmann's cloudy identification and the two sets of fingerprints on the glass!"

"An unsurmountable if, Father."

"Yes, perhaps. I can conceive that under certain provocation Raul might kill—but as for striking Candice, never!"

"He may not have known who it was—just heard a person running toward the archway and struck blindly. You're not exactly icy calm after you've just killed a man."

"I still cannot bring myself to accept it. I have had a sudden thought—it may be fantasy, and yet might lead us to the truth. Yes—I shall test it out. I shall be gone from here until tomorrow evening. And you, you will not be offended? Not think me officious if I make a few suggestions?"

"Why do you suppose I'm here? What are they, Father?"

"I would continue the search for the murder weapon or—what may even be of more importance—try to establish its absence from the place where it might normally be."

"I take it you have an idea what it was?"

"Forgive me if I seem evasive, but to be more specific at this moment might bring grievous injustice upon the innocent. I would suggest that you look for a glove that is perhaps stained with dark grease. Also, it might be advisable to consider the *types* of glasses that contained the orange juice."

"You are confusing me badly, Father."

"Have patience, and a reliance on your own excellent deductive powers. Your department has a plane at its disposal, has it not?"

"Yes."

"Then a flight to Sea Island might also be indicated, and a questioning of the Hoffmann staff."

Stuff looked at the prelate sharply. "Along any particular line?"

"Perhaps as to any unusual visitor who may have called at the Hoffmanns' during the past few weeks."

"Unusual in what way?"

"Let us say in the sense of being a stranger to the servants." Monsignor Lavigny grew deadly serious. "And this is the most important suggestion of all."

"Yes?"

"You might arrange with Mother Superior at the Sacred Heart to permit two women from your department, dressed in nursing habits, to alternate watches in keeping a constant guard over Candice. Never should she be left unattended in the company of *anyone.*"

"There is a man posted there now, but we'll do as you say. Both Candice and Mrs. Hoffmann are under protection. And will be until Fuentes is caught."

"Until," Monsignor Lavigny murmured in polite correction, "the murderer is trapped."

"And you, Father? Where will you be while we're doing all this?"

Monsignor Lavigny's smile was both enigmatic and affectionate. His eyes held what Stuff later described as a beyond-the-horizon look.

"I am considering a pilgrimage accompanied by Saint Jude. He has helped me in the past, and I shall ask him to help me now. Saint Jude, as you know, is the patron saint of the impossible, of the seeming impasse. He is of inestimable assistance at a time when there seems no hope left."

The following evening, again in the patio with its velvet chiaroscuro of moonlight and the night-released scent of jasmine, Monsignor Lavigny sat in troubled contemplation absently sipping his after-dinner brandy and awaiting the arrival of Stuff Driscoll.

The prelate had paused at the Sacred Heart on his way home from the airport and had satisfied himself that Candice was under watchful observation by women from the sheriff's department in their borrowed nursing habits.

He had learned that the girl's condition remained unchanged, that the coma continued unbroken. Elise Hoffmann had been at the hospital and had also telephoned anxious inquiries a number of times, as had many of Candice's young friends. There had been (perhaps understandably) no message or inquiry from Raul Fuentes—this, even though the Hoffmann case continued to be front-page news.

Stuff came. He slumped into a chair, accepted brandy, and went directly to the point.

"Father, your suggestions have opened up a new slant. We

believe now that Elise Hoffmann did the job, but the evidence is slim, entirely circumstantial, and a topflight trial counsel might easily get her off."

"My thoughts lay that way, too. I suspected, and I still suspect, a frame-up. The nature of it is almost clear, but not quite. We will find it exceedingly clever, the work of a truly devious mind. Is Mrs. Hoffmann under arrest?"

"No. She is under surveillance. We won't haul her in until we've got Fuentes. The case against that young buzzard is still too strong. Unless," Stuff added with a friendly grin, "your pilgrimage with Saint Jude cleared his slate?"

"To a certain extent it did—at least to my own satisfaction. I am infinitely grateful. When I flew to New York I carried with me a good photograph of Raul. Now then, I shall ask you for your strict attention. You will remember Elise Hoffmann saying that when she passed the closed door of Candice's bedroom she heard a TV program going on inside?"

"Yes?"

"Well, it occurred to me that the broadcast might have offered a solution to Candice's apparent hallucination—when she told me that she, with herself being here in Halcyon, had *seen* Raul in New York City yesterday morning."

A light broke across Stuff's face. "You've hit it, Father—it was the right hour for the Dave Garroway program 'Today'— people in the street before the exhibition-hall window." (It should be noted that this occurred before the program had been moved to its new, its present quarters.) "Haven't I read, or seen—"

"Yes, there was nothing especially original in my thought, nor in the fact itself. I, too, have read of similar incidents—one in which a spectator in a ringside seat at a televised prizefight was recognized by his wife, who was watching the program at home. She later divorced him, I believe, naming his rather notorious lady companion at the bout as corespondent. No, the thought was nothing new, but it served as a possible lead to casting doubt on Elise Hoffmann's eyewitness identification of Raul."

"What was the result?"

"Mr. Garroway was most courteous, most kind—as were Mr. Lescoulie and Mr. Blair. They studied Raul's picture, and *did remember a man who might have been he.* They had noticed the man because of his gestures."

"But why on earth would Fuentes risk showing himself on a nationwide hookup if he wanted to keep his 'mysterious' absences secret? It doesn't make sense."

"A man in love often makes no sense. He was asking forgiveness."

"Of Candice?"

"Yes, forgiveness for his tantrum with its hotheaded 'or else.' He knew Candice's habit of watching that broadcast, and took a chance on her doing so yesterday morning. Raul's gestures were quite compelling in, Mr. Garroway informed me, an operatic fashion. A Latinesque pantomiming of forgive-me-and-I-love-you, done with bravura."

"Would they make the identification under oath in court, or by sworn affidavit?"

"No. I asked. They would hesitate to do so. There would be in their minds too strong an element of uncertainty. In my own mind there is none."

"At least the kid's got one strike in his favor. Then there's the hotel he must have stayed at, or his friends. He should be able to prove an alibi."

"He might not be willing to."

"Why on earth not, Father?"

"He may flatly refuse to talk about his business in New York or his contacts there."

"He'd better. Because if he doesn't, the two sets of finger-prints on that second glass will knock our case against Elise Hoffmann into the nearest ashcan."

"Just what have you got on her so far?"

Stuff gave the prelate a concise account. The murder weapon had been found. Its place of concealment was in a large clump of star jasmine. It was a jack bar, and had been searched for specifically because of its absence from where it should have been (as Father had suggested), along with the jack in the trunk compartment of Elise Hoffmann's car.

There was more. The two glasses were of different types. No gloves were found, but they could have been disposed of later and at greater leisure than the jack bar.

The Sea Island questioning of the Hoffmann staff revealed that there *had* been a stranger. Ten days ago. He had been closeted with Hoffmann for over half an hour. No name, but the Hoffmann maid who had let him in had given a general description which included a noticeable cast in the man's left eye. Identification had proved simple. The man was a local private investigator, well known to the department and to Stuff personally. Up to the time of Hoffmann's death the man had been in Hoffmann's employ, his assignment to obtain evidence for a divorce. A Miami Beach character, a young muscle-operator of the Hercules type, came into the picture as the "other man." This handsome hulk and a legal separation from the Hoffmann assets by divorce offered plenty of motive for the elimination of Hoffmann . . .

A houseboy interrupted. Mister Stuff was urgently wanted on the telephone.

Monsignor Lavigny, while Stuff went into the house, mused on all human frailty, deploring, yet understanding it very well. It was not for him to judge, certainly not for him to punish. That was within the province of the law, while the ultimate appeal lay in the discretion of God. What malignant germ was it that festered in the brain of murder? Never had it been isolated since the days of Cain. What flaw . . .

"Word from the office," Stuff said, rejoining him. "They caught Fuentes. His plane just landed at the ranch. He clammed up. A 'no comment' to end all 'no comments.' They put him in a car, started for headquarters, and he jumped. Now the boondocks have him, not us." Stuff smashed an angry fist into the palm of his hand. "One other report. The guard we've kept on Elise Hoffmann called in that she left the house and drove off in her convertible. It caught him without warning, too late to check on where she's heading. Father, we're doing just fine!"

Monsignor Lavigny stood up. "It would be wise for us to go to the Sacred Heart. On the way we can discuss the advisability of certain arrangements. I believe I can persuade Mother Superior to give her consent to them. Mrs. Hoffmann will take time to drive about while solidifying her next move. Before," he added softly, "she strikes again."

Owing to a regional wave of the Asian flu with its subsequent complications, and that vague bête noire labeled virus, even some of the corridors of the Sacred Heart held beds, and a suppressed air of tension pervaded the hospital. With it existed a certain laxity of the less imperative regulations, while a greater than usual ebb and flow of traffic—nurses, sisters, interns, orderlies, visiting relatives, an occasional doctor—gave the place a semblance of Grand Central Station during what would have been a normally quiet evening hour.

Candice Hoffmann had been fortunate in having been placed in a private room, one vacated by a fatal case of pneumonia. It was a pleasant, impersonal room, its main furnishings being a hospital bed, a dresser, a locker, and some chairs. There were two doors, one to the corridor, the other to a private bathroom. There was about the room an aseptic openness that made concealment impossible.

Two windows, open to the trade wind with its odors of the flowering night, were frames for pale moonlight, while a shaded night lamp washed faint amber across the bed's white pillow and the white-bandaged head with its contusion-marked face resting motionlessly upon it.

Stuff and Monsignor Lavigny stood in the bathroom, in a state of tense expectancy. The bathroom door was opened a crack, sufficiently for them to have a view that included the bed and the corridor door. The two men were continuing an argument in whispers.

"Father, it is still a crime against the federal government."

"Technically, yes. But isn't it the *intention* that truly constitutes a crime? More so, even, than the crime itself? Remember that Raul has been running guns and ammunition to the rebels at his own expense, paying for them out of his own pocket. There has never been any question of illicit gain. Granted, he is a naturalized citizen, but his roots go back to Cuba. He feels that his family and many of his friends have suffered intolerable injustices from the present regime."

"A case of patriotism once-removed."

"Precisely. And precisely why he would rather suffer death than betray his rebel contacts by revealing the truth about his 'mysterious' disappearances. So far there exists no proof of his activities and he will never speak. Just as I, except for your trusted and confidential ear, shall never speak."

A sudden pressure of Stuff's fingers on Monsignor Lavigny's arm brought immobility and silence.

Elise Hoffmann looked in, satisfying herself that the room, with the exception of the patient, was empty. She had been keeping the door under observation for the past five minutes from an inconspicuous post in the traffic-filled corridor, after having noted the departure from the room of a nurse who presumably had arranged her patient for the night.

She came inside and closed the door. A few hurried footsteps carried her to the bed where in fumbling haste her hands pulled the pillow under the bandage-swathed head, while her dark, abandoned eyes flickered in apprehensive observation between pale windows and the closed corridor door.

She pressed the pillow firmly down on the bruise-marked face.

There was no movement, no struggle. A noise made Mrs. Hoffmann look toward the bathroom door which, remarkably, now stood open with, more remarkably still, that sheriff's man, Mr. Driscoll, framed there with a Leica camera leveled against one eye. Then he was saying, almost casually, "All right, Miss Brown. I have it. You can get up now."

The strong arms of Miss Brown (sheriff's dept., physical ed. grad., adept at judo) gave a practiced shove, knocking Elise Hoffmann backward and into a fortuitously located chair.

Extraordinary, the mind, the nerves of a murderer, with

what fierce egomaniac clinging to avoid punishment, to save his neck until the last ditch failed! Those were Monsignor Lavigny's thoughts as he watched Elise Hoffmann stiffen into an icy rage on the chair while, assisted by Stuff, Miss Brown was unswathed from bandages and cleaned of the grease-paint bruise marks that had camouflaged her face.

"I was rearranging the pillow more comfortably," Elise Hoffmann said in a clear frigid tone. "Seeing you quite naturally gave me a shock. Unconsciously I put the pillow down. That photograph you have just taken, Mr. Driscoll, shall be the basis of a suit I shall bring against your office."

No, there was not even a quiver, much less a break. Elise Hoffmann's control was superb and it was perfectly obvious that she intended to fight right on to the well-known last ditch.

Stuff took over.

Dispassionately, courteously, he outlined the case against her, tracing the probable moves, both physical and mental, that she had gone through.

Her years of oppression under Hoffmann's domination, with a fretful hatred inevitably building up. The threat of imminent divorce proceedings, ruining her share under the community property laws between man and wife.

(*Elise Hoffmann did not even start to break. She sat as a figure of chiseled stone, waiting for an idiot to finish with his maunderings. And Monsignor Lavigny again had that over-the-horizon look.*)

Stuff continued. Opportunity presented itself with the morning of the servant-free house, when the staff would be gone to Sea Island, when Candice would, as was her habit, be breakfasting while watching TV in her bedroom, when Hoffmann would be breakfasting alone in the Florida room.

Opportunity aligned itself with the fortuitous fight overheard among Fuentes and Candice and Hoffmann. Fuentes stepped immediately into the role of being groomed as Suspect Number One for the proposed crime.

Then the actual, and this time the true steps. After passing Monsignor Lavigny with a toot of her horn and a good-morning

hand wave, the car was garaged. The jack bar was removed
from the trunk compartment.

*(Elise Hoffmann's face remained a superciliously interested mask.
Monsignor Lavigny had begun to mutter quietly in his Richelieu
beard.)*

Candice was, as expected, in her bedroom. Hoffmann was,
as expected, breakfasting alone in the Florida room. Not much
of a blow on the head was required to cause death—his rickety
heart contributed to the result. He toppled sideways off the
chair and crashed down to the floor. Then the sound of running
footsteps—Candice. A hasty flattening against the wall beside
the archway and a blow with the jack bar as Candice ran
through—a blow to silence her as an eyewitness to the immediate picture of the crime.

*(Elise Hoffmann smiled. Monsignor Lavigny's muttering grew
faintly feverish.)*

Stuff resolutely went on. Not yet the screams. First, the run
outdoors to conceal the jack bar among the jasmines. Then the
hurried return to the Florida room with the assuming of a
horror-stricken pose. Then the screams.

Stuff's recapitulation was a dud.

In the hush of the room, as Stuff's voice died out, Elise
Hoffmann laughed. A cold, amused, diamond-hard laugh.

"Isn't there a rather important piece of evidence omitted,
Mr. Driscoll? Even the newspaper accounts have played it up
quite strongly. I refer, of course, to the second glass."

Yes, Stuff realized, her bastions of defense still held. She
would never yield while the contradiction offered by the fingerprints remained unresolved. Disheartedly he noticed that
Monsignor Lavigny's mutterings were approaching the deci-
pherable. They seemed to be a murmured supplication to Saint
Jude. Then the prelate's voice exploded with the effect of a
minor bomb.

"I have it! The solution to the second glass. The glass was,"
he said, "a different type from the one beside your husband's
plate, because it came from no set of glassware in your house."

"Merely an odd one, Monsignor," Elise Hoffmann said indifferently. "A leftover from a former set."

Monsignor Lavigny wrapped himself in the full dignity of his high office. His voice might remotely be said to have thundered.

"Madame, we are through with lies! You had determined to make Raul Fuentes the scapegoat. You could not place him physically upon the scene, so you placed an object he had handled upon the scene. I am convinced that you stopped at Raul's house as you started off for Pompano with the direct intention of picking up just such an object. You had the excuse of mediating the quarrel that had shortly occurred. But you did not need the excuse. You found him gone. You were able unobserved to find and take a glass, probably from his bathroom shelf. It is conceivable that its pattern will match a set in use in his house.

"You were wearing driving gloves of chamois, the ones you wore when you waved to me, the ones you have since destroyed. You carried that glass with you to Pompano, guarding and preserving Raul's fingerprints with some protective such as a scarf.

"After you had killed your husband and struck Candice down, you concealed the jack bar, got the glass, poured orange juice into it and set it on the table—*after*, I am convinced, you pressed your dead husband's fingerprints upon it to indicate that he had filled and handed the glass to Raul."

"You are convinced," Elise Hoffmann said. "But will a jury be?"

"They will be because you made one fatal error. When you pressed your husband's fingerprints upon the glass *two of those prints were superimposed upon those of Raul*. Proving that Raul's were on the glass first, and that your husband's were put upon it after his death. You look ill, madame—and well you may!"

She broke completely.

The moon continued its coursing through the scented night.

Raul had been intercepted, and released, in the hospital grounds while on his way to Candice. He was with her now in the room to which she had been transferred when the sheriff's Miss Brown had masqueraded in her place.

Scotch and soda rested on the patio table.

"Father, was it Saint Jude?"

Monsignor Lavigny's voice mellowed with a modest note. "I am gratefully certain that it was. My own poor wits could never have achieved it of themselves."

"And I suppose," said Stuff, "that it was Saint Jude who cracked Elise Hoffmann's nerve? That it was not you, Father, who made the miraculous statement that two of Hoffmann's prints were superimposed upon those of Fuentes?"

Monsignor Lavigny's eyes were the essence of pious innocence as he said, "Well, weren't they?"

"They were not, Father—as you very well know."

THE SANCHEZ SACRAMENTS

Marcia Muller

❧ I was in the basement of the museum un-
packing the pottery figures Adolfo Sanchez had left us when I
began to grow puzzled about the old man and his work. It was
the priest figures that bothered me.

Sanchez had been one of Mexico's most outstanding folk
artists, living in seclusion near the pottery-making center of
Metepec. His work had taken the form of groupings of figures
participating in such religious ceremonies as weddings, feast
days, and baptisms. The figures we'd received from his estate—
actually from the executrix of his estate, his sister, Lucia—
represented an entire life cycle in five of the seven Catholic
sacraments. They'd arrived by truck only yesterday, along with
Sanchez's written instructions about setting them up, and I'd

Marcia Muller, who resides near San Francisco, is one of the new breed
of mystery writers whose female private eyes are challenging the male
dominance of the hardboiled field. Her character Sharon McCone has
appeared in nearly a dozen novels and stories to date. The tale that
follows is about a newer Muller character, Santa Barbara museum
curator Elena Oliverez. It's a blending of religious art and past crime in
a manner Chesterton would have appreciated.

137

decided to devote this morning to unpacking them so we could place them on display in our special exhibits gallery next week.

The crate I'd started with contained the priests, one for each sacrament, and I'd set the two-foot-tall, highly glazed pottery figures at intervals around the room, waiting to be joined by the other figures that would complete each scene. Four of the five figures represented the same man, his clean-shaven face dour, eyes kindly and wise. The fifth, which belonged to the depiction of Extreme Unction—the last rites—was bearded and haggard, with an expression of great pain. But what was puzzling was that this priest was holding out a communion wafer, presumably to a dying parishioner.

I'm not a practicing Catholic, in spite of the fact I was raised one, but I do remember enough of my Catechism to know that they don't give communion during Extreme Unction. What they do is anoint the sense organs with holy oil. Adolfo Sanchez certainly should have known that, too, because he was an extremely devout Catholic and devoted his life to portraying religious scenes such as this.

There was a book on the worktable that I'd bought on the old man's life and works. I flipped through it to see if there were any pictures of other scenes depicting Extreme Unction, but if he'd done any, they weren't in this particular volume. Disappointed, I skimmed backwards through a section of pictures of the artist and his family and found the biographical sketch at the front of the book.

Adolfo had been born seventy-seven years ago in Metepec. As was natural for a local boy with artistic talent, he'd taken up the potter's trade. He'd married late, in his mid-thirties, to a local girl named Constantina Lopez, and they'd had one child, Rosalinda. Rosalinda had married late also, by Mexican standards—in her early twenties—and had given birth to twin boys two years later. Constantina Sanchez had died shortly after her grandsons' birth, and Rosalinda had followed, after a lingering illness, when the twins were five. Ever since the boys had left home, Adolfo had lived in seclusion with only his sister

Lucia as faithful companion. He had devoted himself to his art, even to the point of never attending church.

Maybe, I thought, he'd stayed away long enough that he'd forgotten exactly how things were done in the Catholic faith. But I'd stayed away, and I still remembered.

Senility, then? I flipped to the photograph of the old man at the front of the book and stared into his eyes, clear and alert above his finely chiseled nose and thick beard. No, Sanchez had not been senile. Well, in any event, it was time I got on with unpacking the rest of the figures.

I was cradling one of a baptismal infant when Emily, my secretary, appeared. She stood at the bottom of the steps, one hand on the newel post, her pale-haired head cocked to one side, looking worried.

"Elena?" she said. "There are two . . . gentlemen here to see you."

Something about the way she said "gentlemen" gave me pause. I set the infant's figure down on the work table.

"What gentlemen?"

"The Sanchez brothers."

"Who?" For a moment I didn't connect them with the twins I'd just been reading about. Sanchez is a common Mexican name.

"They're here about the pottery." She motioned at the crates. "One is in your office, and Susana has taken the other to the courtyard."

Susana Ibarra was the Museum of Mexican Art's public relations director—and troubleshooter. If she had elected to take one of the Sanchez twins under her wing, it was because he was either upset or about to cause a scene.

"Is everything all right?"

Emily shrugged. "So far."

"I'll be right up."

"Which one do you want to see first?"

"Can't I see them together?"

"I wouldn't advise it. They almost came to blows in the courtyard before Susana took over."

"Oh." I paused. "Well then, if Susana has the one she's talking to under control, I'll go directly to my office."

Emily nodded and went upstairs.

I moved the infant's figure into the center of the large work table and checked to see if the other figures were securely settled. To break one of them would destroy the effect of the entire work, to say nothing of its value. When I'd assured myself they were safe, I followed Emily upstairs.

Once there, I hurried through the folk art gallery, with its Tree of Life and colorful papier-mâché animals, and peered out into the central courtyard. Susana Ibarra and a tall man wearing jeans and a rough cotton shirt stood near the little fountain. The man's arms were folded across his chest and he was frowning down at her. Susana had her hands on her hips and was tossing her thick mane of black hair for emphasis as she spoke. From the aggressive way she balanced on her high heels, I could tell that she was giving the man a lecture. And, knowing Susana, if that didn't work she'd probably dunk him in the fountain. Reassured, I smiled and went to the office wing.

When I stepped into my office, the young man seated in the visitor's chair jumped to his feet. He was as tall as Susana's companion and had the same lean, chiseled features and short black hair. In his light tan suit, conservative tie, and highly polished shoes, he looked excessively formal for the casual atmosphere of Santa Barbara.

I held out my hand and said, "Mr. Sanchez? I'm Elena Oliverez, director of the museum."

"Gilberto Sanchez." His accent told me he was a Mexican national. He paused, then added, "Adolfo Sanchez's grandson."

"Please, sit down." I went around the desk and took my padded leather chair. "I understand you're here about the Sacraments."

For a moment he looked blank. "Oh, the figures from Tía Lucia. Yes."

"You didn't know they're called the Sanchez Sacraments?"

"No. I don't know anything about them. That is why I'm here."

"I don't understand."

He leaned forward, his fine features serious. "Let me explain. My mother died when my brother Eduardo and I were only five—we are fraternal twins. My father had left long before that, so we had only Grandfather and Tía Lucia. But Grandfather wanted us to see more of the world than Metepec. It is a small town, and Grandfather's village is even smaller. So he sent us to school and then university in Mexico City. After college I remained on there."

"So you never saw the Sacraments?"

"No. I knew Grandfather was working on something important the last years of his life, but whenever I went to visit him, he refused to let me see the project. It was the same with Eduardo; we were not even allowed in his workroom."

"Did he tell you anything about it?"

"No. Tía Lucia did not even know. All she said was that he had told her it was the finish of his life's work. Now he is gone, and even before Eduardo and I could get to Metepec for the funeral, Tía Lucia shipped the figures off to you. She won't talk about them, just says they are better off in a museum."

"And you. . . ?"

"I want to see them. Surely you can understand that, Miss Oliverez. I loved my grandfather. Somehow it will make his death easier to accept if I can see the work of the last ten years of his life." Gilberto's eyes shone with emotion as he spoke.

I nodded, tapping my fingers on the arm of my chair. It was an odd story, and it sounded as if Gilberto's aunt hadn't wanted him or his twin brother to see the figures. To give myself time to order my thoughts, I said, "What do you do in Mexico City, Mr. Sanchez?"

If the abrupt switch in subject surprised him, he didn't show it. "I am a banker."

That explained his conservative dress. "I see."

He smiled suddenly, a wonderful smile that transformed his face and showed me what he might be like without the pall of death hanging over him. "Oh, I am not totally without the family madness, as my grandfather used to call the artistic temperament. I paint in my spare time."

"Oils?"

"Yes."

"Are you talented?"

He considered. "Yes, I think so."

I liked his candor, and immediately decided that I also liked him. "Mr. Sanchez, I understand you and your brother almost came to blows in our courtyard earlier."

The smile dropped away and he colored slightly. "Yes, we met as we were both coming in. I had no idea he was in Santa Barbara."

"What was your argument about?"

"The Sacraments, as you call them. You see, Eduardo also came to Metepec for the funeral. He lives in Chicago now, where he is a film maker—television commercials mainly, but he also does other, more artistic work. The family madness passed down to him, too. Anyway, he was as upset as I was about the Sacraments being gone, but for a different reason."

"And what was that?"

Gilberto laced his long fingers together and looked down at them, frowning. "He thinks Tía Lucia had no right to give them away. He says they should have come down to us. And he wants them back so he can sell them."

"And you don't agree?"

"No, I don't." Quickly he looked up. "We were well provided for in Grandfather's will, but he made Tía Lucia his executrix. She says it was Grandfather's wish that the Sacraments go to a museum. And I feel a man has the right to dispose of his work in any way he chooses."

"Then why are you here?"

"Only because I wish to see the Sacraments."

I decided right then that I had better contact Lucia Sanchez before I went any further with this. "Well, Mr. Sanchez," I said, "the figures just arrived yesterday and haven't been unpacked yet. I plan to have them on exhibit early next week. At that time—"

"Would it be possible to view them privately?"

He looked so eager that I hated to disappoint him, so I said, "I'm sure something can be arranged."

The smile spread across his face again and he got to his feet. "I would appreciate that very much."

Aware that he would not want another run-in with his brother, I showed him the way out through the little patio outside my office, then started out to the central courtyard. Emily was at her desk, doing something to a ditto master with a razor blade.

"Is Susana still talking to Eduardo Sanchez?" I asked her.

"Yes. They seem to have made friends. At least they were sitting on the edge of the fountain laughing when I went past five minutes ago."

"Susana could charm the spots off a leopard." I turned to go, then paused. "Emily, do we have a telephone number for Lucia Sanchez?"

"Yes, I put it in my Rolodex."

"I'll want to talk to her today."

"Then I'd better start trying now. Service to the Metepec area is bound to be poor."

"Right. If I'm not back here by the time the call goes through, come and get me." I turned and went through the doorway to the courtyard.

As Emily had said, Susana and Eduardo Sanchez were sitting on the edge of the blue-tiled fountain, and she appeared to be telling him one of her infamous jokes. Susana loved long jokes, the more complicated the better. The trouble was, she usually forgot the punchlines, or mixed them up with the endings of other jokes. Only her prettiness and girlish charm— she was only seventeen—saved her from mayhem at the hands of her listeners.

When he saw me, Eduardo Sanchez stood up—not as quickly as his brother had, but almost indolently. Up close I could see that his fine features were chiseled more sharply than

Gilberto's, as if the sculptor had neglected to smooth off the rough edges. His hair was longer too, artfully blow-dried, and although his attire was casual, I noted his loafers were Guccis.

Eduardo's handshake, when Susana introduced us, was indolent too. His accent was not so pronounced as his twin's, and I thought I caught a faint, incongruous touch of the Midwest in the way he said hello.

I said, "It's a pleasure to meet you, Mr. Sanchez. I see Ms. Ibarra has been taking good care of you."

He glanced over at Susana, who was standing, smoothing the pleats of her bright green dress. "Yes, she has been telling me a story about a dog who dresses up as a person in order to get the fire department to 'rescue' a cat he has chased up a tree. We have not reached the ending, however, and I fear we never will."

Susana flashed her brilliant smile. "Can I help it if I forget? The jokes are all very long, and in this life a person can only keep so much knowledge in her head."

"Don't worry, Susana," I said. "I'd rather you kept the dates of our press releases in there than the punchline to such a silly story."

"Speaking of the press releases . . ." She turned and went toward the door to the office wing.

Eduardo Sanchez's eyes followed her. "An enchanting girl," he said.

"Yes, we're fortunate to have her on staff. And now, what can I do for you? I assume you've come about the Sacraments?"

Unlike his brother, he seemed to know what they were called. "Yes. Has Gilberto filled you in?"

"A little."

Eduardo reclaimed his seat on the edge of the fountain. "He probably painted me as quite the villain, too. But at least you know why I'm here. Those figures should never have been donated to this museum. Rightfully they belong to Gilberto and me. We either want them returned or paid for."

"You say 'we.' It was my impression that all your brother wants is to see them."

He made an impatient gesture with one hand. "For a banker, Gilberto isn't very smart."

"But he does seem to have respect for your grandfather's wishes. He loved him very much, you know."

His eyes flashed angrily. "And do you think I didn't? I worshipped the man. If it wasn't for him and his guidance, I'd be nobody today."

"Then why go against his wishes?"

"For the simple reason that I don't know if donating those pieces to this museum was what he wanted."

"You think your aunt made that up?"

"She may have."

"Why?"

"I don't know!" He got up and began to pace.

I hesitated, then framed my words carefully. "Mr. Sanchez, I think you have come to the wrong person about this. It appears to be a family matter, one you should work out with your aunt and brother."

"I have tried."

"Try again. Because there's really nothing I can do."

His body tensed and he swung around to face me. I tensed too, ready to step back out of his reach. But then he relaxed with a conscious effort, and a lazy smile spread across his face.

"Clever, aren't you?"

"I have to be, Mr. Sanchez. The art world may seem gentle and nonmaterialistic to outsiders, but—as you know from your work in films—art is as cutthroat a business as any other. To run a museum, you have to be clever—and strong-willed."

"I get your message." The smile did not leave his face.

"Then you'll discuss this with your family?"

"Among others. I'll be in touch." He turned and stalked out of the courtyard.

I stood there, surprised he'd given up so easily, and very much on my guard. Eduardo Sanchez was not going to go away. Nor was his brother. As if I didn't have enough to contend with here at the museum, now I would be dragged into a family quarrel. Sighing, I went to see if Emily had been able to put my call through to Metepec.

The following afternoon, Lucia Sanchez sat across my desk from me, her dark eyes focused anxiously on mine. In her cotton dress that was faded from too many washings, her work-roughened hands clutching a shabby leather handbag, she reminded me of the aunts of my childhood who would come from Mexico for family weddings or funerals. They had seemed like people from another century, those silent women who whispered among themselves and otherwise spoke only when spoken to. It had been hard to imagine them as young or impassioned, and it was the same with Miss Sanchez. Only her eyes seemed truly alive.

When I'd spoken to her on the phone the day before, she'd immediately been alarmed at her great-nephews' presence in Santa Barbara and had decided to come to California to reason with them.

Now she said, "Have you heard anything further from either of the boys?"

"Oh, yes." I nodded. "Gilberto has called twice today asking when the figures will be ready for viewing. Eduardo has also called twice, threatening to retain a lawyer if I don't either return the Sacraments or settle upon a 'mutually acceptable price.'"

Lucia Sanchez made a disgusted sound. "This is what it comes to. After all their grandfather and I did for them."

"I can see where you would be upset by Eduardo's behavior, but what Gilberto is asking seems quite reasonable."

"You do not know the whole story. Tell me, are the figures on display yet?"

"They have been arranged in our special exhibits gallery, yes. But it will not be open to the public until next Monday."

"Good." She nodded and stood, and the calm decisiveness of her manner at once erased all resemblance to my long-departed aunts. "I should like to see the pieces, if I may."

I got up and led her from the office wing and across the

courtyard to the gallery that held our special exhibits. I'd worked all the previous afternoon and evening setting up the figures with the help of two student volunteers from my alma mater, the University of California's Santa Barbara campus. This sort of active participation in creating the exhibits was not the usual province of a director, but we were a small museum and since our director had been murdered and I'd been promoted last spring, we'd had yet to find a curator who would work for the equally small salary we could offer. These days I wore two hats—not always comfortably.

Now, as I ushered Lucia Sanchez into the gallery and turned on the overhead spotlights, I had to admit that the late evening I'd put in had been worthwhile. There were five groupings, each on a raised platform, each representing a Sacrament. The two-foot-tall pottery figures were not as primitive in appearance as most folk art; instead, they were highly representational, with perfect proportions and expressive faces. Had they not been fired in an extremely glossy and colorful glaze, they would have seemed almost real.

Lucia Sanchez paused on the threshold of the room, then began moving counterclockwise, studying the figures. I followed.

The first Sacrament was a baptism, the father holding the infant before the priest while the mother and friends and relatives looked on. Next came a confirmation, the same proud parents beaming in the background. The figure of the bride in the wedding ceremony was so carefully crafted that I felt if I reached out and touched her dress it would be the traditional embroidered cotton rather than clay. The father smiled broadly as he gave her away, placing her hand in that of the groom.

The other two groupings were not of joyous occasions. Extreme Unction—the last rites—involved only the figure of the former bride on her deathbed and the priest, oddly offering her the final communion wafer. And the last scene—Penance—was not a grouping either, but merely the figure of a man kneeling in the confessional, the priest's face showing dimly through the grille. Logically, the order of these two scenes should have been reversed, but Sanchez's written instructions for setting them up had indicated it should be done in this order.

Lucia Sanchez circled the room twice, stopping for a long time in front of each of the scenes. Then, looking shaken, she returned to where I stood near the door and pushed past me into the courtyard. She went to the edge of the fountain and stood there for a long moment, hands clasped on her purse, head bowed, staring into the splashing water. Finally I went up beside her and touched her arm.

"Miss Sanchez," I said, "are you all right?"

She continued staring down for about ten seconds, then raised agonized eyes to mine. "Miss Oliverez," she said, "you must help me."

"With the possibility of a lawsuit? Of course—"

"No, not just the lawsuit. That is not really important. But I do ask your help with this: Gilberto and Eduardo must never see those figures. Never, do you understand? Never!"

At nine o'clock that evening, I was sitting in the living room of my little house in Santa Barbara's flatlands, trying to read a fat adventure novel Susana had loaned me. It was hot for late September, and I wore shorts and had the windows open for cross-ventilation. An hour before the sound of the neighbors' kids playing kickball in the street had been driving me crazy; now everything seemed too quiet.

The phone hadn't rung once all evening. My current boyfriend—Dave Kirk, an Anglo homicide cop, of all things— was mad at me for calling off a tentative date the previous evening so I could set up the Sanchez Sacraments. My mother, who usually checked in at least once a day to make sure I was still alive and well, was off on a cruise with her seventy-eight-year-old boyfriend. Although her calls normally made me think a move to Nome, Alaska, would be desirable, now I missed her and would have liked to hear her voice.

I also would have liked to talk out the matter of the Sanchez Sacraments with her. Mama had a keen intelligence and an ability to sometimes see things I'd missed that were right under my nose. And in the case of the Sacraments, I was missing something very important. Namely, why Lucia Sanchez was so adamant that neither of her great-nephews should ever view the figures.

Try as I might, I hadn't been able to extract the reason from her that afternoon. So, perversely, I hadn't promised that I would bar the brothers from the gallery. I honestly didn't see how I could keep them away from a public exhibit, but perhaps had I known Lucia's reason, I might have been more willing to find a way. As it was, I felt trapped between the pleas of this woman, whom I liked very much, and the well-reasoned request of Gilberto. And on top of that, there was the fear of a lawsuit over the Sacraments. I hadn't been able to talk to the museum's attorney—he was on vacation—and I didn't want to do anything, such as refusing the brothers access to the exhibit, that would make Eduardo's claim against us stronger.

I shifted on the couch and propped my feet on the coffee table, crossing them at the ankles. I gave the novel a final cursory glance, sighed, and tossed it aside. Susana and I simply did not have the same taste in fiction. There was a *Sunset* magazine that she had also given me on the end table. Normally I wouldn't have looked at a publication that I considered aimed at trendy, affluent Anglos, but now I picked it up and began to thumb through it. I was reading an article on outdoor decking— ridiculous, because my house needed a paint job far more than backyard beautification—when the phone rang. I jumped for it.

The caller was Lucia Sanchez. "I hope I am not disturbing you by calling so late, Miss Oliverez."

"No, not at all."

"I wanted to tell you that I had dinner with Gilberto and Eduardo. They remain adamant about seeing the Sacraments."

"So Eduardo now wants to see them also?"

"Yes, I assume so he can assess their value." Her tone was weary and bitter.

I was silent.

"Miss Oliverez," she said, "what can we do?"

I felt a prickle of annoyance at her use of the word "we."

"I don't suppose there's anything you can do. *I*, however,

can merely stall them until I speak with the museum's attorney. But I think he'll merely advise me to let them see the figures."

"That must not be!"

"I don't know what else to do. Perhaps if I knew your reason—"

"We have discussed that before. It is a reason rooted in the past. I wish to let the past die, as my brother died."

"Then there's nothing I can do but follow the advice of our lawyer."

She made a sound that could have been a sob and abruptly hung up. I clutched the receiver, feeling cruel and tactless. The woman obviously had a strong reason for what she was asking, so strong that she could confide in no one. And the reason had to be in those figures. Something I could see but hadn't interpreted . . .

I decided to go to the museum and take a closer look at the Sanchez Sacraments.

The old adobe building which housed the museum gleamed whitely in its floodlights. I drove around and parked my car in the lot, then entered by the loading dock, resetting the alarm system behind me. After switching on the lights, I crossed the courtyard—silent now, the fountain's merry tinkling stilled for the night—and went into the special exhibits gallery.

The figures stood frozen in time—celebrants at three rites and sufferers at two others. I turned up the spots to full beam and began with the baptismal scene.

Father, mother, aunts and uncles and cousins and friends. A babe in arms, white dress trimmed with pink ribbons. Priest, the one with the long jaw and dour lines around his mouth. Father was handsome, with chiseled features reminiscent of the Sanchez brothers. Mother, conventionally pretty. All the participants had the wonderfully expressive faces that had been Adolfo Sanchez's trademark. Many reminded me, as Lucia had initially, of my relatives from Mexico.

Confirmation. Daughter kneeling before the same priest. Conventionally pretty, like her mother, who looked on. Father proud, hand on wife's shoulder. Again, the relatives and friends.

Wedding ceremony. Pretty daughter grown into a young woman. Parents somewhat aged, but prouder than ever. Bridegroom in first flush of manhood. Same family and friends and priest—also slightly aged.

So far I saw nothing but the work of an exceptionally talented artist who deserved the international acclaim he had received.

Deathbed scene. Formerly pretty daughter, not so much aged as withered by illness. No family, friends. Priest—the different one, bearded, his features wracked with pain as he offered the communion wafer. The pain was similar to that in the dying woman's eyes. This figure had disturbed me . . .

I stared at it for a minute, then went on.

Penance. A man, his face in his hands. Leaning on the ledge in the confessional, telling his sins. The priest—the one who had officiated at the first joyful rites—was not easily visible through the grille, but I could make out the look of horror on his face that I had first noted when I unpacked the figure.

I stared at the priest's face for a long time, then went back to the deathbed scene. The other priest knelt by the bed—

There was a sudden, stealthy noise outside. I whirled and listened. It came again, from the entryway. I went out into the courtyard and saw light flickering briefly over the little windows to either side of the door.

I relaxed, smiling a little. I knew who this was. Our ever-vigilant Santa Barbara police had noticed a light on where one should not be and were checking to make sure no one was burglarizing the museum. This had happened so often—because I worked late frequently—that they didn't bother to creep up as softly as they might. If I had been a burglar, by now I could have been in the next county. As it was, I'd seen so much of these particular cops that I was considering offering them an honorary membership in our Museum Society. Still, I appreciated their alertness. With a sigh, I went back and switched out the spots in the gallery, then crossed the courtyard to assure them all was well.

A strong breeze came up around three in the morning. It ruffled the curtains at my bedroom window and made the single sheet covering me inadequate. I pulled it higher on my shoulders and curled myself into a ball, too tired to reach down to the foot of the bed for the blanket. In moments I drifted back into a restless sleep, haunted by images of people at religious ceremonies. Or were they people? They stood too still, their expressions were too fixed. Expressions—of joy, of pain, of horror. Pain . . . horror . . .

Suddenly the dream was gone and I sat up in bed, remembering one thing that had disturbed me about Adolfo Sanchez's deathbed scene—and realizing another. I fumbled for the light, found my robe, and went barefooted into the living room to the bookcase where I kept my art library. Somewhere I had that book on Adolfo's life and works, the one I'd bought when the Sacraments had been donated to the museum. I'd barely had time to glance through it again.

There were six shelves and I scanned each impatiently. Where was the damned book anyway? Then I remembered it was at the museum; I'd looked through it in the basement the other day. As far as I knew, it was still on the worktable.

I stood clutching my robe around me and debated going to the museum to get the book. But it was not a good time to be on the streets alone, even in a relatively crime-free town like Santa Barbara, and besides, I'd already alarmed the police once tonight. Better to look at the book when I went in at the regular time next morning.

I went back to bed, pulling the blanket up, and huddled there, thinking about death and penance.

I arrived at the museum early next morning—at eight o'clock, an hour before my usual time. When I entered the office wing, I could hear a terrific commotion going on in the central courtyard. People were yelling in Spanish, all at once, not bothering to listen to one another. I recognized Susana's voice, and thought I heard Lucia Sanchez. The other voices were male, and I could guess they belonged to the Sanchez brothers. They must have used some ploy to get Susana to let them in this early.

I hurried through the offices and out into the courtyard.

Susana turned when she heard my footsteps, her face flushed with anger. "Elena," she said, "you must do something about them!"

The others merely went on yelling. I had been right: It was Gilberto, Eduardo, and Lucia, and they were right in the middle of one of those monumental quarrels that my people are famous for.

". . . contrived to steal our heritage, and I will not allow it!" This from Eduardo.

"You were amply taken care of in your grandfather's will. And now you want more. Greed!" Lucia shook a finger at him.

"I merely want what is mine."

"Yours!" Lucia looked as if she might spit at him.

"Yes, mine."

"What about Gilberto? Have you forgotten him?"

Eduardo glanced at his brother, who was cowering by the fountain. "No, of course not. The proceeds from the Sacraments will be divided equally—"

"I don't want the money!" Gilberto said.

"You be quiet!" Eduardo turned on him. "You are too foolish to know what's good for you. You could help me convince this old witch, but instead you're mooning around here, protesting that you *only want to see* the Sacraments." His voice cruelly mimicked Gilberto.

"But you will receive the money set aside for you in Grandfather's will—"

"It's not enough."

"Not enough for what?"

"I must finish my life's work."

"What work?" Lucia asked.

"My film."

"I thought the film was done."

Eduardo looked away. "We ran over budget."

"Aha! You've already squandered your inheritance. Before you've received it, it's spent. And now you want more. Greed!"

"My film—"

"Film, film, film! I am tired of hearing about it."

This had all been very interesting, but I decided it was time to intervene. Just as Eduardo gave a howl of wounded indignation, I said in Spanish, "All right! That's enough!"

All three turned to me, as if they hadn't known I was there. At once they looked embarrassed; in their family, as in mine, quarrels should be kept strictly private.

I looked at Lucia. "Miss Sanchez, I want to see you in my office." Then I motioned at the brothers. "You two leave. If I catch you on the premises again without my permission, I'll have you jailed for trespassing."

They grumbled and glowered but moved toward the door. Susana followed, making shooing gestures.

I turned and led Lucia Sanchez to the office wing. When she was seated in my visitor's chair, I said, "Wait here. I'll be back in a few minutes." Then I went downstairs to the basement. The book I'd been looking for the night before was where I'd left it earlier in the week, on the worktable. I opened it and leafed through to the section of pictures of the artist and his family.

When young, Adolfo Sanchez had had the same chiseled features as his grandsons; he had, however, been handsome in a way they were not. In his later years, he had sported a beard, and his face had been deeply lined, his eyes sunken with pain.

I turned the page and found photographs of the family members. The wife, Constantina, was conventionally pretty. The daughter, Rosalinda, took after her mother. In a couple of the photographs, Lucia looked on in the background. A final one showed Adolfo with his arms around the two boys, aged about six. Neither the wife nor the daughter was in evidence.

I shut the book with shaky hands, a sick feeling in the pit of my stomach. I should go to the special exhibits gallery and confirm my suspicions, but I didn't have the heart for it.

Besides, the Sacraments were as clear in my mind as if I'd been looking at them. I went instead to my office.

Lucia Sanchez sat as she had before, roughened hands gripping her shabby leather bag. When I came in, she looked up and seemed to see the knowledge in my eyes. Wearily, she passed a hand over her face.

"Yes," I said, "I've figured it out."

"Then you understand why the boys must never see those figures."

I sat down on the edge of the desk in front of her. "Why didn't you just tell me?"

"I've told no one, all those years. It was a secret between my brother and myself. But he had to expiate it, and he chose to do so through his work. I never knew what he was doing out there in his studio. The whole time, he refused to tell me. You can imagine my shock after he died, when I went to look and saw he'd told the whole story in his pottery figures."

"Of course, no one would guess, unless—"

"Unless they knew the family history and what the members had looked like."

"Or noticed something was wrong with the figures and then studied photographs, like I just did."

She acknowledged it with a small nod.

"Adolfo and his wife had a daughter, Rosalinda," I said. "She's the daughter in the Sacraments, and the parents are Adolfo and Constantina. The resemblance is easy to spot."

"It's remarkable, isn't it—how Adolfo could make the figures so real. Most folk artists don't, you know." She spoke in a detached tone.

"And remarkable how he could make the scenes reflect real life."

"That too." But now the detachment was gone, and pain crossed her face.

"Rosalinda grew up and married and had the twins. What happened to her husband?"

"He deserted her, even before the boys were born."

"And Constantina died shortly after."

"Yes. That was when I moved in with them, to help Rosalinda with the children. She was ill . . ."

"Fatally ill. What was it?"

"Cancer."

"A painful illness."

"Yes."

"When did Adolfo decide to end her misery?"

She sat very still, white-knuckled hands clasping her purse.

"Did you know what he had done?" I asked.

Tears came into her eyes and one spilled over. She made no move to wipe it away. "I knew. But it was not as it seems. Rosalinda begged him to help her end her life. She was in such pain. How could Adolfo refuse his child's last request? All her life, she had asked so little of anyone . . ."

"So he complied with her wishes. What did he give her?"

"An overdose of medicine for the pain. I don't know what kind."

"And then?"

"Gradually he began to fail. He was severely depressed. After a year he sent the boys to boarding school in Mexico City; such a sad household was no place for children, he said. For a while I feared he might take his own life, but then he began to work on those figures, and it saved him. He had a purpose and, I realize now, a penance to perform."

"And when the figures were finished, he died."

"Within days."

I paused, staring at her face, which was now streaked with tears. "He told the whole story in the Sacraments—Rosalinda's baptism, confirmation, and marriage. The same friends and relatives were present, and the same parish priest."

"Father Rivera."

"But in the scene of Extreme Unction—Rosalinda's death— Father Rivera doesn't appear. Instead, the priest is Adolfo, and what he is handing Rosalinda appears to be a communion wafer. I noticed that as soon as I saw the figure and wondered about it, because for the last rites they don't give communion, they use holy oil. And it isn't supposed to be a wafer, either, but a lethal dose of pain medicine. At first I didn't notice the priest's resemblance to the father in the earlier scenes because of the beard. But when I really studied photographs of Adolfo, it all became clear."

"That figure is the least representational of the lot," Lucia said. "I suppose Adolfo felt he couldn't portray his crime openly. He never wanted the boys to know. And he probably didn't want the world to know either. Adolfo was a proud man, with an artist's pride in his work and reputation."

"I understand. If the story came out, it would tarnish the value of his work with sensationalism. He disguised himself in the Penance scene too, by having his hands over his face."

Lucia was weeping into her handkerchief now. Through it she said, "What are we to do? Both of the boys are now determined to see the Sacraments. And when they do they will interpret them as you have and despise Adolfo's memory. That was the one thing he feared; he said so in his will."

I got up, went to the little barred window that overlooked the small patio outside my office, and stood there staring absently at the azalea bushes that our former director had planted. I pictured Gilberto, as he'd spoken of his grandfather the other day, his eyes shining with love. And I heard Eduardo saying, "I worshipped the man. If it wasn't for his guidance, I'd be nobody today." They might understand what had driven Adolfo to his mortal sin, but if they didn't . . .

Finally I said, "Perhaps we can do something after all."

"But what? The figures will be on public display. And the boys are determined."

I felt a tension building inside me. "Let me deal with that problem."

My hands balled into fists, I went through the office wing and across the courtyard to the gallery. Once inside, I stopped, looking around at the figures. They were a perfect series of groupings and they told a tale far more powerful than the simple life cycle I'd first taken them to represent. I wasn't sure I could do what I'd intended. What I was contemplating was—for a curator and an art lover—almost as much of a sin as Adolfo's helping his daughter kill herself.

I went over to the deathbed scene and rested my hand gently on the shoulder of the kneeling man. The figure was so perfect it felt almost real.

I thought of the artist, the man who had concealed his identity under these priestly robes. Wasn't the artist and the life he'd lived as important as his work? Part of my job was to protect those works; couldn't I also interpret that to mean I should also protect the memory of the artist?

I stood there for a long moment—and then I pushed the pottery figure, hard. It toppled backward, off the low platform to the stone floor. Pottery smashes easily, and this piece broke into many fragments. I stared down at them, wanting to cry.

When I came out of the gallery minutes later, Susana was rushing across the courtyard. "Elena, what happened? I heard—" She saw the look on my face and stopped, one hand going to her mouth.

Keeping my voice steady, I said, "There's been an accident, and there's a mess on the floor of the gallery. Please get someone to clean it up. And after that, go to my office and tell Lucia Sanchez she and her great-nephews can view the Sacraments any time. Arrange a private showing, for as long as they want. After all, they're family."

"What about . . . ?" She motioned at the gallery.

"Tell them one of the figures—Father Rivera, in the deathbed scene—was irreparably damaged in transit." I started toward the entryway.

"Elena, where are you going?"

"I'm taking the day off. You're in charge."

I would get away from here, maybe walk on the beach. I was fortunate; mine was only a small murder. I would not have to live with it or atone for it the remainder of my lifetime, as Adolfo Sanchez had.

THE EVIDENCE OF THE ALTAR-BOY

Georges Simenon

A fine cold rain was falling. The night was very dark; only at the far end of the street, near the barracks from which, at half-past five, there had come the sound of bugle calls and the noise of horses being taken to be watered, was there a faint light shining in someone's window—an early riser, or an invalid who had lain awake all night.

The rest of the street was asleep. It was a broad, quiet, newish street, with almost identical one– or two–storied houses such as are to be seen in the suburbs of most big provincial towns.

The whole district was new, devoid of mystery, inhabited by quiet unassuming people, clerks and commercial travellers, retired men and peaceful widows.

Maigret, with his overcoat collar turned up, was huddling

It's a pleasure to include one of Georges Simenon's best short cases about Inspector Maigret in this anthology. Although Simenon ceased writing about Maigret more than a decade ago, editions continue to appear in America and Great Britain, some newly translated into English. "The Evidence of the Altar-Boy" is one of the rare Maigret cases to contain a religious element.

in the angle of a carriage gateway, that of the boys' school; he was waiting, watch in hand, and smoking his pipe.

At a quarter to six exactly, bells rang out from the parish church behind him, and he knew that, as the boy had said, it was the "first stroke" for six o'clock Mass.

The sound of the bells was still vibrating in the damp air when he heard, or rather guessed at, the shrill clamour of an alarm clock. This lasted only a few seconds. The boy must already have stretched a hand out of his warm bed and groped in the darkness for the safety-catch that would silence the clock. A few minutes later, the attic window on the second floor lit up.

It all happened exactly as the boy had said. He must have risen noiselessly, before anyone else, in the sleeping house. Now he must be picking up his clothes, his socks, washing his face and hands and combing his hair. As for his shoes, he had declared:

"I carry them downstairs and put them on when I get to the last step, so as not to wake up my parents."

This had happened every day, winter and summer, for nearly two years, ever since Justin had first begun to serve at Mass at the hospital.

He had asserted, furthermore:

"The hospital clock always strikes three or four minutes later than the parish church clock."

And this had proved to be the case. The inspectors of the Flying Squad to which Maigret had been seconded for the past few months had shrugged their shoulders over these tiresome details about first bells and second bells.

Was it because Maigret had been an altar-boy himself for a long time that he had not dismissed the story with a smile?

The bells of the parish church rang first, at a quarter to six. Then Justin's alarm clock went off, in the attic where the boy slept. Then a few moments later came the shriller, more silvery sound of the hospital chapel bells, like those of a convent.

He still had his watch in his hand. The boy took barely more than four minutes to dress. Then the light went out. He must be groping his way down the stairs, anxious not to waken his parents, then sitting down on the bottom step to put on his shoes, and taking down his coat and cap from the bamboo coat-rack on the right in the passage.

The door opened. The boy closed it again without making a sound, looked up and down the street anxiously and then saw the Superintendent's burly figure coming up to him.

"I was afraid you might not be there."

And he started walking fast. He was a thin, fair-haired little twelve-year-old with an obstinate look about him.

"You want me to do just what I usually do, don't you? I always walk fast, for one thing because I've worked out to the minute how long it takes, and for another, because in winter, when it's dark, I'm frightened. In a month it'll be getting light by this time in the morning."

He took the first turning on the right into another quiet, somewhat shorter street, which led on to an open square planted with elms and crossed diagonally by tramlines.

And Maigret noted tiny details that reminded him of his own childhood. He noticed, for one thing, that the boy did not walk close to the houses, probably because he was afraid of seeing someone suddenly emerge from a dark doorway. Then, that when he crossed the square he avoided the trees in the same way, because a man might have been hiding behind them.

He was a brave boy, really, since for two whole winters, in all weathers, sometimes in thick fog or in the almost total darkness of a moonless night, he had made the same journey every morning all alone.

"When we get to the middle of the Rue Sainte-Catherine you'll hear the second bell for Mass from the parish church . . ."

"At what time does the first tram pass?"

"At six o'clock. I've only seen it two or three times, when I was late . . . once because my alarm clock hadn't rung, another time because I'd fallen asleep again. That's why I jump out of bed as soon as it rings."

A pale little face in the rainy night, with eyes that still

retained something of the fixed stare of a sleepwalker, and a thoughtful expression with just a slight tinge of anxiety.

"I shan't go on serving at Mass. It's because you insisted that I've come today . . ."

They turned left down the Rue Sainte-Catherine, where, as in all the streets in this district, there was a lamp every fifty metres, each of them shedding a pool of light; and the child unconsciously quickened his pace each time he left the reassuring zone of brightness.

The noises from the barracks could still be heard in the distance. A few windows lit up. Footsteps sounded in a side street; probably a workman going to his job.

"When you got to the corner of the street, did you see nothing?"

This was the trickiest point, for the Rue Sainte-Catherine was very straight and empty, with its rectilinear pavements and its street lamps at regular intervals, leaving so little shadow between them that one could not have failed to see a couple of men quarrelling even at a hundred metres' distance.

"Perhaps I wasn't looking in front of me . . . I was talking to myself, I remember . . . I often do talk to myself in a whisper, when I'm going along there in the morning . . . I wanted to ask mother something when I got home and I was repeating to myself what I was going to say to her . . ."

"What did you want to say to her?"

"I've wanted a bike for ever such a long time . . . I've already saved up three hundred francs out of my church money."

Was it just an impression? It seemed to Maigret that the boy was keeping further away from the houses. He even stepped off the pavement, and returned to it a little further on.

"It was here . . . Look . . . There's the second bell ringing for Mass at the Parish church."

And Maigret endeavoured, in all seriousness, to enter into the world which was the child's world every morning.

"I must have looked up suddenly . . . You know, like

when you're running without looking where you're going and find yourself in front of a wall . . . It was just here."

He pointed to the line on the pavement dividing the darkness from the lamplight, where the drizzle formed a luminous haze.

"First I saw that there was a man lying down and he looked so big that I could have sworn he took up the whole width of the pavement."

That was impossible, for the pavement was at least two and a half metres across.

"I don't know what I did exactly . . . I must have jumped aside . . . I didn't run away immediately, for I saw the knife stuck in his chest, with a big handle made of brown horn. I noticed it because my uncle Henri has a knife just like it and he told me it was made out of a stag's horn. I'm certain the man was dead . . ."

"Why?"

"I don't know . . . He looked like a corpse."

"Were his eyes shut?"

"I didn't notice his eyes . . . I don't know . . . But I had the feeling he was dead . . . It all happened very quickly, as I told you yesterday in your office . . . They made me repeat the same thing so many times yesterday that I'm all muddled . . . Specially when I feel people don't believe me . . ."

"And the other man?"

"When I looked up I saw that there was somebody a little further on, five metres away maybe, a man with very pale eyes who looked at me for a moment and then started running. It was the murderer . . ."

"How do you know that?"

"Because he ran off as fast as he could."

"In which direction?"

"Right over there . . ."

"Towards the barracks?"

"Yes . . ."

It was a fact that Justin had been interrogated at least ten times the previous day. Before Maigret appeared in the office the detectives had even made a sort of game of it. His story had never varied in a single detail.

"And what did you do?"

"I started running too . . . It's hard to explain . . . I think it was when I saw the man running away that I got frightened . . . And then I ran as hard as I could . . ."

"In the opposite direction?"

"Yes."

"Did you not think of calling for help?"

"No . . . I was too frightened . . . I was specially afraid my legs might give way, for I could scarcely feel them . . . I turned right-about as far as the Place du Congrès . . . I took the other street, that leads to the hospital too after making a bend."

"Let's go on."

More bells, the shrill-toned bells of the chapel. After walking some fifty metres they reached a crossroads, on the left of which were the walls of the barracks, pierced with loopholes, and on the right a huge gateway dimly lit and surmounted by a clock-face of greenish glass.

It was three minutes to six.

"I'm a minute late . . . Yesterday I was on time in spite of it all, because I ran . . ."

There was a heavy knocker on the solid oak door; the child lifted it, and the noise reverberated through the porch. A porter in slippers opened the door, let Justin go in but barred the way to Maigret, looking at him suspiciously.

"What is it?"

"Police."

"Let's see your card?"

Hospital smells were perceptible as soon as they entered the porch. They went on through a second door into a huge courtyard surrounded by various hospital buildings. In the distance could be glimpsed the white head-dresses of nuns on their way to the chapel.

"Why didn't you say anything to the porter yesterday?"

"I don't know . . . I was in a hurry to get there . . ."

Maigret could understand that. The haven was not the official entrance with its crabbed, mistrustful porter, nor the unwelcoming courtyard through which stretchers were being carried in silence; it was the warm vestry near the chapel, where a nun was lighting candles on the altar.

"Are you coming in with me?"

"Yes."

Justin looked vexed, or rather shocked, probably at the thought that this policeman, who might be an unbeliever, was going to enter into his hallowed world. And this, too, explained to Maigret why every morning the child had the courage to get up so early and overcome his fears.

The chapel had a warm and intimate atmosphere. Patients in the blue-grey hospital uniform, some with bandaged heads, some with crutches or with their arms in slings, were already sitting in the pews of the nave. Up in the gallery the nuns formed a flock of identical figures, and all their white cornets bowed simultaneously in pious worship.

"Follow me."

They went up a few steps, passing close to the altar where candles were already burning. To the right was a vestry panelled in dark wood, where a tall gaunt priest was putting on his vestments, while a surplice edged with fine lace lay ready for the altar-boy. A nun was busy filling the holy vessels.

It was here that, on the previous day, Justin had come to a halt at last, panting and weak-kneed. It was here that he had shouted:

"A man's been killed in the Rue Sainte-Catherine!"

A small clock set in the wainscot pointed to six o'clock exactly. Bells were ringing again, sounding fainter here than outside. Justin told the nun who was helping him on with his surplice:

"This is the Police Superintendent . . ."

And Maigret stood waiting while the child went in, ahead of the chaplain, the skirts of his red cassock flapping as he hurried towards the altar steps.

* * *

The vestry nun had said:

"Justin is a good little boy, who's very devout and who's never lied to us . . . Occasionally he's failed to come and serve at Mass . . . He might have pretended he'd been ill . . . Well, he never did; he always admitted frankly that he'd not had the courage to get up because it was too cold, or because he'd had a nightmare during the night and was feeling too tired . . ."

And the chaplain, after saying Mass, had gazed at the Superintendent with the clear eyes of a saint in a stained glass window:

"Why should the child have invented such a tale?"

Maigret knew, now, what had gone on in the hospital chapel on the previous morning. Justin, his teeth chattering, at the end of his tether, had been in a state of hysterics. The service could not be delayed; the vestry nun had informed the Sister Superior and had herself served at Mass in place of the child, who was meanwhile being attended to in the vestry.

Ten minutes later, the Sister Superior had thought of informing the police. She had gone out through the chapel, and everyone had realized that something was happening.

At the local police station the sergeant on duty had failed to understand.

"What's that? . . . The Sister Superior? . . . Superior to what?"

And she had told him, in the hushed tone they use in convents, that there had been a crime in the Rue Sainte-Catherine; and the police had found nothing, no victim, and, needless to say, no murderer . . .

Justin had gone to school at half-past eight, just as usual, as though nothing had happened; and it was in his classroom that Inspector Besson, a strapping little fellow who looked like a boxer and who liked to act tough, had picked him up at half-past nine as soon as the Flying Squad had got the report.

Poor kid! For two whole hours, in a dreary office that reeked of tobacco fumes and the smoke from a stove that wouldn't draw, he had been interrogated not as a witness but as a suspect.

Three inspectors in turn, Besson, Thiberge and Vallin, had tried to catch him out, to make him contradict himself.

To make matters worse his mother had come too. She sat in the waiting-room, weeping and snivelling and telling everybody:

"We're decent people and we've never had anything to do with the police."

Maigret, who had worked late the previous evening on a case of drug-smuggling, had not reached his office until eleven o'clock.

"What's happening?" he had asked when he saw the child standing there, dry-eyed but as stiffly defiant as a little fighting-cock.

"A kid who's been having us on . . . He claims to have seen a dead body in the street and a murderer who ran away when he got near. But a tram passed along the same street four minutes later and the drivers saw nothing . . . It's a quiet street, and nobody heard anything . . . And finally when the police were called, a quarter of an hour later, by some nun or other, there was absolutely nothing to be seen on the pavement, not the slightest trace of a bloodstain . . ."

"Come along into my office, boy."

And Maigret was the first of them, that day, not to address Justin by the familiar *tu*, the first to treat him not as a fanciful or malicious urchin but as a small man.

He had listened to the boy's story simply and quietly, without interrupting or taking any notes.

"Shall you go on serving at Mass in the hospital?"

"No. I don't want to go back. I'm too frightened."

And yet it meant a great sacrifice for him. Not only was he a devout child, deeply responsive to the poetry of that early Mass in the warm and somewhat mysterious atmosphere of the chapel; but in addition, he was paid for his services—not much, but enough to enable him to get together a little nest-egg. And he so badly wanted a bicycle which his parents could not afford to buy for him!

"I should like you to go just once more, tomorrow morning."

"I shan't dare."

"I'll go along with you . . . I'll wait for you in front of your home. You must behave exactly as you always do."

This was what had been happening, and Maigret, at seven in the morning, was now standing alone outside the door of the hospital, in a district which, on the previous day, he had known only from having been through it by car or in a tram.

An icy drizzle was still falling from the sky which was now paler, and it clung to the Superintendent's shoulders; he sneezed twice. A few pedestrians hurried past, their coat collars turned up and their hands in their pockets; butchers and grocers had begun taking down the shutters of their shops.

It was the quietest, most ordinary district imaginable. At a pinch one might picture a quarrel between two men, two drunks for instance, at five minutes to six on the pavement of the Rue Sainte-Catherine. One might even conceive of an assault by some ruffian on an early passer-by.

But the sequel was puzzling. According to the boy, the murderer had run off when he came near, and it was then five minutes to six. At six o'clock, however, the first tram had passed, and the driver had declared that he had seen nothing.

He might, of course, have been inattentive, or looking in the other direction. But at five minutes past six two policemen on their beat had walked along that very pavement. And they had seen nothing!

At seven or eight minutes past six a cavalry officer who lived three houses away from the spot indicated by Justin had left home, as he did every morning, to go to the barracks.

And he had seen nothing either!

Finally, at twenty-past six, the police cyclists dispatched from the local station had found no trace of the victim.

Had someone come in the meantime to remove the body in a car or van? Maigret had deliberately and calmly sought to consider every hypothesis, and this one had proved as unreliable as all the rest. At No. 42 in the same street, there was a sick woman whose husband had sat up with her all night. He had asserted categorically:

"We hear all the noises outside. I notice them all the more because my wife is in great pain, and the least noise makes her wince. The tram woke her when she'd only just dropped off . . . I can give you my word no car came past before seven o'clock. The dustcart was the earliest."

"And you heard nothing else?"

"Somebody running, at one point . . ."

"Before the tram?"

"Yes, because my wife was asleep . . . I was making myself some coffee on the gas-ring."

"One person running?"

"More like two."

"You don't know in which direction?"

"The blind was down . . . As it creaks when you lift it I didn't try to look out."

This was the only piece of evidence in Justin's favour. There was a bridge two hundred metres further on. And the policeman on duty there had seen no car pass.

Could one assume that barely a few minutes after he'd run away the murderer had come back, picked up his victim's body and carried it off somewhere or other, without attracting attention?

Worse still, there was one piece of evidence which made people shrug their shoulders when they talked about the boy's story. The place he had indicated was just opposite No. 61. Inspector Thiberge had called at this house the day before, and Maigret, who left nothing to chance, now visited it himself.

It was a new house of pinkish brick; three steps led up to a shiny pitchpine door with a letter-box of gleaming brass.

Although it was only 7.30 in the morning, the Superintendent had been given to understand that he might call at that early hour.

A gaunt old woman with a moustache peered through a

spy-hole and argued before letting him into the hall, where there was a pleasant smell of fresh coffee.

"I'll go and see if the Judge will see you."

For the house belonged to a retired magistrate, who was reputed to have private means and who lived there alone with a housekeeper.

Some whispering went on in the front room, which should by rights have been a drawing-room. Then the old woman returned and said sourly:

"Come in . . . Wipe your feet, please . . . You're not in a stable."

The room was no drawing-room; it bore no resemblance to what one usually thinks of as such. It was very large, and it was part bedroom, part study, part library and part junk-room, being cluttered with the most unexpected objects.

"Have you come to look for the corpse?" said a sneering voice that made the Superintendent jump.

Since there was a bed, he had naturally looked towards it, but it was empty. The voice came from the chimney corner, where a lean old man was huddled in the depths of an armchair, with a plaid over his legs.

"Take off your overcoat, for I adore heat and you'll not be able to stand it here."

It was quite true. The old man, holding a pair of tongs, was doing his best to encourage the biggest possible blaze from a log fire.

"I had thought that the police had made some progress since my time and had learnt to mistrust evidence given by children. Children and girls are the most unreliable of witnesses, and when I was on the Bench . . ."

He was wearing a thick dressing-gown, and in spite of the heat of the room, he had a scarf as broad as a shawl round his neck.

"So the crime is supposed to have been committed in front of my house? And if I'm not mistaken, you are the famous Superintendent Maigret, whom they have graciously sent to our town to reorganize our Flying Squad?"

His voice grated. It was that of a spiteful, aggressive, savagely sarcastic old man.

"Well, my dear Superintendent, unless you're going to accuse me of being in league with the murderer, I am sorry to tell you, as I told your young inspector yesterday, that you're on the wrong track.

"You've probably heard that old people need very little sleep. Moreover there are people who, all their life long, sleep very little. Erasmus was one such, for instance, as was also a gentleman known as Voltaire . . ."

He glanced smugly at the bookshelves where volumes were piled ceiling-high.

"This has been the case with many other people whom you're not likely to know either . . . It's the case with me, and I pride myself on not having slept more than three hours a night during the last fifteen years . . . Since for the past ten my legs have refused to carry me, and since furthermore I've no desire to visit any of the places to which they might take me, I spend my days and nights in this room which, as you can see for yourself, gives directly on to the street.

"By four in the morning I am sitting in this armchair, with all my wits about me, believe me . . . I could show you the book in which I was deep yesterday morning, only it was by a Greek philosopher and I can't imagine you'd be interested.

"The fact remains that if an incident of the sort described by your over-imaginative young friend had taken place under my window, I can promise you I should have noticed it . . . My legs are weak, as I've said, but my hearing is still good.

"Moreover, I have retained enough natural curiosity to take an interest in all that happens in the street, and if it amuses you I could tell you at what time every housewife in the neighbourhood goes past my window to do her shopping."

He was looking at Maigret with a smile of triumph.

"So you usually hear young Justin passing in front of the house?" the Superintendent asked in the meekest and gentlest of tones.

"Naturally."

"You both hear him and see him?"

"I don't follow."

"For most of the year, for almost two-thirds of the year, it's broad daylight at six in the morning . . . Now the child served at six o'clock Mass both summer and winter."

"I used to see him go past."

"Considering that this happened every day with as much regularity as the passing of the first tram, you must have been attentively aware of it . . ."

"What do you mean?"

"I mean that, for instance, when a factory siren sounds every day at the same time in a certain district, when somebody passes your window with clockwork regularity, you naturally say to yourself: Hello, it must be such and such a time.

"And if one day the siren doesn't sound, you think: Why, it's Sunday. And if the person doesn't come past you wonder: What can have happened to him? Perhaps he's ill?"

The judge was looking at Maigret with sharp, sly little eyes. He seemed to resent being taught a lesson.

"I know all that . . ." he grumbled, cracking his bony finger-joints. "I was a magistrate before you were a policeman."

"When the altar-boy went past . . ."

"I used to hear him, if that's what you're trying to make me admit."

"And if he didn't go past?"

"I might have happened to notice it. But I might have happened not to notice it. As in the case of the factory siren you mentioned. One isn't struck every Sunday by the silence of the siren . . ."

"What about yesterday?"

Could Maigret be mistaken? He had the impression that the old magistrate was scowling, that there was something sullen and savagely secretive about his expression. Old people sometimes sulk, like children; they often display the same puerile stubbornness.

"Yesterday?"

"Yes . . ."

Why did he repeat the question, unless to give himself time to make a decision?

"I noticed nothing."

"Not that he had passed?"

"No . . ."

"Nor that he hadn't passed?"

"No . . ."

One or the other answer was untrue, Maigret was convinced. He was anxious to continue the test, and he went on with his questions:

"Nobody ran past your windows?"

"No."

This time the *no* was spoken frankly and the old man must have been telling the truth.

"You heard no unusual sound?"

"No" again, uttered with the same downrightness and almost with a note of triumph.

"No sound of trampling, of groaning, no sound of a body falling?"

"Nothing at all."

"I'm much obliged to you."

"Don't mention it."

"Seeing that you've been a magistrate I need not of course ask you if you are willing to repeat your statement under oath?"

"Whenever you like."

And the old man said that with a kind of delighted impatience.

"I apologize for disturbing you, Judge."

"I wish you all success in your enquiry, Superintendent."

The old housekeeper must have been hiding behind the door, for she was waiting on the threshold to show out the Superintendent and shut the front door behind him.

Maigret experienced a curious sensation as he re-emerged into everyday life in that quiet suburban street where housewives were beginning their shopping and children were on their way to school.

It seemed to him that he had been hoaxed, and yet he could

have sworn that the judge had not withheld the truth except on one point. He had the impression, furthermore, that at a certain moment he had been about to discover something very odd, very elusive, very unexpected; that he would only have had to make a tiny effort but that he had been unable to do so.

Once again he pictured the boy, he pictured the old man; he tried to find a link between them.

Slowly he filled his pipe, standing on the curb. Then, since he had had no breakfast, not even a cup of coffee on rising, and since his wet overcoat was clinging to his shoulders, he went to wait at the corner of the Place du Congrès for the tram that would take him home.

Out of the heaving mass of sheets and blankets an arm emerged, and a red face glistening with sweat appeared on the pillow; finally a sulky voice growled:

"Pass me the thermometer."

And Madame Maigret, who was sewing by the window—she had drawn aside the net curtain so as to see in the gathering dusk—rose with a sigh and switched on the electric light.

"I thought you were asleep. It's not half an hour since you last took your temperature."

Resignedly, for she knew from long marital experience that it was useless to cross the big fellow, she shook the thermometer to bring down the mercury and slipped the tip of it between his lips.

He asked, meanwhile:

"Has anybody come?"

"You'd know if they had, since you've not been asleep."

He must have dozed off though, if only for a few minutes. But he was continually being roused from his torpor by that blasted jingle from down below.

They were not in their own home. Since his mission in this provincial town was to last for six months at least, and since Madame Maigret could not bear the thought of letting her husband eat in restaurants for so long a period, she had followed him, and they had rented a furnished flat in the upper part of the town.

It was too bright, with flowery wallpaper, gimcrack furniture and a bed that groaned under the Superintendent's weight. They had, at any rate, chosen a quiet street, where, as the landlady Madame Danse had told them, not a soul passed.

What she had failed to add was that, the ground floor of the house being occupied by a dairy, the whole place was pervaded by a sickly smell of cheese. Another fact which she had not revealed but which Maigret had just discovered for himself, since this was the first time he had stayed in bed in the daytime, was that the door of the dairy was equipped not with a bell but with a strange contraption of metal tubes which, whenever a customer came in, clashed together with a prolonged jingling sound.

"How high?"

"38.5 . . ."

"A little while ago it was 38.8."

"And by tonight it'll be over 39."

He was furious. He was always bad-tempered when he was ill, and he glowered resentfully at Madame Maigret, who obstinately refused to go out when he was longing to fill himself a pipe.

It was still pouring with rain, the same fine rain that clung to the windows and fell in mournful silence, giving one the impression of living in an aquarium. A crude glare shone down from the electric light bulb which swung, unshaded, at the end of its cord. And one could imagine an endless succession of streets equally deserted, windows lighting up one after the other, people caged in their rooms, moving about like fishes in a bowl.

"You must have another cup of tisane."

It was probably the tenth since twelve o'clock, and then all that lukewarm water had to be sweated away into his sheets, which ended up as damp as compresses.

He must have caught flu or tonsillitis while waiting for the boy in the cold early morning rain outside the school, or else afterwards while he was roaming the streets. By ten o'clock, when he was back in his room in the Flying Squad's offices, and while he was poking the stove with what had become almost a ritual gesture, he had been seized with the shivers. Then he had felt too hot. His eyelids were smarting and when he looked at himself in the bit of mirror in the cloakroom, he had seen round staring eyes that were glistening with fever.

Moreover his pipe no longer tasted the same, and that was a sure sign.

"Look here, Besson: if by any chance I shouldn't come back this afternoon, will you carry on investigating the altar-boy problem?"

And Besson, who always thought himself cleverer than anybody else:

"Do you really think, Chief, that there is such a problem, and that a good spanking wouldn't put an end to it?"

"All the same, you must get one of your colleagues, Vallin for instance, to keep an eye on the Rue Sainte-Catherine."

"In case the corpse comes back to lie down in front of the judge's house?"

Maigret was too dazed by his incipient fever to follow Besson on to that ground. He had just gone on deliberately giving instructions.

"Draw up a list of all the residents in the street. It won't be a big job, because it's a short street."

"Shall I question the kid again?"

"No . . ."

And since then he had felt too hot; he was conscious of drops of sweat beading on his skin, he had a sour taste in his mouth, he kept hoping to sink into oblivion but was constantly disturbed by the ridiculous jingle of the brass tubes from the dairy.

He loathed being ill because it was humiliating and also because Madame Maigret kept a fierce watch to prevent him from smoking his pipe. If only she'd had to go out and buy something at the pharmacist's! But she was always careful to take a well-stocked medicine chest about with her.

He loathed being ill, and yet there were moments when he almost enjoyed it, moments when, closing his eyes, he felt ageless because he experienced once again the sensations of his childhood.

Then he remembered the boy Justin, whose pale face already showed such strength of character. All that morning's scenes recurred to his mind, not with the precision of everyday reality nor with the sharp outline of things seen, but with the peculiar intensity of things felt.

For instance he could have described almost in detail the attic room that he had never seen, the iron bedstead, the alarm clock on the bedside table, the boy stretching out his arm, dressing silently, the same gestures invariably repeated . . .

Invariably the same gestures! It seemed to him an important and obvious truth. When you've been serving at Mass for two years at a regular time, your gestures become almost completely automatic . . .

The first bell at a quarter to six . . . The alarm clock . . . The shriller sound of the chapel bells . . . Then the child would put on his shoes at the foot of the stairs, open the front door and meet the cold breath of early morning.

"You know, Madame Maigret, he's never read any detective stories." For as long back as they could remember, possibly because it had begun as a joke, they had called one another Maigret and Madame Maigret, and they had almost forgotten that they had Christian names like other people . . .

"He doesn't read the papers either . . ."

"You'd better try to sleep."

He closed his eyes, after a longing glance at his pipe, which lay on the black marble mantelpiece.

"I questioned his mother at great length; she's a decent woman, but she's mightily in awe of the police . . ."

"Go to sleep!"

He kept silence for a while. His breathing became deeper; it sounded as if he was really dozing off.

"She declares he's never seen a dead body . . . It's the sort of thing you try to keep from children."

"Why is it important?"

"He told me the body was so big that it seemed to take up the whole pavement . . . Now that's the impression that a dead body lying on the ground makes on one . . . A dead person always looks bigger than a living one . . . D'you understand?"

"I can't think why you're worrying, since Besson's looking after the case."

"Besson doesn't believe in it."

"In what?"

"In the dead body."

"Shall I put out the light?"

In spite of his protests, she climbed on to a chair and fastened a band of waxed paper round the bulb so as to dim its light.

"Now try to get an hour's sleep, then I'll make you another cup of tisane. You haven't been sweating enough . . ."

"Don't you think if I were to have just a tiny puff at my pipe . . ."

"Are you mad?"

She went into the kitchen to keep an eye on the vegetable broth, and he heard her tiptoeing back and forth. He kept picturing the same section of the Rue Sainte-Catherine, with street lamps every fifty metres.

"The judge declares he heard nothing . . ."

"What are you saying?"

"I bet they hate one another . . ."

And her voice reached him from the far end of the kitchen:

"Who are you talking about? You see I'm busy . . ."

"The judge and the altar-boy. They've never spoken to one another, but I'll take my oath they hate each other. You know, very old people, particularly old people who live by themselves, end up by becoming like children . . . Justin went past every morning, and every morning the old judge was behind his window . . . He looks like an owl."

"I don't know what you're trying to say . . ."

She stood framed in the doorway, a steaming ladle in her hand.

"Try to follow me. The judge declares that he heard nothing, and it's too serious a matter for me to suspect him of lying."

"You see! Try to stop thinking about it."

"Only he dared not assert that he had or had not heard Justin go past yesterday morning."

"Perhaps he went back to sleep."

"No . . . He daren't tell a lie, and so he's deliberately vague. And the husband at No. 42 who was sitting up with his sick wife heard somebody running in the street."

He kept reverting to that. His thoughts, sharpened by fever, went round in a circle.

"What would have become of the corpse?" objected Madame Maigret with her womanly common sense. "Don't think any more about it! Besson knows his job, you've often said so yourself . . ."

He slumped back under the blankets, discouraged, and tried hard to go to sleep, but was inevitably haunted before long by the image of the altar-boy's face, and his pallid legs above black socks.

"There's something wrong . . ."

"What did you say? Something wrong? Are you feeling worse? Shall I ring the doctor?"

Not that. He started again from scratch, obstinately; he went back to the threshold of the boys' school and crossed the Place du Congrès.

"And this is where there's something amiss."

For one thing, because the judge had heard nothing. Unless one was going to accuse him of perjury it was hard to believe that a fight could have gone on under his window, just a few metres away, that a man had started running off towards the barracks while the boy had rushed off in the opposite direction.

"Listen, Madame Maigret . . ."

"What is it now?"

"Suppose they had both started running in the same direction?"

With a sigh, Madame Maigret picked up her needlework and listened, dutifully, to her husband's monologue interspersed with wheezy gasps.

"For one thing, it's more logical . . ."

"What's more logical?"

"That they should both have run in the same direction . . . Only in that case it wouldn't have been towards the barracks."

"Could the boy have been running after the murderer?"

"No. The murderer would have run after the boy . . ."

"What for, since he didn't kill him?"

"To make him hold his tongue, for instance."

"He didn't succeed, since the child spoke . . ."

"Or to prevent him from telling something, from giving some particular detail . . . Look here, Madame Maigret."

"What is it you want?"

"I know you'll start by saying no, but it's absolutely necessary . . . Pass me my pipe and my tobacco . . . Just a few puffs . . . I've got the feeling that I'm going to understand the whole thing in a few minutes—if I don't lose the thread."

She went to fetch his pipe from the mantelpiece and handed it to him resignedly, sighing:

"I knew you'd think of some good excuse . . . In any case tonight I'm going to make you a poultice whether you like it or not."

Luckily there was no telephone in the flat and one had to go down into the shop to ring up from behind the counter.

"Will you go downstairs, Madame Maigret, and call Besson for me? It's seven o'clock. He may still be at the office. Otherwise call the *Café du Centre*, where he'll be playing billiards with Thiberge."

"Shall I ask him to come here?"

"To bring me as soon as possible a list, not of all the residents in the street but of the tenants of the houses on the left side of it, between the Place du Congrès and the Judge's house."

"Do try to keep covered up . . ."

Barely had she set foot on the staircase when he thrust both legs out of bed and rushed, barefooted, to fetch his tobacco pouch and fill himself a fresh pipe; then he lay back innocently between the sheets.

Through the flimsy floorboards he could hear a hum of voices and Madame Maigret's, speaking on the telephone. He smoked his pipe in greedy little puffs, although his throat was very sore. He could see raindrops slowly sliding down the dark panes, and this again reminded him of his childhood, of childish illnesses when his mother used to bring him caramel custard in bed.

Madame Maigret returned, panting a little, glanced round the room as if to take note of anything unusual, but did not think of the pipe.

"He'll be here in about an hour."

"I'm going to ask you one more favour, Madame Maigret . . . Will you put on your coat . . ."

She cast a suspicious glance at him.

"Will you go to young Justin's home and ask his parents to let you bring him to me . . . Be very kind to him . . . If I were to send a policeman he'd undoubtedly take fright, and he's liable enough to be prickly as it is . . . Just tell him I'd like a few minutes' chat with him."

"And suppose his mother wants to come with him?"

"Work out your own plan, but I don't want the mother."

Left to himself, he sank back into the hot, humid depths of the bed, the tip of his pipe emerging from the sheets and emitting a slight cloud of smoke. He closed his eyes, and he could keep picturing the corner of the Rue Sainte-Catherine; he was no longer Superintendent Maigret, he had become the altar-boy who hurried along, covering the same ground every morning at the same time and talking to himself to keep up his courage.

As he turned into the Rue Sainte-Catherine:

"Maman, I wish you'd buy me a bike . . ."

For the kid had been rehearsing the scene he would play for

his mother when he got back from the hospital. It would have to be more complicated; he must have thought up subtler approaches.

"You know, maman, if I had a bike, I could . . ." Or else, "I've saved three hundred francs already . . . If you'd lend me the rest, which I promise to pay back with what I earn from the chapel, I could . . ."

The corner of the Rue Sainte-Catherine . . . a few seconds before the bells of the parish church rang out for the second time. And there were only a hundred and fifty metres of dark empty street to go through before reaching the safe haven of the hospital . . . A few jumps between the pools of brightness shed by the street lamps . . .

Later the child was to declare:

"I looked up and I saw . . ."

That was the whole problem. The judge lived practically in the middle of the street, half way between the Place du Congrès and the corner of the barracks, and he had seen nothing and heard nothing.

The husband of the sick woman, the man from No. 42, lived closer to the Place du Congrès, on the right side of the street, and he had heard the sound of running footsteps.

Yet, five minutes later, there had been no dead or injured body on the pavement. And no car or van had passed. The policeman on duty on the bridge, the others on the beat at various spots in the neighbourhood, had seen nothing unusual such as, for instance, a man carrying another man on his back.

Maigret's temperature was certainly going up but he no longer thought of consulting the thermometer. Things were fine as they were; words evoked images, and images assumed unexpected sharpness.

It was just like when he was a sick child and his mother, bending over him, seemed to have grown so big that she took up the whole house.

There was that body lying across the pavement, looking so long because it was a dead body, with a brown-handled knife sticking out of its chest.

And a few metres away a man, a pale-eyed man who had begun running . . . Running towards the barracks, whereas Justin ran for all he was worth in the opposite direction.

"That's it!"

That's what? Maigret had made the remark out loud, as though it contained the solution of the problem, as though it had actually been the solution of the problem, and he smiled contentedly as he drew on his pipe with ecstatic little puffs.

Drunks are like that. Things suddenly appear to them self-evidently true, which they are nevertheless incapable of explaining, and which dissolve into vagueness as soon as they are examined coolly.

Something was untrue, that was it! And Maigret, in his feverish imagining, felt sure that he had put his finger on the weak point in the story.

Justin had not made it up . . . His terror, his panic on arriving at the hospital had been genuine. Neither had he made up the picture of the long body sprawling across the pavement. Moreover there was at least one person in the street who had heard running footsteps.

What had the judge with the sneering smile remarked? "You haven't yet learned to mistrust the evidence of children?" . . . or something of the sort.

However the judge was wrong. Children are incapable of inventing, because one cannot construct truths out of nothing. One needs materials. Children transpose maybe, they don't invent.

And that was that! At each stage, Maigret repeated that self-congratulatory *voilà*!

There had been a body on the pavement . . . And no doubt there had been a man close by. Had he had pale eyes? Quite possibly. And somebody had run.

And the old judge, Maigret could have sworn, was not the sort of man to tell a deliberate lie.

He felt hot. He was bathed in sweat, but nonetheless he left his bed to go and fill one last pipe before Madame Maigret's return. While he was up, he took the opportunity to open the cupboard and drink a big mouthful of rum from the bottle. What did it matter if his temperature was up that night? Everything would be finished by then!

And it would be quite an achievement; a difficult case solved from a sick-bed! Madame Maigret was not likely to appreciate that, however.

The judge had not lied, and yet he must have tried to play a trick on the boy whom he hated as two children of the same age can hate one another.

Customers seemed to be getting fewer down below, for the ridiculous chimes over the door sounded less frequently. Probably the dairyman and his wife, with their daughter whose cheeks were as pink as ham, were dining together in the room at the back of the shop.

There were steps on the pavement; there were steps on the stair. Small feet were stumbling. Madame Maigret opened the door and ushered in young Justin, whose navy-blue duffel coat was glistening with rain. He smelt like a wet dog.

"Here, my boy, let me take off your coat."

"I can take it off myself."

Another mistrustful glance from Madame Maigret. Obviously, she could not believe he was still smoking the same pipe. Who knows, perhaps she even suspected the shot of rum?

"Sit down, Justin," said the Superintendent, pointing to a chair.

"Thanks, I'm not tired."

"I asked you to come so that we could have a friendly chat together for a few minutes. What were you busy with?"

"My arithmetic homework."

"Because in spite of all you've been through you've gone back to school?"

"Why shouldn't I have gone?"

The boy was proud. He was on his high horse again. Did Maigret seem to him bigger and longer than usual, now that he was lying down?

"Madame Maigret, be an angel and go and look after the vegetable broth in the kitchen, and close the door."

When that was done he gave the boy a knowing wink.

"Pass me my tobacco pouch, which is on the mantel-piece . . . And the pipe, which must be in my overcoat pocket . . . Yes, the one that's hanging behind the door . . . Thanks, my boy . . . Were you frightened when my wife came to fetch you?"

"No." He said that with some pride.

"Were you annoyed?"

"Because everyone keeps saying that I've made it up."

"And you haven't, have you?"

"There was a dead man on the pavement and another who . . ."

"Hush!"

"What?"

"Not so quick . . . Sit down . . ."

"I'm not tired."

"So you've said, but I get tired of seeing you standing up . . ."

He sat down on the very edge of the chair, and his feet didn't touch the ground; his legs were dangling, his bare knobbly knees protruding between the short pants and the socks.

"What sort of trick did you play on the judge?"

A swift, instinctive reaction:

"I never did anything to him."

"You know what judge I mean?"

"The one who's always peering out of his window and who looks like an owl?"

"Just how I'd describe him . . . What happened between you?"

"In winter I didn't see him because his curtains were drawn when I went past."

"But in summer?"

"I put out my tongue at him."

"Why?"

"Because he kept looking at me as if he was making fun of me; he sniggered to himself as he looked at me."

"Did you often put out your tongue at him?"

"Every time I saw him . . ."

"And what did he do?"

"He laughed in a spiteful sort of way . . . I thought it was because I served at Mass and he's an unbeliever . . ."

"Has he told a lie, then?"

"What did he say?"

"That nothing happened yesterday morning in front of his house, because he would have noticed."

The boy stared intently at Maigret, then lowered his head.

"He was lying, wasn't he?"

"There was a body on the pavement with a knife stuck in its chest."

"I know . . ."

"How do you know?"

"I know because it's the truth . . ." repeated Maigret gently. "Pass me the matches . . . I've let my pipe go out."

"Are you too hot?"

"It's nothing . . . just the flu . . ."

"Did you catch it this morning?"

"Maybe . . . Sit down."

He listened attentively and then called:

"Madame Maigret! Will you run downstairs? I think I heard Besson arriving and I don't want him to come up before I'm ready . . . Will you keep him company downstairs? My friend Justin will call you . . ."

Once more, he said to his young companion:

"Sit down . . . It's true, too, that you both ran . . ."

"I told you it was true . . ."

"And I believe you . . . Go and make sure there's nobody behind the door and that it's properly shut."

The child obeyed without understanding, impressed by the importance that his actions had suddenly acquired.

"Listen, Justin, you're a brave little chap."

"Why do you say that?"

"It was true about the corpse. It was true about the man running."

The child raised his head once again, and Maigret saw his lip quivering.

"And the judge, who didn't lie, because a judge would not dare to lie, didn't tell the whole truth . . ."

The room smelt of flu and rum and tobacco. A whiff of vegetable broth came in under the kitchen door, and raindrops were still falling like silver tears on the black window pane beyond which lay the empty street. Were the two now facing one another still a man and a small boy? Or two men, or two small boys?

Maigret's head felt heavy; his eyes were glistening. His pipe had a curious medical flavour that was not unpleasant, and he remembered the smells of the hospital, its chapel and its vestry.

"The judge didn't tell the whole truth because he wanted to rile you. And you didn't tell the whole truth either . . . Now I forbid you to cry. We don't want everyone to know what we've been saying to each other . . . You understand, Justin?"

The boy nodded.

"If what you described hadn't happened at all, the man in No. 42 wouldn't have heard running footsteps."

"I didn't make it up."

"Of course not! But if it had happened just as you said, the judge would not have been able to say that he had heard nothing . . . And if the murderer had run away towards the barracks, the old man would not have sworn that nobody had run past his house."

The child sat motionless, staring down at the tips of his dangling feet.

"The judge was being honest, on the whole, in not daring to assert that you had gone past his house yesterday morning. But he might perhaps have asserted that you had not gone past. That's the truth, since you ran off in the opposite direction . . . He was telling the truth, too, when he declared that no man had run past on the pavement under his window . . . For the man did not go in that direction."

"How do you know?"

He had stiffened, and was staring wide-eyed at Maigret as

he must have stared on the previous night at the murderer or his victim.

"Because the man inevitably rushed off in the same direction as yourself, which explains why the husband in No. 42 heard him go past . . . Because, knowing that you had seen him, that you had seen the body, that you could get him caught, he ran *after* you . . ."

"If you tell my mother, I . . ."

"Hush! . . . I don't wish to tell your mother or anyone else anything at all . . . You see, Justin my boy, I'm going to talk to you like a man . . . A murderer clever and cool enough to make a corpse disappear without trace in a few minutes would not have been foolish enough to let you escape after seeing what you had seen."

"I don't know . . ."

"But I do . . . It's my job to know . . . The most difficult thing is not to kill a man, it's to make the body disappear afterwards, and this one disappeared magnificently . . . It disappeared, even though you had seen it and seen the murderer . . . In other words, the murderer's a really smart guy . . . And a really smart guy, with his life at stake, would never have let you get away like that."

"I didn't know . . ."

"What didn't you know?"

"I didn't know it mattered so much . . ."

"It doesn't matter at all now, since everything has been put right."

"Have you arrested him?"

There was immense hope in the tone in which these words were uttered.

"He'll be arrested before long . . . Sit still; stop swinging your legs . . ."

"I won't move."

"For one thing, if it had all happened in front of the judge's house, that's to say in the middle of the street, you'd have been aware of it from further off, and you'd have had time to run away . . . That was the only mistake the murderer made, for all his cleverness . . ."

"How did you guess?"

"I didn't guess. But I was once an altar-boy myself, and I served at six o'clock Mass like you . . . You wouldn't have gone a hundred metres along the street without looking in front of you . . . So the corpse must have been closer, much closer, just round the corner of the street."

"Five houses past the corner."

"You were thinking of something else, of your bike, and you may have gone twenty metres without seeing anything."

"How can you possibly know?"

"And when you saw, you ran towards the Place du Congrès to get to the hospital by the other street. The man ran after you . . ."

"I thought I should die of fright."

"Did he grab you by the shoulder?"

"He grabbed my shoulders with both hands. I thought he was going to strangle me . . ."

"He asked you to say . . ."

The child was crying, quietly. He was pale and the tears were rolling slowly down his cheeks.

"If you tell my mother she'll blame me all my life long. She's always nagging at me."

"He ordered you to say that it had happened further on . . ."

"Yes."

"In front of the judge's house?"

"It was me that thought of the judge's house, because of putting out my tongue at him . . . The man only said the other end of the street, and that he'd run off towards the barracks."

"And so we very nearly had a perfect crime, because nobody believed you, since there was no murderer and no body, no traces of any sort, and it all seemed impossible . . ."

"But what about you?"

"I don't count. It just so happens that I was once an

altar-boy, and that today I'm in bed with flu . . . What did he promise you?"

"He told me that if I didn't say what he wanted me to, he would always be after me, wherever I went, in spite of the police, and that he would wring my neck like a chicken's."

"And then?"

"He asked me what I wanted to have . . ."

"And you said a bike . . . ?"

"How do you know?"

"I've told you, I was once an altar-boy too."

"And you wanted a bike?"

"That, and a great many other things that I've never had . . . Why did you say he had pale eyes?"

"I don't know. I didn't see his eyes. He was wearing thick glasses. But I didn't want him to be caught . . ."

"Because of the bike?"

"Maybe . . . You're going to tell my mother, aren't you?"

"Not your mother nor anyone else . . . Aren't we pals now? . . . Look, you hand me my tobacco pouch and don't tell Madame Maigret that I've smoked three pipes since we've been here together . . . You see, grown-ups don't always tell the whole truth either . . . Which door was it in front of, Justin?"

"The yellow house next door to the delicatessen."

"Go and fetch my wife."

"Where is she?"

"Downstairs . . . She's with Inspector Besson, the one who was so beastly to you."

"And who's going to arrest me?"

"Open the wardrobe . . ."

"Right . . ."

"There's a pair of trousers hanging there . . ."

"What am I to do with it?"

"In the left hand pocket you'll find a wallet."

"Here it is."

"In the wallet there are some visiting-cards."

"Do you want them?"

"Hand me one . . . And also the pen that's on the table . . ."

With which, Maigret wrote on one of the cards that bore his name: *Supply bearer with one bicycle.*

"Come in, Besson."

Madame Maigret glanced up at the dense cloud of smoke that hung round the lamp in its waxed-paper shade; then she hurried into the kitchen, because she could smell something burning there.

As for Besson, taking the chair just vacated by the boy, for whom he had only a disdainful glance, he announced:

"I've got the list you asked me to draw up. I must tell you right away . . ."

"That it's useless . . . Who lives in No. 14?"

"One moment . . ." He consulted his notes. "Let's see . . . No. 14 . . . There's only a single tenant there."

"I suspected as much."

"Oh?" An uneasy glance at the boy. "It's a foreigner, name of Frankelstein, a dealer in jewellery."

Maigret had slipped back among his pillows; he muttered, with an air of indifference:

"A fence."

"What did you say, Chief?"

"A fence . . . Possibly the boss of a gang."

"I don't understand."

"That doesn't matter . . . Be a good fellow, Besson, pass me the bottle of rum that's in the cupboard. Quickly, before Madame Maigret comes back . . . I bet my temperature's soaring and I'll need to have my sheets changed a couple of times tonight . . . Frankelstein . . . Get a search warrant from the examining magistrate . . . No . . . At this time of night, it'll take too long, for he's sure to be out playing bridge somewhere . . . Have you had dinner? . . . Me, I'm waiting for my vegetable broth . . . There are some blank warrants in my desk—left hand drawer. Fill one in. Search the house. You're sure to find the body, even if it means knocking down a cellar wall."

Poor Besson stared at his Chief in some anxiety, then glanced at the boy, who was sitting waiting quietly in a corner.

"Act quickly, old man . . . If he knows that the kid's been here tonight, you won't find him in his lair . . . He's a tough guy, as you'll find out."

He was indeed. When the police rang at his door, he tried to escape through backyards and over walls; it took them all night to catch him, which they finally did among the roof-tops. Meanwhile other policemen searched the house for hours before discovering the corpse, decomposing in a bath of quicklime.

It had obviously been a settling of accounts. A disgruntled and frustrated member of the gang had called on the boss in the small hours; Frankelstein had done him in on the doorstep, unaware that an altar-boy was at that very instant coming round the street corner.

"What does it say?" Maigret no longer had the heart to look at the thermometer himself.

"39.3 . . ."

"Aren't you cheating?"

He knew that she was cheating, that his temperature was higher than that, but he didn't care; it was good, it was delicious to sink into unconsciousness, to let himself glide at a dizzy speed into a misty, yet terribly real world where an altar-boy bearing a strong resemblance to Maigret as he had once been was tearing wildly down the street, sure that he was either going to be strangled or to win a shiny new bicycle.

"What are you talking about?" asked Madame Maigret, whose plump fingers held a scalding hot poultice which she was proposing to apply to her husband's throat.

He was muttering nonsense like a feverish child, talking about the first bell and the second bell.

"I'm going to be late . . ."

"Late for what?"

"For Mass . . . Sister . . . Sister . . ."

He meant the vestry-nun, the sacristine, but he could not find the word.

He fell asleep at last, with a huge compress round his neck, dreaming of Mass in his own village and of Marie Titin's inn, past which he used to run because he was afraid.

Afraid of what? . . .

"I got him, all the same . . ."

"Who?"

"The judge."

"What judge?"

It was too complicated to explain. The judge reminded him of somebody in his village at whom he used to put out his tongue. The blacksmith? No . . . It was the baker's wife's stepfather . . . It didn't matter. Somebody he disliked. And it was the judge who had misled him the whole way through, in order to be revenged on the altar-boy and to annoy people . . . He had said he had heard no footsteps *in front of his house* . . .

But he had not said that he had heard two people running off in the opposite direction . . .

Old people become childish. And they quarrel with children. Like children.

Maigret was satisfied, in spite of everything. He had cheated by three whole pipes, even four . . . He had a good taste of tobacco in his mouth and he could let himself drift away . . .

And tomorrow, since he had flu, Madame Maigret would make him some caramel custard.

CHANCE AFTER CHANCE

Thomas Walsh

Padre, everybody in Harrington's called him. Year after year he dropped in from his furnished room about seven at night, then drank steadily until three in the morning, closing time; and one Christmas Eve, very drunk, he curled both arms around his shot glass, put his head down, and began chanting some kind of crazy gibberish. Nobody in Harrington's knew what it was—but maybe, Harrington himself thought later on, maybe it was Latin. Because little by little, from remarks he let drop about his earlier life, it became rumored that he had once been a Roman Catholic priest in a small New England town somewhere near Boston.

He was perhaps in his fifties and in youth must have been a lusty and physically powerful man. Now, however, the

Thomas Walsh (1908–1984) began writing for *Black Mask* and other magazines in the 1930s and did not make the transition to mystery novels until 1950. Though his books were successful, he seemed to prefer the short story and returned to it exclusively during the last decade of his life. He was twice a winner of the Mystery Writers of America Edgar Award, for his first novel *Nightmare in Manhattan* and for the story that follows, a moving portrait of a fallen priest.

whiskey had almost finished him. His hands trembled; his face was markedly lined, weary, and sunken; his shabby alcoholic's jauntiness had a forced ring to it; and he was almost never without a stubble of dirty gray beard on his cheeks.

One night Jack Delgardo on the next stool inquired idly as to why they had kicked him out of the church. Was it the whiskey, Jack wanted to know, or was it women? Did he mean to say they never even gave him a second chance?

"Well, a chance," Padre admitted, always a bit genially boastful in man-of-the-world conversation. "They found out about a certain French girl over in Holyoke, Massachusetts, and because of her and the booze they told me I'd have to go down to a penitential monastery in Georgia for two years. But bare feet and long hours of prayerful communion with the Lord God would be the only ticket for me in that place, not to mention the dirtiest sort of physical labor day after day. They had no conception at all, however, about the kind of man they were dealing with. So naturally, when I told the monsignor straight out where to go, since I discovered that I had lost the faith by that time, there was no more point in discussing the matter. A long time past, Jack—twenty-odd years."

But Jack Delgardo was not much interested in the Lord God. Besides which, he had just seen his new girl bob in, very dainty and elegant, through Harrington's front door.

"Yeah," he said, rising briskly. "Can't blame you a bit, Padre, for getting the hell out. See you around, huh?"

"Very probably," Padre said, blessing him with humorously overdone solemnity for the free drink. "Always here, Jack. Could you spare me a dollar or two until the first of the month?"

Because the first of the month was when his four checks arrived. In Harrington's he never mentioned that part of his life, but he came from a large and very prosperous family of Boston Irish—Robert the surgeon, Michael the chemist, Edward the engineer, and Kevin Patrick the businessman; and three married sisters and their families who had all settled down years ago in one or another of the more well-to-do Boston suburbs.

But Padre had eventually found himself unable to endure

his family anymore than he had been able to endure his
monsignor. He never failed to detect a slight but telltale flush of
shame and apology when they had to introduce him to some
friend who dropped by, and he could all too easily imagine the
sly knowledge of him that would be whispered from mouth to
mouth later on—the weakling of the family, the black sheep, the
spoiled youngest of them, and now the drunken, profligate,
defrocked priest.

Although having been the spoiled youngest, Padre occasionally thought, might have been the beginning of all his
troubles. Like Robert he might well have been the surgeon, or
like Michael the chemist; but as little Joey, always too much
loved, always dearest and closest of anyone to the mother, he
seemed never once to have had his own life in his hands. As far
back as he could remember anything, he could remember Mama
and him in a church pew, with sunlight streaming in over them
through a stained-glass window, her face lifted up to the high
dim altar before them, her lips moving silently, and the rosary
beads slipping one by one through her fingers.

Only three or four years old then, Padre had been young
enough to believe anything he was told; young enough, in fact,
to have believed everything. Only in seminary days had come
his first questioning, his first resentment, his first rebellion. So
he had written a long letter to his favorite uncle, Uncle Jack, and
announced dramatically that he was unable to take the life
anymore. So if Uncle Jack could not get Mama to see some
sense, he had made up his mind to run away, or even to kill
himself.

But in the end he had done neither. He had gone on, and he
could also remember, if he ever wanted to, a winter night soon
afterward in the kitchen at home, with Uncle Jack and his
mother shouting angrily at each other from opposite sides of the
table.

"Don't try to make the boy do what he has no inclination at
all for," Uncle Jack had cried out to her. "Damn it to hell,
Maggie, can't you understand there's nothing half so contempt-
ible in this world as a bad priest? Where in God's name are your

brains? It's his life, don't you see? It's not yours. Then let him do what he wants with it, or you'll have to answer for that yourself. It's just the pride you'd feel at having a son in the church—that's why you're bound and determined on it! Why, you're forcing him to—"

Leaning forward shakily, his mother had rested both hands on the table in front of her.

"He'll do what I say!" she had cried back. "He'll have the only true happiness there is in the world. He'll have the collar, I tell you! And you daring to come here tonight and lead him on like this when you never once had the faith that I do, and you never will! What were you all your days but a shame and disgrace to yourself and to the Holy Roman Catholic Church? I know what he wants and what he needs, and better than you. I've prayed to the Blessed Lady every night of my life for it—and she'll answer me! And you'll change that, will you, with your mad carrying on here tonight, and your cursing and swearing at us! Then I take my vow on the thing here and now. From this day on I swear to Almighty God that you and yours will never again enter this house, as I swear to Almighty God that I and mine will never again enter yours! Is that the answer you want? Then there it is. Never again!"

But after that had come the sudden horrible twist of her whole face to one side and her clumsy lurch forward halfway across the table. And after that, Padre could also remember, there had been the family doctor hurriedly summoned, and old Father O'Mara, and up in her bedroom a few minutes after, all the family down on their knees, with Bonnie and Eileen and Agnes all crying, and Father O'Mara leading them on solemnly and gravely in the Litany for the Dying. But Padre had been closest of all to her, as he knew from the day of his birth he had always been, and holding her hand. So. . . .

So. He had gone on. He had done what he had promised her in that moment, if without words. He had got the collar at last. But now, on the first of every month, what he got were the fifty-dollar checks mailed in, one apiece, from the surgeon and the chemist and the engineer and the businessman. To earn them, tacitly understood, he had only to keep himself well away from the city of Boston for as long as he lived. So Harrington's as the finale of all; so his regular stool at the end of the bar, nearest the rest rooms; so Padre, now hardly more than a shaky and alcoholic shadow of his former self, at the age of not quite fifty-three years old.

There, year after year, he troubled no one and bothered no one, making no friends and no enemies. So he was rather surprised when he was invited up to Jack Delgardo's apartment on Lexington Avenue one January night to meet two of Jack's friends, with a promise that the whiskey would be free and liberally provided for him. And it was. They all had a lot to drink, one after another—a lot even for Padre; and then in half an hour or so, surprisingly enough, it appeared that the conversation had turned to theology.

"But at least you have to believe in God," Jack argued, refilling the glass for him. "You can't kid me, Padre—because a guy has to believe in something, that's all, no matter what he says. And I can still remember what they taught me in parochial school. Once a priest always a priest, the way I got it."

"Quite true," Padre had to agree, smacking his lips over the fine bourbon. "Although I believe the biblical terminology is a priest forever, according to the order of the high priest Melchizedek."

"Yeah, I guess," Eddie Roberts grinned—Steady Eddie, as Jack often referred to him. "Only how do you mean high, Padre? The way you get every night in the week down at Harrington's?"

At that they all laughed, including Padre, although the third man, Pete, did not permit the laugh to change his expression in any way. He had said little so far. He appeared to be studying Padre silently and intently, though not openly, dropping his eyes down to the cigarette in his hand every time Padre happened to glance at him.

"No, not quite like me," Padre said, very jovial about it. "In seminary we used to paraphrase a poem about him, or at least I did. 'Melchizedek, he praised the Lord and gave some wine to

Abraham; but who can tell what else he did is smarter far than what I am.'"

"Oh, sometimes you seem smart enough," Steady Eddie put in. "Almost smart enough to know the right score, Padre. I wonder, are you?"

"Classical education," Padre assured him. "Only the best, Eddie, Latin, Greek, and Advanced Theology."

"Yeah, but I thought the theology never took," Jack said, exchanging a quick glance with Pete. "That's what you're always claiming around at Harrington's, isn't it?"

"Well, yes," Padre had to agree once more. "At least these days. Years ago it just happened to strike me all of a sudden that the Lord God Almighty, granting that He exists at all, isn't what most of us are inclined to believe about Him. Look at His record for yourself. Who else, one by one, has killed off every life that He ever created?"

"Yeah, but Sister Mary Cecilia," Jack objected, "used to tell us that no human being ever died, actually. They were transported."

"No, no," Padre corrected grandly. "Transformed, Jack. Into a higher and more superior being into the spirit; or else, conversely, down into eternal and everlasting hell. And very useful teaching too, let me tell you. Nothing like it for keeping in line everyone who still believes."

"Only you don't believe it anymore?" Pete asked softly.

Padre finished his drink, again smacking his lips over it with great relish. He was very cunning in defending himself at these moments. He'd had much practice.

"I believe," he said, indicating the glass to them, "in what a man sees, hears, tastes, touches, and feels. That's what I believe, gentlemen, and all I believe. Is your bourbon running out, Jack?"

"Yeah, sure," Steady Eddie grinned. "But of course lots of guys talk real big with a few drinks in them. Sometimes you never know whether to believe them or not, Padre."

"So you don't believe in nothing," Pete said, while Jack

hurriedly refilled Padre's glass. "Nothing at all. How about money, though? You believe in that?"

"Oh, most emphatically. And in God too. Or at least," Padre amended, trying his new drink, "at least God in the bottle. Which of course means God in the wallet too."

"Yeah, but old habits," Pete said, even more softly. "Hard to break, Padre. Let's suppose somebody ast you to hear a guy's confession, say—and for maybe five or ten thousand dollars? Your specialty too. Right up your alley. Only it wouldn't bother you even one bit?"

"Shrive the penitent," Padre beamed, knowing that he was somewhat overdoing it, as always in discussions of this kind, but unable to restrain himself. Why? He did not know. He did not, as a matter of fact, want to know. It simply had to be done, that was all. Someone had to know the kind of a man He was dealing with. "Solace the afflicted and comfort the dying. I've heard many a confession in my day, and for nothing at all. Very juicy listening too, some of them. You wouldn't believe the things that—"

Pete and Jack exchanged quick glances. Steady Eddie inched forward a bit.

"And then tell us," he whispered, "tell us what the guy said to you afterwards?"

Padre, hand up with the refilled glass, felt an altogether absurd catch of the heart. He had broken many vows in his time, but there was one he had not. He looked over at Eddie, as if a bit startled, then up at Jack, then around at Pete. But this was not fair, something whispered in him. This was active and deliberate malevolence. All his life he had been tried and tried, and beyond his strength; tested and tested; but now at last to betray the only thing he had never betrayed. . . .

Yet he managed to nod calmly. There had to be considered, after all, the kind of man that he was, and what five or ten thousand dollars would mean to him. Could he admit now that he had lied and lied even to himself all these years, and lied to everyone else too? Never! It was not to be thought of for one instant.

"I see," he murmured. "And tell you afterwards. So that's the condition?"

"That's the condition," Pete said. "You still got a priest's shirt and a Roman collar, Padre?"

"Here or there," Padre said, still smiling brightly at them, which was very necessary now; nothing but the bold face for it. "Only it's been a very long time, of course. As the old song has it, there's been a few changes made. So I don't know that I could quite—"

Jack Delgardo rubbed a savage hand over his mouth. Steady Eddie replaced his grin with a cold ominous stare. But Pete proved much more acute than either of them. He understood at once why the protest had been made by Padre—not out of strength, but from sudden shrinking weakness; the hidden and unadmitted desire, probably, to be persuaded now even against himself.

"Easiest thing in the world," Pete remarked quietly. "Guy you know, too—so no question about you being a priest, Padre. All you'd have to say is that you've gone back to the church and he'd believe it. Remember Big Lefty Carmichael?"

And Padre did—four or five years ago from Harrington's— but not clearly. He was trying to get the name straight in his head when Jack Delgardo leaned forward to him.

"Well, they let him out," Jack whispered, resting his right hand on Padre's arm, then shaking it, as if to give the most perfect assurance of what he said. "He got sick up in Dannemora Prison, Padre, and now he's dying in a cheap little furnished room over on Ninth Avenue. They can't do a damned thing for him anymore now. They can't even operate. He's just sick as hell and ready to holler cop, see? A friend of his told us. He said that Lefty asked him to bring a priest tomorrow night. So where's any problem?"

That time Padre decided only to sip from his glass. He had begun to feel all drunkenly confused.

"Because what happened," Pete drawled, apparently observing that Padre could not quite place the name, "is that Lefty and two other guys got away with a potful of money three years ago—only they piled up into a trailer truck on Second Avenue, and no one but Lefty got out alive.

"Then the cops grabbed him that night, soon as they identified the two dead guys he always worked with. Grabbed him, Padre—but not the bank money. Well, he couldn't have spent it, of course. No time. And he wouldn't have given it to anyone to hold for him, because he wasn't that stupid. He must have stashed it away somewhere real cute, and wherever he put it, it's still there. They only let him out of Dannemora yesterday morning and he ain't left the house on Ninth Avenue since he got there. He couldn't have. We've been watching it. We'd have seen.

"OK. So now he wants somebody like you, old Lefty does. No more of the old zip in him, Padre. So if we have the friend tell him about you rejoining the church and all, he's gonna believe it. You're the kind of a priest he wouldn't mind telling his confession to, you know what I mean? You're just like him, the way he'll look at it. You're both losers. Then when he confesses about the bank holdup, all you have to do is tell him he's got to make restitution for what he stole. That's what you'd do, anyway, isn't it? Only this time, of course, soon as he tells you where the money is hid—"

Padre picked up his drink from the coffee table and this time he emptied it. His mind still worked slowly, which irritated him. He could not understand why. So he took good care to conceal whatever he felt, and to smile back at Pete even more arrogantly than before. He reached over to the bourbon bottle with his right hand, lifted it, and solemnly blessed the assembly.

"*Absolvo te*," he announced then, and in a tone that successfully gave just the right touch of derisive priestly unction to what he said. "'Blessed is he that comes in the name of the Lord.' If it's as simple as that, gentlemen, then I think we're just about agreed on the matter. Let's say somewhere about nine o'clock tomorrow night, then. What's the address?"

Pete was behind the steering wheel, Eddie beside him. Jack Delgardo was crouched forward in the middle of the back seat.

It was 9:30 the next night and they were all watching the entrance to a tenement house directly opposite.

About fifteen minutes later Padre came out of the house. He was now shaved cleanly; he wore the black shirt and the Roman collar; and Steady Eddie at once reached back to open the rear door.

"Hey, Padre," he called guardedly. "Over here. We decided to wait for you."

It was a cold January night, with misty rain in the air, but Padre removed his hat a bit wearily in the vestibule doorway. They could see his gray hair then, and the thinly drawn pale face under it—the alcoholic's face. He glanced about, right and left, but did not move until Pete impatiently tapped on the car horn.

Even then, when Jack Delgardo had made room on the back seat, there was a kind of funny look on his face, Steady Eddie thought—a look, for a couple of long seconds, just like he had never seen them before and did not know who they were.

"So how did it go?" Jack Delgardo whispered. "Come on and tell us, Padre. He make his confession to you?"

But for another moment or so Padre only fingered the black hat on his knees, lightly and carefully.

"Yes," he said then. "Yes, he did. He made his confession."

"Then open up," Steady Eddie urged. "What did he tell you? Where's the money, Padre?"

"What?" Padre said. He appeared to be thinking of other matters; like in some damn fog, Jack thought furiously. He did not answer the question. All he did was to keep smoothing the black hat time after time while looking down at it, as if he had never seen that before either. "But first," he added, "I decided that I'd better talk to him a little— to get him into the right mood for the thing. And I had to think up the words to do that, of course—only pretty soon they seemed to be coming out of me all by themselves. Father, he kept calling me—" and he had to laugh here, with a kind of shakily nervous unsteadiness. "It's almost thirty years since anybody called me that, in that way.

With respect, I mean. With a certain kind of dependence on me . . . Father."

Eddie got hold of him by the throat angrily and yanked his head up.

"You listen to me, you old lush! Jack asked you something. Where's the money?"

"What?" Padre repeated. He did not seem to understand the question. He was frowning absently. "I had to tell him I'd be around first thing tomorrow morning with the Host," he said. "I think I may have helped him a little. When I gave him Absolution afterwards, he kissed my hand. He actually—"

Pete, who had been staring fixedly ahead through the windshield, his lips compressed, started the car. Nothing more was said. It must have been all decided between them, just as they had decided to wait for Padre while he was still in the house.

They drove into a dingy street farther west under the shadows of an overhead roadway that was being constructed, and there they drove up and around on a half-finished approach ramp. There was a kind of platform at the top of it, with lumber and big concrete mixers scattered about; before them a waist-high stone parapet; and beyond that the river.

No other cars could be seen, and no other people; no illumination except the intermittent gleam of a blinker light down on the next corner. Red, dark, red, dark. Padre found himself thinking with a curious and altogether aimless detachment of mind. Bitter cold cheer this night against the January rain and against the cluster of faint lights way over on the Jersey side—or not cheer at all, really . . . Father.

"Padre," Pete said, and unlike Eddie in a calm, perfectly controlled manner. "Where's the money?"

Padre might not have heard him at all.

"I had to—comfort him," he said. "But the only thing that came to me was what I had read once in the words of a French Jesuit priest—that a Christian must never be afraid of death, that he must welcome it, that it was the greatest act of faith he would ever make in this life, and that he must plunge joyfully into death as into the arms of his living and loving God. Then I led him on into the Act of Contrition—after I remembered it myself. And somehow I did remember it. Hoist by my own petard, then—" and once more he had to laugh softly. "'Oh, my God, I am heartily sorry for having offended Thee—' That's how it starts, you know. And once I'd repeated that for him—would any of you have a drink for me?"

Pete got out of the car. So did Eddie. So did Jack Delgardo. One of them opened the door for Padre and took his arm. He got out obediently and then stood there.

"Padre," Pete said. "Where's the money?"

"What?" Padre said. The third time.

There were no more words wasted, just Eddie and Jack Delgardo closing in on him. They were quick about it and very efficient. They got Padre back against the stone parapet, which was some eighty or ninety feet above the river at this point, and there Eddie used his hands, and Jack Delgardo the tip of his right shoe.

There were almost no sounds, just the quick scrape of their feet on the paving, then a gasp, and then Padre falling. After that they allowed him to sit up groggily, muddy brown gutter water all over his black suit, his hat knocked off so that his gray hair could again be seen, and blood on his mouth.

"Now you just come on," Steady Eddie gritted. "We ain't even started on you. You ain't getting away with this, not now. We didn't make you come in with us. You promised you would. So do what we tell you, you phony old lush, or we'll—*Where's that money?*"

By then Padre had straightened against the parapet, supporting himself by his two hands, and breathing with shallow and labored effort.

"But it was never fair," he cried out. "Never fair! I was tempted not in one way during my life but in every possible way—and time after time! And now tonight up in that room back there, I had to listen to myself saying something—whatever kept coming into my head. And not for him either—but for myself, don't you see? That it didn't matter how often we failed. That we only had to succeed at the end! That it wasn't trial after trial that was given to us. That it was chance after chance after chance! And that if only once, if only once and at the very finish of everything, we could say to Almighty God that we accepted the chance—"

Pete gestured Eddie and Jack Delgardo off and then moved back himself into somewhat better light so that the knife in his hand became clearly visible.

"You know what this is?" he said. "This is a knife. And you know, if you want to go ahead and make me, what I can do with it?"

He proceeded to say. He spoke in a clinically detached manner of various parts of the human body, of their extreme vulnerability to pain, and of what he could do with the knife—if he was forced. Very soon Padre, still hanging onto the parapet, had to turn shuddering away from that voice, and in blind panic. But on one side there was Steady Eddie waiting for him. On the other was Jack Delgardo.

"We'll even give you a square count," Steady Eddie urged, obviously thinking that part important, and at the same time offering a pint bottle of whiskey out of his overcoat pocket. "Honest to God, Padre. Just take a good long drink for yourself—and then think for a minute. Nothing like it, remember? God in a bottle."

And Padre needed that drink. He was beginning to feel the pain now—in his face, in the pit of his stomach, in his right knee. Which would be nothing at all, he realized, to the pain of the knife. Yes, then, he would tell. In the end, knowing himself, he knew he would have to tell.

But was it test after test that had always been demanded of him, venomously and to no purpose? Or was it, as he had found himself saying earlier tonight, chance after chance after chance that was offered—and the chance even now, it might be, to admit finally and for the first time in his life a greater love which, being the kind of man he was, or had insisted he was, he had always denied?

He still could not say. But how queer, it came to him, that

the last denial of all, the only promise he had never violated, was now being demanded of him. But as proof of what? Of a thing he believed in his heart even yet, or of a thing he did not believe?

His hands were shaking. He looked at them, at the pint bottle they held, and then at the jagged cluster of rocks almost a hundred feet straight down that he could see at the very edge of the river. He had not drunk from the bottle yet. Now he attempted to and it rolled out of his hands, as if accidentally, onto the parapet.

He wailed aloud, scrambling up desperately for the bottle, and before Steady Eddie could lose his contemptuous grin, before Jack Delgardo, turning his back to the wind, could light the match for the cigarette, and before Pete, now more distant than either of them, could move, Padre was standing erect on top of the parapet.

Pete shouted a warning. Steady Eddie rushed forward. But plunge joyfully, Padre was thinking—the chance taken, the trust maintained, the greater love at last and beyond any question admitted to him. Plunge joyfully!

That was the final thought in his head. After it, avoiding a frantic outward grab for his legs by Steady Eddie, Father Joseph Leo Shanahan moved quickly but calmly to the edge of the parapet, crossed himself there, put up the other hand in a last moment of weakness to cover his eyes—and stepped straight out.

Then the blinker light shone down on a stone ledge empty save for the still corked whiskey bottle, and there were left only the three men, but not the fourth, to gape stupidly and unbelievingly from back in the shadows.

BIBLIOGRAPHY

❧ (This is not meant to be a complete bibliography, even of the authors listed, but rather an annotated checklist of some novels and short story collections which might interest readers of the present volume.)

Aird. Catherine. *The Religious Body*. New York: Doubleday, 1966. Murder in an English convent, solved by Inspector Sloan.

Boucher, Anthony. *Exeunt Murderers*. Carbondale, IL: Southern Illinois University Press, 1983. Twenty-two short mysteries, including two of the Sister Ursula stories, with introduction and bibliography by Francis M. Nevins, Jr. The third Sister Ursula tale, "Vacancy with Corpse," is a long novelette which has never been collected.

———. *Nine Times Nine*. New York: Duell, 1940.

———. *Rocket to the Morgue*. New York: Duell, 1942. The two Sister Ursula novels, originally published as by "H.H. Holmes," but reprinted under the Boucher name in later editions.

Catalan, Henri. *Soeur Angele and the Bell Ringer's Niece*. New York: Sheed, 1957.

———. *Soeur Angele and the Embarrassed Ladies.* New York: Sheed, 1955.

———. *Soeur Angele and the Ghost of Chambord.* New York: Sheed, 1956. Three French novels about a nun detective,.

Chesterton, G.K. *The Incredulity of Father Brown.* New York: Dodd, 1926.

———. *The Innocence of Father Brown.* New York: Lane, 1911. The first and best of the five Father Brown collections.

———. *The Man Who Was Thursday.* New York: Dodd, 1908. Chesterton's religious allegory in the form of a thriller.

———. *The Scandal of Father Brown.* New York: Dodd, 1935.

———. *The Secret of Father Brown.* New York: Harper, 1927.

———. *Thirteen Detectives.* New York: Dodd, 1987. Thirteen stories including a "lost" Father Brown tale written in collaboration with a magazine editor.

———. *The Wisdom of Father Brown.* New York: Lane, 1915.

Davis, Dorothy Salisbury. *A Gentle Murderer.* New York: Scribner, 1951.

———. *Where the Dark Streets Go.* New York: Scribner, 1959. Two novels about two quite different priest detectives.

Eco, Umberto. *The Name of the Rose.* New York: Harcourt, 1983. Murder in a 14th century monastery.

Evans, John. *Halo for Satan.* Indianapolis: Bobbs, 1948. Private eye Paul Pine is hired by a bishop to find a priceless religious manuscript.

Fraser, Antonia. *Jemima Shore's First Case.* New York: Norton, 1987. Thirteen stories, five about the title character, whose first case is included in this anthology.

———. *Quiet as a Nun.* New York: Viking, 1977 Murder in a convent, solved by Jemima Shore.

Gash, Joe. *Priestly Murders.* New York: Holt, 1984.

Gash, Jonathan. *The Vatican Rip.* New York: Ticknor, 1982. A Lovejoy novel, about an attempt to steal antique treasures from the Vatican.

Greely, Andrew M. *Happy Are the Clean of Heart.* New York: Warner, 1986.

———. *Happy Are the Meek.* New York: Warner, 1985.

————. *Happy Are Those Who Thirst For Justice*. New York: Mysterious, 1987.

————. *Virgin and Martyr*. New York: Warner, 1985. Four novels about Father Greeley's clerical protagonist Father Blackie Ryan. The first three are mysteries. The final title, a mainstream novel about a martyred former nun, contains strong elements of mystery and detection.

Green, F.L. *Odd Man Out*. New York: Reynal, 1947. Crime and murder in northern Ireland, basis for the well-known film.

Greene, Graham. *Brighton Rock*. New York: Viking, 1938.

————. *A Burnt-Out Case*. New York: Viking, 1961.

————. *The End of the Affair*. New York: Viking, 1951.

————. *The Heart of the Matter*. New York: Viking, 1948.

————. *The Honorary Consul*. New York: Simon, 1973.

————. *Monsignor Quixote*. New York: Simon, 1982.

————. *The Power and the Glory*. New York: Viking, 1940. First U.S. edition published as *The Labyrinthine Ways*.

————. *The Quiet American*. New York: Viking, 1956.

————. *A Sense of Reality*. New York: Viking, 1963. Four short stories, with three stories added to later editions.

————. *Twenty-one Stories*. New York: Viking, 1962. Virtually all of Greene's 23 novels and three collections (as well as his plays) could be listed, but these seem to have the greatest religious interest among the novels and stories.

Haymon, S.T. *Ritual Murder*. New York: St. Martin's, 1982.

Herr, Dan & Joel Wells, eds. *Bodies and Souls*. New York: Doubleday, 1961. Fourteen mystery and fantasy stories of Catholic interest. Especially notable for Frank Ward's long novelette "The Dark Corner" and Agatha Christie's "The Apples of the Hesperides," in which Hercule Poirot mentions that he was a Catholic by birth.

Hoch, Edward D. *The Quests of Simon Ark*. New York: Mysterious, 1984. Nine stories about a mystic detective who sometimes claims to be an ageless Coptic priest. The early stories especially have strong religious elements.

Holton, Leonard. *A Corner of Paradise*. New York: St. Martin's, 1977.

———. *Deliver Us from Wolves*. New York: Dodd, 1963.

———. *The Devil to Play*. New York: Dodd, 1974.

———. *Flowers by Request*. New York: Dodd, 1964.

———. *The Mirror of Hell*. New York: Dodd, 1972.

———. *Out of the Depths*. New York: Dodd, 1966.

———. *A Pact with Satan*. New York: Dodd, 1960.

———. *A Problem in Angels*. New York: Dodd, 1970.

———. *The Saint Maker*. New York: Dodd, 1959.

———. *Secret of the Doubting Saint*. New York: Dodd, 1961.

———. *A Touch of Jonah*. New York: Dodd, 1968. Eleven mysteries solved by Father Joseph Bredder.

Hubbard, Margaret Ann. *Murder at St. Dennis*. Milwaukee: Bruce, 1952.

———. *Murder Takes the Veil*. Milwaukee: Bruce, 1950.

———. *Sister Simon's Murder Case*. Milwaukee: Bruce, 1959.

Hughes, Richard. *Unholy Communion*. New York: Doubleday, 1982. A former priest encounters ritual murders at a ski resort.

Johnson, Grace & Harold. *The Broken Rosary*. Milwaukee: Bruce, 1959.

———. *Roman Collar Detective*. Milwaukee: Bruce, 1953.

Kienzle, William X. *Assault with Intent*. Kansas City: Andrews, 1982.

———. *Death Wears a Red Hat*. Kansas City: Andrews, 1980.

———. *Kill and Tell*. Kansas City: Andrews, 1984.

———. *Mind Over Murder*. Kansas City: Andrews, 1981.

———. *The Rosary Murders*. Kansas City: Andrews, 1979.

———. *Shadow of Death*. Kansas City: Andrews, 1983.

———. *Sudden Death*. Kansas City: Andrews, 1985. The first seven novels in the continuing series about Father Bob Koesler.

Lord, Daniel A. *Murder in the Sacristy*. St. Louis: Queen's Work, 1941.

Ludlum, Robert, *The Road to Gandolfo*. New York: Dial, 1975. A plot to kidnap the Pope. First published as by "Michael Shepherd."

McConnell, Frank. *Blood Lake*. New York: Walker, 1987.

————. *Murder Among Friends*. New York: Walker, 1986. Two novels about Bridget O'Toole, an elderly ex-nun who runs a private detective agency.

McGivern, William P. *The Big Heat*. New York: Dodd, 1952. A tough cop's Catholic faith is tested.

McInerny, Ralph. *Bishop as Pawn*. New York: Vanguard, 1978.

————. *Getting a Way with Murder*. New York: Vanguard, 1984.

————. *The Grass Widow*. New York: Vanguard, 1983.

————. *Her Death of Cold*. New York: Vanguard, 1977.

————. *A Loss of Patients*. New York: Vanguard, 1982.

————. *Lying Three*. New York: Vanguard, 1979.

————. *Second Vespers*. New York: Vanguard, 1980.

————. *The Seventh Station*. New York: Vanguard, 1977.

————. *Thicker Than Water*. New York: Vanguard, 1981. The first nine novels in the continuing series about Father Roger Dowling. See also "Monica Quill" below.

McMahon, Thomas Patrick. *The Issue of the Bishop's Blood*. New York: Doubleday, 1972.

McNamara, Kena. *The Penance Was Death*. Milwaukee: Bruce, 1964.

Moore, Brian. *The Color of Blood*. New York: Dutton, 1987. A Cardinal in an Eastern European country is hunted by assassins.

O'Marie, Sister Carol Anne. *Advent of Dying*. New York: St. Martin's, 1986.

————. *A Novena for Murder*. New York: St. Martin's, 1984. The first two novels in a continuing series about Sister Mary Helen.

Peters, Ellis. *Dead Man's Ransom*. New York: Morrow, 1985.

————. *The Devil's Novice*. New York: Morrow, 1984.

————. *The Leper of Saint Giles*. New York: Morrow, 1982.

————. *Monk's Hood*. New York: Morrow, 1981.

————. *A Morbid Taste for Bones*. New York: Morrow, 1978.

————. *One Corpse Too Many*. New York: Morrow, 1980.

————. *Saint Peter's Fair*. New York: Morrow, 1981.

————. *The Sanctuary Sparrow*. New York: Morrow, 1983.

————. *The Virgin in the Ice*. New York: Morrow, 1982. The first nine novels in a continuing series about Brother Cadfael, a 12th century Benedictine monk.

Quill, Monica. *And Then There Was Nun*. New York: Vanguard, 1984.

———. *Let Us Prey*. New York: Vanguard, 1982.

———. *Not a Blessed Thing*. New York: Vanguard, 1981.

———. *Nun of the Above*. New York: Vanguard, 1985.

———. *Sine Qua Nun*. New York: Vanguard, 1986. The first five novels in a continuing series about Sister Mary Teresa Dempsey. "Monica Quill" is a pen name for Ralph McInerny.

Shepherd, Eric. *More Murder in a Nunnery*. New York: Sheed, 1954.

———. *Murder in a Nunnery*. New York: Sheed, 1940. Two cases solved by Superintendent Pearson of Scotland Yard.

Webb, Jack. *The Bad Blonde*. New York: Rinehart, 1956.

———. *The Big Sin*. New York: Rinehart, 1952.

———. *The Brass Halo*. New York: Rinehart, 1957.

———. *The Broken Doll*. New York: Rinehart, 1955.

———. *The Damned Lovely*. New York: Rinehart, 1954.

———. *The Deadly Sex*. New York: Rinehart, 1959.

———. *The Delicate Darling*. New York: Rinehart, 1959.

———. *The Gilded Witch*. Evanston, IL: Regency, 1963.

———. *The Naked Angel*. New York: Rinehart, 1953. Nine cases solved by Father Joseph Shanley and Sergeant Sammy Golden.

Whalen, Will. *The Priest Who Vanished*. Ozone Park, NY: Catholic Literary Guild, 1942.